LET GO THE REINS

· JOHN D. HUGHES ·

LET GO THE REINS

~SPOTLESS BOOKS~

Let Go the Reins, a novel by John D. Hughes.

Published by Spotless Books, PO Box 25, Vancouver, WA, 98666

ISBN: 978-1-7322426-3-0
        978-1-7322426-2-3 (ebook)

Library of Congress Control Number: 2019902869

Cover design by Damonza.

Printed in the United States of America

First Edition

For anyone who desires to surrender.

PROLOGUE

They sprang up from nowhere along the Central Pacific Railroad after line workers hammered the final spike into place in the spring of 1869—towns scattered along the full length of the railway that ran from Ogden, Utah, to Sacramento, California, and across the barren deserts of northern Nevada. Western states and territories boomed as the Central Pacific connected with the Union Pacific of the east, bringing labor and materials to the gold and silver mines of Nevada, as well as easterners seeking riches and adventure. The towns of northern Nevada epitomized the Wild West as much as any other. These were ghost towns in the making—towns with stories as true as any ever told, even those stretched and tethered to outright falsehoods. Palisade, Nevada, was one of these towns, and this is one of its stories.

1

Palisade, Nevada—July 1878

THE SHERIFF MOVED from the Lind house onto the dry dirt road, his nerves weakened but steady. Allie Lind slowed as she approached the sheriff, then stopped a few feet from him. The sheriff knew that in Palisade, Nevada, even at seven years old, you learn to read faces. The vile. The greedy. The desperate. The honest. The hurt. He stood before her, a shield between the blood and the innocence. The dress Allie wore stilled itself. He'd seen her in that same baby-blue dress with the white sash around the waist every Sunday for as long as he could remember. It once fit large and baggy and nearly to the ground—now small and tight and to her knees.

Allie dropped her Bible and ran past the sheriff toward her home. He reached out and grabbed her waist and pulled her back, into himself. He knelt to her side and held her close. He'd done this dozens of times, hundreds maybe—taking someone's life away with his words, wishing he never had to. A lawman's job was to prevent these moments, but they happened. This one felt different, though. He'd had these feelings before but was always able to bury them. This time it dug deep. Unwanted images flashed in him. He shook them away.

"She's gone," he whispered to her. As soon as he said those words, the images returned—memories of Savery Creek rushed through him. He shoved them out again and forced his thoughts back to the present, back to Allie.

He could see that she already knew. He watched her senses shut off to prevent further harm. Her eyes blank and staring ahead at nothing, no attention given to the people creeping in around them and murmuring among themselves, her arms hanging limp even as he held her close.

The sheriff felt her body tighten as she worked to protect herself from his words—words she was too young to hear. He felt her tears on his cheek. She gave a small gasp and then a failed attempt to scream as the unimaginable sank in: her mother was gone.

He held her away as a neighbor approached, ready to take her. He had a killing to investigate. Evidence to gather. Interviews to hold. He had a job to do.

Allie again darted toward her home, to her mother, but he pulled her back in once more.

"Allie. You don't... You don't want to go in." He knew his words gave her no comfort.

She wrestled to pull herself free, but the sheriff held tight. She screamed for her mother again and again, then pounded him with her fists, fighting hard to take back that which was just taken from her.

Finally, she settled and whispered, "Mommy..."

The sheriff knew Allie's love for her mother. He'd seen

it as they walked hand in hand in town, and on those occasions, official all of them, when he'd visited their home and she sat on her mother's lap as if they were one. He knew that she was too young to contemplate her life after today—let alone grasp the scene inside—but old enough to feel the loss.

Esther Jorgensen, the Linds' neighbor across the road, took Allie from the sheriff.

"I can get her to my house so you can focus on your work inside," she said. "I don't mind."

"Thank you, Esther. Much appreciated."

He watched as Esther ushered Allie over to her home, a well-tended place that contrasted with the mostly unkempt and rough-hewn homes of Palisade. Only the crumbling rock wall in front of her house, partially spilling over to the ground, permitted her house among the others. The sheriff looked around and watched as more townspeople gathered, making the long walk from town to the east edge of Palisade, and then up a side road near half a mile. They eased closer to hear everything, or anything. He heard their mingling whispers. Like flies attracted to a carcass, they buzzed and weaved around and among themselves. Fact and gossip mixed and joined. Meg Lind's death spread.

"Her old man done it," said a neighbor.

"Ain't no bigger truth than that," said another.

"I seen it comin'," a third responded. "I'm surprised he didn't take the girl too."

"He ain't long for this earth," the first added.

The sheriff looked over the crowd as if he was both judge and jury, then shook his head at their gossip and moved back to the house.

A small, two-story frontier home—its unpainted boards worn and splintered by the brutality of the seasons—the Lind house held the deadly scene that cut into the kitchen. The smell of death and must met the warmth of coffee and fresh-baked bread.

Inside, Meg hadn't been moved. She lay still and cold on the floor, up against the cabinets of the kitchen, eyes half-shut and blank. Her legs shot straight out, body leaning forward, arms to each side, palms down as if trying to push her lifeless body back up. Blood painted the front of her white apron. The bare wood floors and cabinets caught what the apron couldn't.

Five men stood nearby: two of the sheriff's deputies, James and Jeb; the two scraggly men they'd cuffed; and Doc Smith, who stood across the room, against the far wall, taking notes.

The deputies and Doc were inexpressive and serious, not so much out of respect for the dead, but out of duty to their roles and professions.

"Should we get 'em out of here, Sheriff… maybe to the back so we can make 'em talk?" James asked.

"Yeah. But don't hurt 'em. Dammit, don't hurt 'em." The sheriff kept his stare on Meg, hands on his hips, thoughts on why and how, on Allie and what would become of her the following days… years. Her mother gone, her dad soon gone at the end of a rope, maybe just a prison—*If he's lucky.*

*

The two deputies each grabbed one of the cuffed men and forced them through the back door and around the small barn and out of sight from the growing crowd. James handled the first man, who was taller and bigger and at least a couple years older than the second. Both had dark hair, the second wearing a cowboy hat pushed down enough to hide his eyes; the younger deputy, Jeb, handled him.

Dirt and rocks led out beyond the yard to the brown of the desert, then up a hill and out against the clear blue sky. No one noticed the conflicting image as the harshness of the brown hit against the softness of the blue. A few pigs gathered, then scattered to the far corner of the pen as the men passed by.

"You smell like them fat, shit-covered pigs," the younger man in cuffs said to Jeb.

Ignoring him, Jeb pushed the man hard and forward to beyond the pen and barn.

James spoke up, his tone matching the toughness of the two cuffed men: "You two gonna talk to the sheriff or to the judge?"

Quiet.

"Don't matter. Either way you'll get hung."

"I didn't do it," the bigger man said matter-of-fact like. His height and build overshadowed the other three men, his beard a week from a razor, his face even more from a wash.

"Sit down," James said, shoving him to the ground and against a water trough.

The man fell to one side, scraping his elbow to keep from falling all the way over. He forced himself up and leaned back, hands still cuffed behind him.

James knelt down to see his face. "What you done to Meg, only a coward would do. She never hurt you or no one.

I'll be there to watch you die, just like you got to see her die. You didn't care, and I surely won't either."

"I didn't do it," he said, besting the deputy's serious tone.

Jeb, still holding the younger man by his arm, jerked him around till the sweat of their noses merged and each tasted the other's breath. "James," Jeb said, "I got five dollars says this one done it. Pulled the trigger and killed that woman."

The young man snorted and spit into Jeb's face. Jeb shoved his hand to the man's throat and squeezed. James stepped in and pulled Jeb away.

"The sheriff said not to hurt 'em," James said.

Jeb grabbed the man's shirt and pushed him down and onto the ground. The man spit again. The deputy stood and fisted and reached back to punch him, but James grabbed his arm before he could follow through.

The sheriff arrived at that moment and walked up to his two deputies. He looked hard at them, and they stepped away. He lightened and looked down at the two men sitting on the ground. He knew them and knew their ways. He wasn't surprised they were sitting cuffed on the ground. *Guilt never squealed so loud,* he thought.

"Daniel," the sheriff said, kicking at the bigger man's dusty boots. "Daniel Lind." He kicked harder. The dirt smoked. "You finally did it, huh? Killed her. Shot your wife. Killed Allie's momma. How's it feel to have her dead? Satisfy you enough? Taste better than that whiskey you drowned in last night?"

Daniel didn't speak. He just stared ahead, past the sheriff, out across the barren desert. The sheriff knew Daniel, and knew men like him. In situations like this they went quiet, pushing all thoughts from their mind, forcing themselves vacant and detached. It helped them look innocent, kept them from saying something stupid, anything that might reveal a hint of guilt. Men like this made their mistakes in their teens and twenties when they were young and arrogant. The sheriff could see that, at thirty-five years old, Daniel was reaping the rewards of those mistakes. No pride. No arrogance. No words. It forced a lawman to have to work for justice.

"Your daughter will be gone too. You never gonna see her again," he said. "You'll be rotting away in prison, maybe neck-jerked at the end of a rope. You proud of that, tough guy?"

"He ain't said nothin' but that he didn't do it," Jeb said. "He's a damned liar, Sheriff."

The sheriff ignored his deputy's words. "She ain't hell ever had a father, has she, Daniel? Now ain't hell got a mother."

Daniel looked up. Stared at the sheriff. Cold. His eyes didn't waver; they didn't confess.

The sheriff locked on Daniel. "A few years back we could take you a couple miles out, to that oak along the dry run. You and I both seen a man or two hangin' there, haven't we? Remember Virg Blocker? No wind to even cool him baking in that hot July sun."

The sheriff paused. "Hey, James. What month is it?" he asked.

"July, sir."

"Damned if it ain't. That tree held some big men, Daniel. You're big, but you lookin' mighty small about now."

The sheriff looked up and out beyond the hills, squinted as if he could see that oak. "A rope. A horse. A rifle shot.

I'd love to spare this town a trial—a sure waste of time. A piss-poor way to spend a couple days." Back to Daniel. "But I can't think of a better way to waste a round."

"Let's do it, Sheriff," the younger deputy said. "No one would fault us for what he done."

The sheriff shook his head. "Jeb, I'm here to bring law to this hellhole of a county, especially this town, though I can't reckon a good reason why. Seems like everyone's given up on it, except maybe the buzzards. Palisade, Nevada—they say the deadliest place there is up and down this rail line. It's shoot or be shot, ain't it, Daniel?"

That long steel line of the Central Pacific Railroad flashed in the sheriff's mind. Wells and Carlin and Palisade and the other twenty-some odd towns spread across northern Nevada would still be nothing but dirt and rocks and rattlers if it wasn't for the Central Pacific. And he'd still be a US marshal, not standing in front of lowlifes the likes of the Lind brothers. For certain he'd be chasing bigger game across a larger territory, and with it praise from the White House. *Now President Hayes doesn't know who the hell the sheriff of Elko County is.*

Daniel wasn't going to talk, and the sheriff knew it. He was a tough man; he'd been through this before. And a smart man in a tough way, but not smart enough to stop himself when he's full of whiskey. The turpentine will eat your insides just as fast as the liquor will turn you drunk.

The sheriff eyed the other man. Clay Lind. He stepped in front of him and looked down. Clay's hat covered his eyes.

"Well," the sheriff said, "here sits scum if I ever seen a pile of it. Why the hell you messed up in this, Clay? Oh yeah—you the younger Lind boy, got the same wicked blood in you."

The sheriff kicked Clay's leg and waited. Nothing. He kicked again. Clay didn't move. The sheriff carefully set the bottom of his boot under Clay's hat and onto his forehead, then lifted the hat and knocked it backward into the water trough.

Clay looked up at the sheriff without a hint of sorrow or care for what had happened that morning.

"Watch it, Sheriff," Jeb said. "He's a spitter."

"Two brothers," the sheriff said. "Two son-of-a-bitch brothers full of drinkin' and fightin' and stealin'. Never a good thing come out of either of you. Only thing come out of you is bad."

The sheriff thought of Meg and Allie and the town he was supposed to protect. His rage flashed. He forced himself to pause and wrangle down his anger. A drink would have helped—a shot would calm him for certain. He found it harder and harder to pull back in these moments, though. He used to have the patience, but he learned that men like this were all the same—liars. No sense in having patience, just a waste of time. He also knew that beating up a man that hadn't been proven guilty put himself in the same cage the brothers were headed for.

Clay kept his eyes up and on the sheriff. Daniel kept his head down and held his quiet.

"The judge'll be here in about a week," the sheriff said. "He won't take but five seconds to pound his gavel and claim you guilty, Daniel. Just about the time Bertie's potato salad's ready for the hangin' party."

"That'll be quite a show, won't it, Sheriff?" Jeb exclaimed.

The sheriff cut his eyes at the young deputy. "Jeb, one more word and I'll take *you* out to that dry run."

Sensing movement behind him, the sheriff turned to see the townspeople creeping alongside and around the house. They were sneaking peeks in the windows and leaning over each other to look around the back of the house, the back of the barn. He knew they were easterners, all of them, not a one born or bred in the west. Westerners knew to keep to their own business, help a neighbor when needed, fight to protect that same neighbor when necessary. Easterners didn't. *Cowards.* They ran when the fighting started, nosed in when it was done. They fancied themselves brave heading west to settle or to pick for gold or silver like they knew what the hell they were doing, a fit of pure luck when they hit on something. He liked to think that most left big strikes behind, not able to even make out what they were looking for. He learned early as a lawman in the west that easterners wouldn't do their own fighting; the likes of the Lind brothers would. He respected that but despised it at the same time.

He looked back to his two deputies. "Jeb, why don't you do something useful for once in your squirrely life. Get those damned nosy people back to the road and home. James, give him a hand."

Clay laughed. "You a squirrel, Deputy? You scrawny like one."

Jeb headed toward the crowd.

"Hey, Deputy," Clay said, nodding his head at James. "I didn't kill that woman. The sheriff here'll have to let me go. Then maybe you and I can get out and do some squirrel huntin'." He laughed again.

James turned and followed his partner. For his young age James had a natural, almost cool way about him. The sheriff appreciated that. He wished he'd show more toughness at times, though. A loaded gun needed to have its trigger pulled every so often to remind itself what it was.

The sheriff let the brothers sit and think and bake in the sun. He liked this part of his job. No one saying anything. Not many men could keep their mouth shut in the heat of a July day in northern Nevada. He knew Clay would shoot off his mouth, didn't figure Daniel would. *Same parents, same raising. Don't make sense.*

Jeb returned after a few minutes, back to the sheriff and the brothers.

"Esther has somethin' to tell ya, Sheriff. I think you should hear it. She said Clay couldn't have done it."

He looked over and saw the woman standing beyond the pen, her look begging him over. He had known Esther for several years. Strong and sweet mixed together as a matter of rule, separate when called for. Bitter coffee had its time and reason; sweet did too. He watched her get them right every time. She hadn't taken sides in the war. "You take sides," she would say, "and just when you do, the damn fools remind you who they are and then kick your backside to remind you who you are. You can't let them yoke you and drive you like an ox; you have to stand your ground, stay true to yourself." The sheriff wished for more bitter coffee like Esther Jorgensen.

"Tell her to come to the jail in a couple hours. She can tell me herself there."

"Yessir, Sheriff."

"Told ya I didn't kill her," Clay said to the sheriff, then smirked and nodded his head up. "Looks like I'll be gettin' out for some squirrel huntin'."

Jeb started to move toward Clay, but the sheriff blocked him. James returned at that moment and said they'd gotten all the townspeople headed home. "All yappin' and gossipin' like a band of crows chasing off a hawk," he said.

The sheriff nodded. "Go inside and get Doc's notes for me, James. I want everything he seen. Look yourself. Write everything down; don't miss nothin'. Draw pictures of how she sits and where and what's in the kitchen. Floor, counters, table, everything. We ain't gonna mess this up. We need this all done quick, hanging or otherwise, to teach this town a lesson, send a message they haven't damn learned yet."

"Got it, Sheriff," James said.

"And don't forget the guns and ammunition, where it is and where it ain't. Get it all. Let's give the judge and jury more than they need."

The sheriff watched his deputy head back to the house. He knew James liked this part of his job. Not the killing, but the detail work and learning the profession. James certainly felt bad for Allie, and for Meg, but a bit for Daniel too. A no-good man for sure, but human nonetheless. He knew James felt that way about most people—*Figured the good Lord put a heart in all of us for a reason.* And he didn't mind looking at the body lying there in the kitchen, or the blood, or the death. James told him once that he'd wake in the middle of the night and wish to God that he was doing something else, something easier, but once his boots hit the floor and the dirt outside, he couldn't think of another way he wanted to make his living.

"Jeb, let's get these boys to the jailhouse," the sheriff said.

They each grabbed a man tight by his shirt and against their neck and stood them up and off the ground. The sheriff had Daniel; Jeb took Clay again. They shoved the brothers forward and began walking them to the jailhouse, taking the back way out behind the houses and barns, hidden enough for most people not to see them. The sheriff knew that having to let Clay go would keep fear in the town, but he also knew that only the man who shot Meg deserved to be punished, no matter how guilty of something Clay might be. Daniel shot her for certain. The sheriff just needed the evidence so the prosecutor could prove it to a jury. *No reason to think on it much. Guilty is guilty.* His thoughts went from Daniel to Allie. There'd been a lot of killing in Palisade throughout her short life, too many to count, but he was certain they'd numbed her, at least until now. *When an innocent life's shot down it changes you and echoes sharp, for a lifetime.* He knew that all too well. *Nothing you can do but move on. But the echo follows.*

As the sheriff was lost in his thoughts, Clay bumped Jeb and knocked him sideways, then took off running the other way. The sheriff pushed Daniel away as he bent right and reached for his revolver, rammed it up against his left palm to cock the hammer back, and triggered a shot at Clay's feet. The bullet cracked against the rocks and ricocheted away. Clay stopped flat.

The sheriff straightened and pulled his gun up in sync, keeping it pinpointed on Clay. His left arm relaxed. He stood there. Confident. Arrogant. As much a gunfighter as a lawman in that moment. He cocked the hammer back again. The cylinder turned, clicked, and locked into place. Another cartridge chambered.

Rocks that had kicked up settled to a stop. The sun burned and baked the ground and the men. The heat, with no wind to challenge it, crawled up and around and between them. The sheriff held. Clay froze, gripped by the shot at his feet, wondering if there would be a second. Jeb and Daniel stood quiet and motionless.

"The next one's in your back if you take another step, Clay. You got nowhere to go, no one out there to help you."

Clay looked right, calculating his chances of beating a bullet to the corner of a building. Then he leaned his head back, closed his eyes, and clenched his jaw tight.

"If you so innocent, why you runnin'?" the sheriff asked. "What ya got to hide, Clay? Or you just a chicken that can't stand bein' cooped up?"

"I'm innocent, Sheriff. You know it. You gotta let me go."

"Now you guilty, boy. Runnin' from the law like that. Worth at least ten days. Now you gonna be smart or stupid? I'm hoping you pick stupid. Run like that again and I'll put you down and let the turkey buzzards pick you clean. Now you gonna walk and make my job hard, or run and make it easy?"

Clay hesitated. Then turned and dragged his feet slowly forward, head still back, then down.

"Okay, Jeb, let's get 'em in," the sheriff, settling his revolver into its holster.

Jeb shoved Clay's back to pick up his pace. His feet still dragged and scuffed against the stones and dirt.

The sheriff turned his attention back to Daniel and pushed him forward toward the jailhouse. But Daniel's look was off in a different direction. He'd kept quiet even as his brother tried to run. The sheriff had seen that look before, disconnected from the moment. A man caught red-handed with no way of escape could only reflect on the decisions that brought him to that point. They'd search for an escape, a way out—not from being cuffed, but from their life. These men all knew that one day they'd be here, dragged to jail, and then to a rope. The sheriff had met hundreds of men like this. Most, if they were honest, told him they wished for the rope or a bullet in the back, an end to it all—they wished everything would just stop. But mostly they wished they would stop, either their ways or their life. Didn't matter much to them which way the lot fell. But they didn't have the courage to take either path. They only had the courage to kill another human being, but not the courage to stop themselves. The sheriff could see regrets already slipping into Daniel. They would certainly be strange and unfamiliar thoughts to him, and he'd be uncertain what to do with them. The regrets couldn't change what he'd done in his life, but they were there nonetheless.

The sheriff's thoughts returned to Allie. He knew first-hand that the healing would take years, maybe a lifetime. She certainly couldn't stay here. *Shouldn't have been here anyway. No place to raise a child.* He needed to get her out of Palisade, out of Nevada. Far from this waste of a town. The law would take care of Daniel; someone needed to take care of Allie.

2

"C'MON IN, ESTHER," the sheriff said.

Stepping from the doorway into the jailhouse, her white kerchief over her nose and mouth, Esther immediately looked into the cell at the brothers. She half expected to see evil demons caged inside, having shed their human shells for their more natural, beastly appearance. But instead she saw the same two dirty brothers bent on nothing but trouble from one sunup to the next. She would never choose to live in a place like Palisade, full up of vicious and vulgar men the likes of the Lind brothers, but her husband ran three silver mines across Elko and Eureka Counties, and they needed to be central to them. The pay was good, but the living wasn't.

As Esther stepped into the jailhouse, Daniel ignored her. But Clay stared at her in a way that forced a gasp in her breath. She couldn't escape his look. She felt his threat—*Tell the truth or else.* She was resolute in her purpose, though. In times like these everyone had a job to do, and this was hers.

The sheriff politely broke their stare by laying his hand soft against her elbow and guiding her to his desk.

"Ma'am, we can meet in the hotel lobby, if you prefer," the sheriff offered.

"I'm not afraid of him. I can see he's afraid of me, though."

The sheriff laughed and flipped a belittling look at Clay.

Esther had dressed up in her Sunday best for the meeting out of respect for the sheriff, but more for the law itself. She watched him slide a chair to his desk and set it at an angle so she could easily sit without a fuss. She appreciated his attention to her. He moved behind the desk to his chair and sat. The chair creaked as he settled in. He pushed his coffee to the side and leaned his forearms on the desk. He looked over at the brothers and back to Esther. She breathed in the coffee. Bitter and burned. It covered the smell of the men good enough, though, so she dropped her handkerchief and folded it into her purse.

She turned her head slightly and peeked at the brothers, not wanting to actually see them but instead gauge how softly she needed to speak. Clay's look sent a chill through her body. It felt like he'd grabbed her hair tight and jerked her head back hard.

The sheriff reached and touched her hand to pull her focus back to their conversation.

"Esther," the sheriff said gently, "what did you want to tell me?"

She broke Clay's look and returned her focus to the sheriff. "Well, I hate to say this, but Clay didn't do it. He couldn't have. I sure don't want to be the one to see him set free, but I can't give a false witness either."

"What makes you think he didn't do it?"

"Well, I heard just one shot. I was in the front yard tending my flowers—what's left of them anyway in this heat. Clay was walking up the road and says hi to me when he got close. I turned and looked but didn't say nothing. You know, I ain't mixing with his kind. I just went back to my flowers. I didn't even finish turning when I heard a gun fire. I turned again and there was Clay, still standing in the road. Unless he's faster than lightning, he didn't pull that trigger. No way he could've gone in and been back out to the road."

The sheriff closed his eyes and rubbed his forehead, then ran his fingers hard across the top of his head and through his graying hair.

"Damn," the sheriff said. "I was just hopin' to get both of these boys out of this town, out of this county, in a prison, and chip away at the wicked spread throughout this corner of the state."

"I for one would welcome a clean town, Sheriff. My husband knows I don't take to living across from a man like Daniel Lind. And now with Meg shot dead, no one's safe anymore."

"I'm confident we'll get Daniel out of Palisade. But Clay—are you sure you saw him in the road when you heard that shot, or maybe... maybe there was a delay from the shot and you seein' Clay on the road? Maybe he was already in the house?"

Esther looked Clay's way and saw that he continued his

glare on her, but the glare slipped to a grin, showing that he was pleased with her words for the sheriff.

"I'm certain, Sheriff. As much as I want to see this town rid of that man, he was outside when I heard the shot. It was all quick-like, the shot and me seeing Clay there in the road, his grimy body and ratty hair and all. I thought maybe Daniel was out back shooting at crows or rabbit for dinner. I didn't think anything bad about it at first."

"What'd Clay do after the shot?"

"Well, he looked at me, then back at the house. Maybe it was the other way around; I can't remember. Like I said, it was all real fast. He had fear in his eyes right there, like he knew something bad happened. He ran to the house. That's when I got scared too."

"I'm listenin', Sheriff," Clay interrupted. He'd crossed his arms and leaned his shoulder into the bars like he was chatting with a friend on a lazy Saturday afternoon. "I heard what she said. You gotta let me go. Esther is tellin' the truth, less'n you think she's a liar. You ain't lyin', are you, ma'am?"

Esther looked at the sheriff like she didn't know whether to keep talking to him or answer Clay. But the sheriff looked at Clay and without saying a word told him to shut up. He kept his stare on him and talked on with Esther. "Ignore him. He's staying right where he is till I telegraph the judge and see what he wants to do with him."

"You know what he's gonna tell ya, Sheriff," Clay said. "'Do your job and let the boy go.' So do your job, old man. I'll change my ways, I promise. You and me can be friends here on out. I'll testify for you, help you clean up this town. Meg was family and she didn't deserve to die. What ya say,

Sheriff? You and me and Esther together can make all this go away real quick."

Esther pushed her chair back a couple inches and lined herself up with the door of the jailhouse. She was ready to be done, ready to escape Clay's presence and threats.

The sheriff looked back to Esther. "Go on. What'd Clay do after the shot?"

"Well…" she started, her voice finally starting to quiver, "he ran into the house and come out almost as fast as he went in, yellin' at me to go get you and Doc."

"But Rose Marten's boy came and got me," the sheriff said.

"I know. I had to send someone else. I don't have a way to get into town easily and can't walk fast neither. I went over next door and told Thomas to run quick and get you and Doc."

"I got the rest," the sheriff said. "And you didn't see anyone else go in or come out of the Lind house?"

"Well, I watched you and your deputies and Doc go in. The only one that came out was you when Allie come up the road."

The sheriff leaned back in his chair and studied Esther. She knew he read her as telling the truth. She didn't mind the once-over, as it gave her comfort that he was doing his job.

"Is Allie at your place now?" the sheriff asked her.

"No, Rose Marten took her in. Said she can watch her for a few days, but not much more. I can't take her in neither, Sheriff."

"I appreciate what you've done, Esther. You're mighty brave to go through with this. I'll wire the law in Frisco and marshals in the Utah territory to see if they know of any schools or places that might be able to help with Allie."

*

Clay turned and sat on the floor against the cage as the sheriff walked Esther out of the jailhouse. He was pleased with himself, confident he'd be set free. He looked at his brother, who continued to sit on a cot in silence.

"What you gonna do?" Clay asked his brother. "This don't look good for you. I'll do all I can to help, but you know I wasn't mixed up in this. You gotta answer for what you done."

Clay could see that Daniel was troubled by the situation. His eyes were red, but he knew there would be no tears—Lind boys didn't cry.

Daniel looked at Clay. "We've had a tough life. We fought a lot. Sometimes together and sometimes against each other. And you know we done some bad things. Nothing good ever come to me but Meg, and nothing good ever come outta me but Allie. Meg tried to settle me down, but I fought her too. I even cussed her for it, cussed her to leave me alone. Guess mean is just buried deep in me, in my blood. This is my fault—why I'm sittin' here—not yours. I deserve whatever's comin' to me. You don't need to help none."

Daniel looked away. Clay knew his brother, knew he'd been a strong man all his life, strong-willed as much. He'd never seen quit in him before. He didn't know this weak and surrendered man. He studied him for a while, then moved his thoughts to his niece.

"Whaddaya think will happen to Allie?" Clay asked.

Daniel shook his head. "I don't know. Our momma and pop dead; none of our kin can take on another."

Clay could see emotion well up in Daniel.

"I don't know what'll happen to her. She sure as hell deserved better than me. Meg did too."

Leaning back, Clay set his head against the cage. He looked out the back window, small and high and lined with iron bars. Neither spoke. The quiet held them.

Clay soon broke the silence. "Do you remember the last time we sat in a jail together? Near three years now. Down in Tucson. The farthest south we'd ever been. We rode into town, tied up our horses, then spent the next four hours in a saloon." He laughed. "Somewhere in the middle of the second bottle we come up with a plan to steal a couple shotguns and rifles strapped to the horses next to ours. It would pay for the trip south and then some. We woulda gotten away with it if we'd just rode out, but you couldn't help but stop for one more drink. Got caught red-handed by the owners of those guns. We sat in that Tucson jail cell for two days. Your talkin' eventually convinced them it was all a mistake. You just kept at it, kept fightin' for our freedom. Not sure how you did it, but you sure saved us."

Daniel smiled, remembering the adventure.

"You're gonna fight your way out of this one too, right?" Clay asked.

Daniel lost his smile and went quiet.

Clay looked at his brother and whispered to himself, *where'd your fight go, brother?*

*

Out front of the jailhouse James rode up with Jeb's and the sheriff's horses in tow, having ridden them back from the Lind house. The sheriff and Esther lingered on the porch, continuing their discussion. James slipped off Sky—the mustang he'd roped in the wild himself, broke, trained, and happily ridden for five years—then wrapped the reins of all three horses around the post.

"Got the notes and all from the Doc," he said, walking to the porch and looking up at the sheriff. "Not much to share. Just a couple things we don't already know."

The sheriff nodded. "Good work. We can go over them later. Get Esther back home. She already walked up here. Don't want her walkin' back too."

James headed to the side of the jailhouse and around to the back. He hitched another horse, Scout, to a buckboard wagon and walked back to the front. All the time he thought of the notes and the two brothers and Meg sitting on the floor as dead and innocent as they come. On his way back into town he'd seen Allie standing in the Martens' doorway looking at him, begging him to bring her mother back. He kept her look as long as he could as he passed by, but eventually had to look away. Another reminder that a lawman was of little use after the fact.

James brought Scout and the wagon to the front of the jailhouse. The sheriff had shifted his conversation to Jeb. James always found their interactions amusing and worked hard not laugh out of respect for both of them. He knew the sheriff had a quick temper with Jeb and kept the younger deputy on a short rope. Jeb had a lot to learn, but no doubt the learning had been slow coming.

"Jeb, you go in and keep an eye on those boys," the sheriff said. "Don't say a word no matter what they say. You hear me? Don't talk, don't move, don't even think. Just sit in your chair. And you better damn well not touch your revolver. Those boys ain't goin' nowhere."

"Will do, sir," Jeb said, saluting.

James caught the sheriff shaking his head at the salute. He knew what was going through the sheriff's head; he'd heard it from him dozens of times—that he should have picked another deputy besides Jeb, one that knew where the hell he was and what the hell he was doing.

Fighting off a laugh, James helped Esther up and onto the front seat of the wagon. She scooted to the opposite side. James jumped up and moved to the middle, then reached down for the reins and tapped Scout into a trot.

"Don't worry," James said to Esther. "Clay may get out, but he won't hurt no one... for certain not you. You're the reason he'll be gettin' out anyway. It's like you did him a favor. But he can't leave town since he'll be called at the trial. We'll watch him close. He can't even walk crooked or the sheriff will drag him back in quicker'n a rattlesnake bite."

Esther frowned. "I'm not worried for me. I'm worried for Allie. Such a shame. An orphan, poor girl. A sad shame. This town has had too much killing 'n' dying. When's it all gonna stop, James?"

He didn't respond; he couldn't. James could only stare ahead and wonder himself when it was all going to stop. He tapped Scout again and moved the wagon out to the road.

The rocky, rutty street jostled them all the way back to Esther's home. Only the wheels crunching the gravel and sandy dirt of the road broke the quiet between them. James brought Scout to a halt, hopped off the wagon, then helped Esther down and into her house. She thanked him for the ride and closed the door. He heard the latch fall into place as he turned back to the road and Scout. Across at the Lind house the activity was ending. Doc was helping Eli Bankston carry the coffin out and onto Eli's funeral wagon. The weight banged hard on the wood of the wagon. It hung over the edge halfway before the men finally shoved it the full way in, which took four or five strong efforts. Eli jumped to his seat, grabbed the reins, and began the ride to his place to prepare Meg for her burial. James wondered how he could work on such hot days moving heavy boxes all around town dressed in that dark black suit.

James hopped back onto his wagon just as Eli rode off. James heard Doc call out, "Just a wood marker, Eli. The family can't afford anything more."

After turning his wagon around, James followed Eli's dust trail back to town, with Meg in view the full way.

*

Still standing on the jailhouse porch, the sheriff leaned his head to the door and listened. Nothing. "First thing that boy's done right all day… maybe all year," he whispered to himself. He moved a few feet over and sat on the bench, then leaned forward and stared at the Palisade Hotel across Main Street. People walked in and others out, never giving the stairs a break, just like the men at Millie's on a Saturday night. Three wood columns stood tall and spread across the front of the hotel. They reached high above the hotel's boardwalk, carrying the full weight of the balcony above, which leaned crooked to the right. Several people stood outside the hotel entrance, staring across at him and pointing. He knew what they were thinking and saying—wondering if their sheriff could ever bring a man to justice, wondering if he knew what the hell *he* was doing. He wondered the same thing.

Gunshots popped loud and hard at the end of the street and disturbed their staring and the sheriff's thoughts. He looked back to the people. They scurried into the safety of the hotel. Rowdy miners having fun on a Sunday afternoon. Nothing more, he was certain. He looked up again to the balcony. *Seems like everything leans crooked in this town,* he thought. And he couldn't decide which was more crooked: Daniel, Clay, or that balcony.

3

THE SHERIFF LEFT the jailhouse porch and walked across the street to the Palisade Hotel, right under that crooked balcony he'd been staring at, and up the steps. The aroma of steak and fried chicken and fresh-baked biscuits drifted out to meet him. He knew that if it wasn't for Bertie's cooking, he'd be a starving lawman. He could butcher a deer or cow or lamb faster and cleaner than any man he knew, but he didn't know what to do with a fresh cut of meat except kill it again in a hot skillet.

He headed for his regular table at the back corner of the dining room, took off his hat, and slung it soft across the table until it slid to a stop at the edge. Bertie walked over and asked if he needed dinner, dessert, or a drink.

Bertie had built the Palisade Hotel with her own money and nearly with her own two hands. She came from eastern wealth—family riches earned by acquiring and selling land in New York and Connecticut—but you'd never know it by her lifestyle. She didn't flaunt her abundance and was more likely to give a dinner away to someone in need than charge full price. And she was as strong a woman as you'd find in the west, and certainly the smartest he'd ever known. Her establishment was the first of its kind in Palisade... all of Elko County for that matter. To the sheriff, that showed vision, and surviving the town showed fortitude. She dressed the western part too, no evidence that she flowed from eastern affluence—though she didn't bear the simplicity of the western woman, her face made up each day fresh and new, and her hair an opulent style more likely to impress in New York City than Palisade, Nevada. He deemed her an attractive woman, as much for her good heart as her physical features, though he gave no sign of it.

Bertie knew very well what he wanted but always asked just to poke at him. He'd certainly desire a whiskey but never wanted to be seen drinking in public. And he wasn't much of a dessert man, even if she had the best damned apple pie in the west. No, the sheriff always wanted dinner.

He looked up at her and laughed. She tossed her hands on her hips and cocked her foot out. The sheriff knew that look. She was serious but, at the same time, not. She teased him like that when she saw he needed it, but there was always a taint of truth to her, as if she knew the full story already and he didn't. She was smarter than he was, and she fancied staying out in front and playing with him the full way.

"What's wrong with you, Marshal? Jeb fall off his horse again?"

"Bert, ya know you're the only one that still calls me 'Marshal.'"

"You were a marshal for so long... and besides, you ain't worn out the name yet."

"I appreciate it. But I haven't been a marshal since right after Lincoln sewed that Nevada star on the flag. We weren't near ready for a state, but he needed us for reelection. He got that alright. And then for some damn reason I chose to give up bein' a marshal. Thought maybe I could settle down and start a family."

"Never too late to start that family, Sheriff," Bertie said, smiling and winking at him."

The sheriff grinned and shook his head.

"You had a tough job as marshal, the whole Nevada Territory to cover, just you and Monroe and Martinez. You sacrificed what you loved to stay here and be a county sheriff. We sure as pumpkin pie need you with the likes of the Lind brothers around."

The sheriff looked down and ran those memories through his mind, those years as a marshal. He knew he lost something of himself when he quit and took the sheriff's position—lost something that he was certain he'd never get back. He went from the freedom of riding a territory alone to watching over a small county with two little boys as deputies trailing along behind. Being a county sheriff felt like a prison sentence—but one he knew he deserved.

Bertie interrupted, "So hell, Marshal, what sorta county are you running here? We got Meg lying dead in a box over at Eli's and a hole half-dug at the cemetery for that fellow from Cincinnati who got shot just for bumping the wrong man in the street. Most times it's a drunk man dead that no one knew, and no one cared about neither. Meg getting killed is a different situation."

"I know the situation better than anyone, Bert."

"Eli's getting rich burying my customers. Don't know if you noticed but dying kinda takes a person's appetite away. I like them hungry, not dead."

"I got them Lind boys locked up, don't you worry none."

"Ha! You sure do have them boys locked up, but I suspect not for long. You might want to turn over more rocks if you want to get to the truth."

The sheriff looked up at her, curious and mad at the same time. "You know somethin' I don't, Bert?"

"I know everything you don't, Marshal."

"Dammit, Bertie, I got a job to do. If you know something about—"

"Whoa, Marshal! You best settle your bronco down. All I'm saying is, do your work. Those Lind boys ain't the only bad around these parts."

"Okay, got it. Thanks for the deep insight on Elko County crime."

Bertie huffed a sigh. "Marshal, you been coming in here since the day I opened and fried my first steak. You always enjoy this back-and-forth. Gives us some entertainment without anyone getting shot. We don't get this with most others around here. Now you're riding my hump for it? What's gotten into you?"

"Sorry, but this one hurts. I'm not sure if it's an innocent woman like Meg gettin' killed on my watch that bothers me most, or that little girl whose life is pretty much over. Either way it cuts deep."

"Sorry this one's eating at ya, Marshal. You wait here. I got what you need."

Bertie walked to the kitchen and returned a couple

minutes later with a cup of coffee. She set it on the table in front of him.

"Coffee ain't what I need, Bert."

"I know," she said, winking and nodding at the cup. "Gave ya two long shots. Just sip it like it's hot and black."

The sheriff smiled and relaxed.

She eyed him. "You just remember who your friends are next time, okay?"

"I will. Thanks for the drink... and the friendship."

"I got all you need of both."

"Much obliged. Now I do need some supper. For me, James, and Jeb, and those two cow piles sittin' in my jail. Three steaks with beans and fried potatoes, and two fried chicken dinners with beans and rice. Throw in three slices of apple pie. And cornbread—*warm*. Not those cold bricks you sent over last time."

"You sure are particular for a low-brand county sheriff."

"Low-brand's the only kind there is, Bert."

"Dinner will be there about six o'clock."

"Thanks. And let me know if you hear anything else I don't already know."

Bertie laughed and headed back to the kitchen.

The sheriff slouched low in his chair and stared into his drink, tapping his fingers. A steam whistle screamed from down the tracks. Another train rolling in. An unrelenting sound in Palisade. Most town folks didn't hear them anymore. They eventually faded to the background just like the drifters who would show up for a few days, pretend to look for work, waste their money on whiskey, and move on.

The whistle blew a second time, but the only thing the

sheriff heard was Allie's screams for her mother. Then Meg's body on the floor flashed in his mind. Then Daniel saying he didn't do it. The sounds and images and words mixed and twisted in his head—from Allie's screams to Meg's lifeless body to Daniel's denial.

What else is a liar—and a thief—going to say? the sheriff thought. *Anything to stay out of jail.* After all, for Daniel, this wasn't about Meg or Allie, but about himself. The sheriff was certain of that. At that thought he slapped the tabletop, grabbed his hat, and headed for the door.

Before returning to the jailhouse he walked over to the telegraph office at the train depot to have Henry send messages to the sheriff's office in San Francisco and to Marshal Luck, who rode the Utah Territory around Salt Lake City. He needed to find a place for Allie to go, likely for good. An orphanage, but hopefully a school for girls where she could get a more proper education than the killing she'd been learning in the godforsaken streets of Palisade. He figured that he would hear back in a day or two from Frisco, but it could be a couple weeks before Luck responded; he'd likely be out deep in the territory. He thought maybe to try Denver as well, but that would be twice the trip for Allie.

As the sheriff approached the depot, he watched an eagle soar high in the distance to the west. *Easy pickings of trout in the Humboldt River, or rabbits running happy and free among the sage of the desert.* He hoped to set Allie free, free from all the bad of Palisade, and preferably as quickly and easily as that eagle flew west. Unless he found Allie a way out, she would have no chance but to end up—

He stopped himself and forced the thought from his mind, but it remained there, at a distance, taunting him to act fast.

The rat-a-tat of the telegraph grew louder as he walked into Henry's tiny office. He was jotting down a message that had just arrived. Meg's parents already received word that their daughter had been shot and killed that morning. Henry read their response for the sheriff. They demanded that she not be buried until they returned from Omaha in five days. And:

WE EXPECT THAT MAN TO BE HANGED AND BURIED
BEFORE SUNDOWN.

He had Henry message back and agree to their request to delay the funeral, but only for three days. A body wouldn't last much longer in this heat. He had Henry respond to the second request saying that it would be a matter for the judge and jury to decide, not them. He sent another message asking if they could take Allie on, that she needed somewhere to go. He knew they wouldn't. Not couldn't. *Wouldn't.* A few minutes later their response tapped in:

CAN'T TAKE HER. NO SPACE OR TIME. CAN ASSIST WITH
FUNDS IF NEEDED. TROUBLED BY HER PROSPECTS.
HOPE SHE FINDS A SAFE PLACE.

The sheriff wasn't surprised by their response, but it pushed his frustration further to the edge. He knew they had the time and money to help Allie. What they didn't have was love, or a heart for that matter. They spent their time traveling the rails between Omaha and San Francisco, passing through Palisade regularly but barely stopping long enough to say hello to their daughter and granddaughter, and only when it suited them. Meg's father, Walter Franks, owned the store in town where Daniel first saw Meg. Franks was an original investor in the Central Pacific Railroad and then an executive whose sole job, it seemed, was riding up and down the line—purposeless—he and his wife safely sheltered in their coach at the end, far from the noise of the whistle and from those who had to pay. Meg told the sheriff once, during an official visit to her home, that she had to promise her parents that Daniel would never be around when they came to see her. He was far beneath their class, and they'd warned her in the beginning not to get involved with him. Meg said that his rugged nature and life of adventure appealed to her. It was mysterious and inviting, so different from the repressed home she'd grown up in. She acknowledged to the sheriff that Daniel easily stripped away all that her parents had worked to breed into her. But for a brutish man with some bad ways about him, he showed a kind heart at times. Even before they were married, she'd seen him sneak a dollar piece to a stranger in need. She didn't understand why he hid such beautiful gestures, but he did. And worse, why he failed to have that same heart and compassion for his own wife and daughter.

The sheriff stepped out of the telegraph office and onto the narrow side street that led back to the center of town and to the jailhouse. He looked up and whispered, "No, please don't give this to me. I can't handle it. It'll just remind me…" He closed his eyes and shook his head as he felt the full weight of saving Allie fall on him.

4

THE JAILHOUSE WAS quiet when Bertie walked in with dinner. The three lawmen were busy at their desks; Daniel and Clay lay silent in their cell. Daniel caught Bertie's look as she stared at him and Clay. He turned away but watched as his brother returned her gaze.

"Thanks for bringin' dinner over, Bert," the sheriff said.

"They can eat my food here," she said, still keeping her eye on the brothers, "but I don't wanna see 'em in my place again. Ever. I'm not afraid to pull Chester out and put some buckshot in my walls just to scare 'em out the door either. And if they get a little lead in 'em, well, that'd be fine with me."

James and Jeb let out a laugh, but the sheriff gave them a look that stopped them quick, then returned his attention to Bertie.

"These men ain't been proved guilty of anything yet," the sheriff said.

"Marshal, there's guilty according to the law and there's guilty according to Bertie. And I say they're guilty. Of killing

Meg, I'm willing to wait and see, but certainly guilty of something worth a little buckshot up their backside."

The sheriff didn't respond. He just thanked her again for the dinner and escorted her out. Jeb picked up two plates and headed over to the cage. James stood by and kept his revolver on the brothers as he ordered them to the back of the cell. Jeb opened the cage and set the food on the floor, keeping his head up the whole time, then went back for the coffees, slid them in, and clanged the door shut. Except for the chewing, the men ate in silence.

After the meal the sheriff split his pie in half and gave a piece each to the brothers. Clay stood up and leaned his head back, then dropped the half slice fully into his mouth and began smacking and talking at the same time. "Thank ya, Sheriff, for being so kind to give up your dessert. We'll be friends in no time, you and me. We can go to Bertie's place for dinner and more of this d'lish pie. Tomorrow night good for you?"

"Shut the hell up, Clay," the sheriff responded.

James broke in, "Sheriff, you wanna talk about the notes Doc and I took down?"

"Yeah. Let's visit Allie, then get out to my place where we'll have some peace and quiet."

The sheriff then turned and glared at Jeb.

"I know, I know." Jeb sighed. "Watch 'em. Don't do nothin'. Don't even talk to 'em. I got it."

The sheriff stared at Jeb even as he opened the door, then he and James left for the ride out to his house.

*

Clay didn't hesitate to take advantage of having only Jeb in the jailhouse with them. "Hey, Deputy Squirrel. How about some more coffee for me and my brother?"

Jeb leaned forward in his chair and started to get up, then sat back down. "Oh no you don't. You think I'm dumb. You can have more coffee when they get back."

"You need to get these plates outta here," Clay said. "They're messy. I like a clean room."

"Clay, leave the deputy alone," Daniel said. "I'd welcome some quiet myself."

Daniel noticed that Jeb had ignored Clay's request. He looked over at the deputy. Jeb had pulled out his revolver, then pushed open the cylinder and rolled it, allowing the unspent cartridges to fall out, each knocking onto his desk. He flicked the cylinder closed and stood up and away from the desk. He began practicing twirling the gun and holstering it, seemingly not thinking a thing about Meg or Allie or the Lind brothers. Clay lay back down on his cot. He picked up a drumstick from his plate on the floor, stuck it in his mouth, and sucked on it like it was a piece of hard candy.

Daniel watched his brother. He knew Clay wasn't involved in Meg's death, but still worried how this might unfold for him—the prospect of being found guilty of something. Daniel looked up to the ceiling, then lay an arm over his eyes. He heard some townspeople outside the window whispering and shushing each other, their voices mixing with Jeb's, who was now fantasizing that he was a gunfighter. Daniel ignored him and the townspeople.

"Clay, whaddaya think will happen to Allie?" Daniel asked.

Looking over at Daniel, Clay for once didn't have a response.

Not hearing a reply, Daniel lifted his arm up enough to look over and see Clay's face. He was staring back as if to remind Daniel that this was his fault.

"I don't know nothin' about handlin' kids, especially girls," Clay said.

He looked away from Daniel and followed a fly as it buzzed around the cell and down to the food on the floor, then freely in flight again as it circled in and out and around the bars without pattern or reason, only to end up back at the food.

Daniel closed his eyes and rested his arm again. "I don't think Meg and me were the only ones in that house," he said from under his arm.

"I sure as hell wasn't there," Clay responded.

"I know. But the back door was open. Not like Meg to do that."

"She probably went out and tossed the breakfast you were too drunk to eat at them pigs, come back in, and then to the pigs again with more."

"Maybe," Daniel said. "Do you believe me, Clay? That I didn't kill her?"

Clay went quiet.

Daniel was hoping for support from his brother. He felt alone without it. As brothers, they'd always had each other's back, from the time they were little until this very moment. There was never a time when they didn't. But that was with stealing and fighting, not a killing. Clay now seemed to be distancing himself from him and the situation.

"I just know I didn't do it," Clay finally responded. "And I ain't goin' to prison for somethin' I didn't do."

Daniel nodded. "I'll make sure everyone knows you weren't there. I'll protect you."

Clay ignored his brother's words. "You were drunk the night before, and people know you had been complaining and yelling at her. But you gotta convince the judge and jury you're innocent, not me. I was outside when I come in and you were standin' over her in the kitchen. You weren't cryin' or anything. Just starin' at her. Kinda like when you shot your horse outside that saloon in Reno. You didn't look like you was happy about it, but didn't look sad neither. That won't sit well with those men on a jury, Daniel. And you got nothin' that says someone else was there. It just don't look good is all I'm sayin'."

Daniel didn't hear him. His thoughts were on Meg: the first time he saw her—eight years earlier at her father's general store in Palisade, he and Clay's first time in town. Daniel had asked the clerk if he could look at any swayback knives they might have. The man walked to the end of the counter to get what they had. Daniel took off his hat and scanned the store to see who might be around to watch him. A young lady—not much more than eighteen, twenty at most—was looking over the dry goods. She put a sack of flour in her carrying basket, which already held some sugar and other items, as best he could remember. She was petite, but not so much to show herself weak and frail. Skin white and soft like a lily, her dress yellow and flowered, reminding him of a garden he'd seen once farther east toward Kansas, where they actually had enough rain and flowers had a fair chance at blooming. Out of place in the hard desert life of Palisade was the best way he could sum her up. That simple.

She moved about the store unaware of him. Made sense, a man of his condition, layered in dirt picked up on the ride from Eureka and the trails and hills and camps in between, clothes soaked in fire smoke, breath of whiskey and coffee, natty hair flattened by his hat—like a dog back in the house from a day out in the rain, then mud, then sun, breath of possum flowing from him.

He and Clay were riding through Palisade looking for work, though for them stealing was more amusement than work, and it paid better. They were entrepreneurs, simply middlemen transporting merchandise from one owner to another, enough to get them to the next town or territory and keep them fed and the law off their tail. And they never stole from a woman, as that would be unprincipled, an affront to their strong moral fiber, as thin as it was. Daniel was satisfied that they weren't all bad. Only shot a couple men who questioned their business operations. No one died, just left with a limp at worst. He did ride off with a man's horse once, worse than a killing to some, but he'd shot his own horse dead after a night of drinking, thinking it was a deer. And a man always needed a horse—walking was for people who didn't have the common sense to hold on to their horse anyway, and a miserable way to ruin a good pair of boots and take on blisters and sores worse than anything one might succumb to in a bar fight. Cuts and bruises sure healed faster than boot blisters. And he'd been in a few barroom fights, the kind where you give up your beer, strap your gun tight, and hope to give more licks than you get. Either way cuts and bruises sure beat dragging boot blisters from here to creation and back.

The store clerk soon returned with several swaybacks and laid them on a piece of cloth on the counter. "You take a look and let me know what ya like. They're four dollars each. 'Cept that one. That one's seven dollars due to the pearl in the handle. I'll be right back to help you."

As the clerk walked to the far side of the store to help another customer, Daniel turned his look from Meg, scanned the store again, then swept the cloth and knives off the counter and into his hat and walked out.

Clay was outside, waiting.

"Let's ride over to Carlin," Daniel said as they both quickly mounted up. "We can get cleaned up and sell these knives."

"And find a good place for dinner," Clay added.

Daniel ignored his brother. His thoughts were still on the girl in the store and how she made him feel. He wanted to ride back to Palisade for dinner.

A couple miles outside of town, Daniel finally spoke. "Get anything yourself?"

"I got us twenty dollars workin' at the trains," Clay said. "Those folks from Chicago 'n' New York sure will fall for anything."

"What'd ya cook up this time?"

"I told 'em I knew where a gun duel was gonna be at one o'clock. They could stand a safe distance and watch a man die over a spilled beer. For two dollars they could see somethin' they never seen in the big city. They happily handed over their money. I told 'em the fight would be outside the

Gold Dust Tavern at the west edge of town. Then I found two men to act out the gunfight. Paid 'em just a dollar each. They were so excited, they woulda done it for free!"

Daniel smiled at his brother's daring cleverness; Clay whooped and hollered and laughed out loud.

"Let's get cleaned up and come back," Daniel said. "No one will know us clean shaven or what we done here. It's small stuff anyway. Palisade—hell, this whole state—is full of killin' enough to keep any lawman busy."

"Why do you wanna come back here?" Clay asked, surprised at Daniel's idea. "Even shaved and washed good, we still might get caught. We never go back to a town we worked for a good while, you know that."

Daniel couldn't disagree. He knew Clay was thinking straighter and smarter than he was, but he couldn't shake that young lady from his mind.

"You ever think about finding someone and settlin' down, maybe get married?" Daniel asked his brother.

"What in hell's name are you talkin' about? We're havin' fun, not hurtin' no one much, makin' a livin'. Now you talkin' about marrying and stayin' in one place and going straight? You don't sound like the brother I know. You sound like a settler with big plans of gold or ranchin' and puttin' down roots."

"I didn't say nothin' about goin' straight—just marrying, that's all. That's all I'm talkin' about."

Clay looked at his brother like he'd just asked which end a horse eats from.

"Maybe we should get some new Saturday night clothes too," Daniel suggested.

Clank! Clank! Clank!

The loud sounds jarred Daniel back to reality, to his jail cell, and from his memory of meeting Meg for the first time.

Now alert, the brothers both looked over at Jeb. The deputy was reaching down to the floor for his gun, which he had spun hard off his finger and against the iron stove. Still bent down and now red-faced, he looked over at the brothers.

"I'd sure hate to face ol' Deputy Squirrel in a gunfight," Clay said. "He might whip out his gun and throw it—hit me right square between the eyes and kill me dead on the spot."

Daniel snickered, though more at his brother than at his joke or at the deputy.

"You got us scared, Deputy," Clay said. "We ain't movin' an inch, worried you might drop your gun and shoot us. Though, I reckon you might just as quick shoot yourself." Clay laughed even harder.

Jeb stood and looked at the two men, not knowing what to say or do.

"Why don't you get us some coffee, Jeb?" Daniel said. "The sheriff won't hear a word from us, right, Clay?"

"Can't talk if my mouth's fulla coffee," Clay responded.

"Slide your cups out as far as you can, boys, and I'll fill 'em for ya. It ain't hot anymore, but it's still coffee."

They both tipped their cups back, drank in the last few drops they had, and pushed them outside the cage. Jeb filled the cups and slid them back to the brothers.

Clay took a sip and winced. "Holy... This is damn bad coffee, Deputy. Ain't you got none hotter sittin' out there?"

"It's all we got. And I ain't never made coffee, so you'll

have to wait for the sheriff or James to return if you want fresh made."

"Maybe you could pour in a little of the sheriff's whiskey," Clay said. "I seen him sneak it out of his desk. He won't miss a little. That'll sure keep me quiet."

Jeb thought for a moment, then opened the sheriff's desk and pulled out a bottle and poured some in the two coffee cups.

"That ain't enough! C'mon, Jeb," Clay said, adding a little whine to his voice.

Daniel ignored Clay's bickering. He lay down again and pulled his thoughts back to his memory of Meg. She once told him that she looked up in the store and saw this big, mangy man. She turned away from him, neither seeing nor smelling anything she wanted. Daniel told her that he'd noticed her right off and that he couldn't get her out of his thoughts. He remembered walking out with the knives that day but also with a feeling he'd never known before, like he was sick but happy about it.

He and Clay rode to Carlin that afternoon and returned to Palisade in the early evening, clean and mostly sober. As they rode by the store, Meg was standing on the porch. She had on the same flowered dress and held a parasol above her head, looking like that white lily was in full bloom and swaying in the afternoon breeze.

As Daniel rode by, he saw Meg peek out from under her parasol and grace him with a twirl and a smile. Not wanting to make known his intentions, Daniel kept his pace and only lightly smiled and nodded in return. Her perfume easily won out over the horse droppings drying in the dust of the street in the hot summer sun. It was like she had just soaked in a tub of a thousand lilies and each one surrendered their full aroma over to her. He surrendered as well, as if he had no say in the matter. Like she had lassoed him with her perfume and was slowly wrangling him back. He closed his eyes and breathed her in.

Daniel was now pleased that their trip over to Carlin had proved a good decision. He wondered why such a refined lady would be in a dirty town like Palisade. Figured maybe she was just passing through on her way to San Francisco, or back east to home, where he judged her a better fit.

Clay stopped his ride in front of where Meg stood and leaned forward onto his saddle horn. He looked toward his brother and then up at Meg. "Howdy, miss," Clay said, tipping his hat back. "I apologize for my brother's manners. We just rode in way over from Tulasco today. His belly missed lunch, so he's feeling light and, well, maybe even a bit out of sorts."

Daniel heard their voices but kept riding. His brother sure had the gift of gab, able to speak with anyone, anywhere, anytime, about anything. Daniel was more measured in his words. When he realized that Clay wasn't going to follow him, but instead keep the conversation with the young lady going, he stopped. He knew what Clay was up to, forcing him into a conversation he wasn't ready for. Maybe he'd be ready after a drink or two, but not now. Daniel wanted to meet her to be sure, but he already felt the anxiety of having to come up with something to say. His throat started to tighten as he made the decision to turn back to Clay and the lady.

"Dammit, Clay," he muttered to himself.

"Daniel," Clay called out to him, "this here pretty young lady is Meg Franks. Meg, this handsome young gentleman is my brother, Daniel Lind. A finer man you will not find."

Meg smiled. Daniel lightly tipped his hat while throwing Clay an "I'm gonna kill you" look.

Clay went on, "Meg says that Bertie at the Palisade Hotel has the best steak in town."

Daniel nodded his appreciation. "Thank you, miss. Let's go, Clay."

"Why you in such a hurry, Daniel? Miss Meg, would you honor us with your presence for dinner?"

Daniel began to get agitated with his brother. He wasn't ready to talk with Meg. A drink first would soothe his nerves.

He watched as Meg's soft, white skin turned bright pink. She smiled at him and took a step closer. Even as she answered Clay, her eyes were on Daniel: "My momma warned me about boys like you. Riding in with no purpose but bad, especially with the women."

Her voice seemed a wisp of wind blowing solely for him. Daniel lost his breath and his words.

Clay broke in, "Miss Meg, we have the best of intentions. We're searching for a town to settle in, work on the line, maybe do a little mining ourselves. And right now just lookin' for a good steak and friendly company."

"The Palisade is just up the street on your right." Meg nodded in that direction. "Like I said, ask for Bertie; she'll take care of you."

"It surely would be our pleasure to have you join us, Miss Meg," Clay said again.

"That wouldn't be proper," she said. "Maybe a little stroll around town later... and a lemonade."

"Well, okay then," Clay said. "It's settled. We'll see you after dinner."

The brothers headed to the hotel, Daniel's eyes still burning on his brother.

"You a ruttin' steer, Daniel... a ruttin' steer and don't even know it. You can have your stroll and lemonade with Meg after dinner. I'll head off for a beer and whiskey."

As they tied their horses to the post in front of the hotel, Clay yelled out, "A whiskey for me and a *sweeet* lemonade for my brother!"

Daniel shoved Clay into the street and walked up the steps and into the hotel, with his brother following and laughing the whole way.

The brothers did settle in Palisade and carried on with their business up and down the rail line, from the Utah Territory to California, and even down to southern Nevada and the Arizona Territory—but never again in Palisade, as the town was now their home. Six months after they met, Meg and Daniel married. He trusted that his love for her was permanent, challenged only by his raw nature. Allie arrived a year later. And just as quick as Meg and Allie came into his life, they faded, giving way to the man he seemed destined to be—coldhearted with no room for anybody or anything but himself and his brother... and their drinking and fighting and stealing ways. The drive for bad was baked hard into him—a team of oxen always striving forward, pulling hard, full strength, never stopping, never letting up. Driven. Relentless. Out of control.

For the next several years Daniel, Meg, and Allie fell into a spiraling life of three people who just happened to live in the same house, nothing more—with Meg and Allie frozen in fear, always wondering which man would walk through the door, and when.

5

ALLIE STOOD AT the window of Rose Marten's house and watched as the sheriff and James dismounted and walked to the front door. Rose had taken Allie into her home earlier in the day, when Esther Jorgensen made the trip to the jailhouse. Allie knew Rose and her family well and felt comforted being with her. Her comfort fell to anguish, though, as the lawmen walked up and knocked on the door. Her mother was dying all over again.

"Good afternoon, Rose," the sheriff said. "We'd like to speak with Allie for a few minutes, if you don't mind."

Allie looked up at the two men standing in the doorway. Her eyes told them no. That she wanted to be done with the day. That she was too hurt and scared and tired. She wondered why they couldn't see that, why they couldn't just leave her alone.

The sheriff smiled at her. "Hi, Allie. Can James and I talk with you a bit?"

She took in a tiny breath and gathered what strength she had left. "Okay."

Rose pulled the sheriff aside. "Just a few minutes. It's getting late and she's not done well since this morning. I know you have a job to do, but for now, so do I. Someone needs to protect her."

The sheriff gave a nod. "I appreciate what you're doing, Rose. I promise, we'll only be a few minutes."

The three walked into the front room. Allie moved to the couch and leaned back against the armrest, lacing her fingers together and looking down, ashamed to be standing before the sheriff and his deputy, as if she'd done something wrong and caused their visit. Hurt and fear and anguish washed over her, unsure of how to take in the loss of her mother, and anger at her father, and wondering what would become of her. Thoughts and feelings twisted and wrenched and knotted inside her. Allie went numb.

The two men stood in front of her as a pair of menacing giants. Neither of the men spoke. They looked at the floor and fumbled with their hats.

Rose walked in with a glass of water each for the sheriff and James. Allie watched them take a drink. The sheriff rapped his fingernails against his glass, the clinking sound breaking the lengthy silence. James looked uncomfortable. He wore the same awkward expression he'd worn when he rode past her earlier in the day. Then, as now, he seemed unsure of how to look at her. She wondered what was taking them so long to talk. Maybe they'd brought more bad news. Tears dripped from her eyes.

The sheriff knelt down. "Allie... James and I sure are sorry for what happened. Your momma was kind and caring and, well..." He cleared his throat and moved on. "Your father is in jail and he'll stay there, maybe for good, so you don't need to worry about him."

Allie let herself relax. She slid over and sat on the edge of the couch. Her shoulders dropped from their high and tight hold. She nodded, giving the sheriff permission to continue.

"This morning, Allie—other than seeing me walk out of your house toward you on the road, did you see or hear anything else?"

She shook her head. "No, just you."

"What about earlier in the morning, before you went to Sunday school? Was there anything different? Did you see or hear anything?"

Allie paused as she worked to collect memories of that morning, to remember something that might be of help, or that might get these menacing giants to leave her alone. But instead of helpful thoughts, the image of her mother lying dead in the house kept forcing its way in. She slammed her eyes closed and shook her head and fought the image off. It reappeared and she fought it off again. She fixed her mind on moments from earlier that morning. Her mother slowly returned to her thoughts, alive, standing before her in the gray dress she wore nearly every day, black shoes, and white apron. They kissed good-bye as Allie left for Sunday school. Something was different, though; she felt it now.

With her eyes still shut Allie spoke to the sheriff. "My mom was quiet. She didn't want to talk or go to church like she always does. I think she was crying." Allie opened her eyes and looked at the sheriff, begging to be done already.

"That's helpful, Allie," he said, continuing. "Did she look sick or act like she wasn't feeling good?"

Allie cried. The memories and hurt of that morning weighed heavy inside her. She felt her stomach and heart stretch and twist and knot together.

She managed to shake her head again. "No, it just seemed like she'd been crying, that's all."

"Where was your pa?"

"I don't know. Maybe asleep upstairs."

"So you went to Sunday school and came home?"

Allie took in a deep breath and let it out, then wiped the tears from her eyes and face. "Yes, sir."

"How about the night before—was there anything different?"

"No, I don't think so."

"Who was in the house when you went to bed?"

"Just my mom. Dad was gone like always."

"Did you hear him come home?"

"No, I usually don't since I'm asleep and he comes late. And sometimes not at all."

"And over the last few days, did anything bad happen... anything you can remember?"

"No, just normal, like I said. My mom cried a lot, but just because Dad was always mad at her and threw things that broke. Sometimes... he hurt her a bit."

Tears poured out of Allie. This was too much for her, talking about her mom as she lay dead while her father got to live on. Probably happy about the whole thing too. Anger snuck in. Then it built to a rage. *It isn't fair!* she screamed to herself. She tensed her face and jaw as she thought about her father sitting in a jail cell, smiling and laughing. Her anger seemed wrong, but it also felt real. She looked away from the sheriff as she let her anger and rage take root.

"Did you ever see that happen?" he asked. "Did you ever see him hurt your mom?"

"No!" she yelled, her eyes now wide and piercing the sheriff's. "I hated what he always did to her! I didn't want to see it or hear it. I held my ears closed and prayed for it to stop."

At those words she hardened her heart toward her father. She didn't plan to, or even know how—it just happened. He took her mother from her, and with these questions he was taking her away all over again. She hated her father and now wished him dead.

James leaned to the sheriff. "What about Clay?" he whispered, as if keeping a secret from Allie.

"Allie, when was the last time you saw your uncle?"

"He was at the house yesterday."

"Does he visit often?"

Allie finally lost control. She fought to take a breath, then buried her face in her hands and screamed. "I don't know! I don't know! I don't know! I want to be done!"

Rose ran in and held Allie. "We're done, Sheriff. No more."

"Yes, I can see," he said, standing up. "Thank you, Allie. You were very helpful."

She ignored his words. Forcing her to talk about her mom felt cruel. She wished someone had shot her dad and they were talking about him being dead instead.

Allie sunk her face in the couch and cried as the sheriff,

James, and Rose walked to the front door. She knew they'd be talking about her, so she quieted herself and listened.

"What next for her, Sheriff?" Rose asked.

The sheriff sighed. "I've already sent telegraphs to San Francisco and Salt Lake. We need to get her out of here. We'll find a place where she'll be safe and taken care of."

"And her grandparents? Where are they? Won't they step in and help?" she asked.

"They won't help her. They'll be here for the funeral, though—nothing more."

"I'm not surprised. Taking her in would mean time away from themselves and their comfortable life on that damn train.... Sorry, Sheriff. I've just no patience for folks who put themselves first, especially above family. And Allie needs family, desperately so at this time. But they don't need her, and I guess that's that. Daniel didn't exist to them, and once they married, neither did Meg or Allie."

"We'll do all we can for her, Rose," the sheriff said.

He and James walked out the front door and to their horses for the ride back into town.

Allie finally relaxed. The menacing giants were gone, the questions that tore at her were done. Rose returned and sat on the couch alongside her and rubbed her back. Allie remembered the sheriff's words to Rose, about getting her out of here, out of Palisade.

Nobody wants me now, she thought. And at that the anger and rage at her father hardened.

*

At the front of Rose's house, the sheriff grabbed Gal's reins and started to mount, then stopped. He took in a breath and held it as he wrapped the reins hard and tight around his hand. He felt sick to his stomach but reminded himself that he was a lawman.

"You okay, Sheriff?" James asked.

"That was… difficult. I hurt for her. I hurt bad. Sorry to say that. As a lawman I shouldn't ever feel that way. It just felt wrong to be doing that to Allie. We forced her to experience her mother's death all over again. We shoulda known we wouldn't get much from her—coulda saved her from more pain."

"You're a lawman alright, but you're human too. Can't hide from those feelings if they're there."

"I been hidin' from feelings my whole life, James. Just keep shovin' 'em down. They're like ghosts, though. They stay hidden and act like they ain't around anymore, and then without warning they bust out and throw your life into turmoil. And they keep comin' at ya and comin' at ya and there ain't nothing you can do about 'em. This one will ride me right into the ground, I'm sure of it."

He looked up at James, who had already mounted. He knew what he was thinking, knew he was now worried about his boss.

"I'm okay, so don't ask," the sheriff said.

He loosened the reins he'd squeezed around his hand, then mounted without looking at James again.

"Let's get out to my place to talk about the notes," he said. "I'll see about talkin' to Daniel in the next couple of days, see what we can get out of him."

They turned and headed back through town and out to

the sheriff's place, a small spread far west and then north of town. Not another place within a few miles in any direction, and likely wouldn't ever be. He chose the location because nothing would dare grow that far out in the desert. The only thing that could grow out that way would need to be wild to survive.

As they rode through town, Palisade had settled to a quiet hum, typical of a Sunday evening. The last trains of the day had finished their runs in and out, and the stagecoaches had also ended their runs for the day. Saloons were still open, with only a few customers in each, thwarting the yelling and fighting, which also meant less gunfire to disturb the yelling and fighting. It was as if a traveling evangelist had ridden into Palisade and, with just a stroll through the streets, stolen its soul. Oil lamps glowed in the hotels and some of the shops, then in the homes as they edged farther out of town.

The two men, in no hurry, stuck to their own thoughts, the horses as quiet as their riders.

"What ya thinking, Sheriff?" James asked, finally breaking the silence.

"Just wondering why I took this damn job. I feel trapped here. I miss the freedom, roamin' a full territory, no jail or deputies to watch over and no one to watch over me. Gone for days without seein' no one. Huntin' for one outlaw, chasin' 'em from town to town. Then another and another. This here, this ain't fun. We got so much bad, we ignore half of it. And I gotta see people I know, friends, gettin' shot and killed. Out there I had no friends. No one to question your ways or motives or remind you of your past."

"You really don't need no one to talk to out there? No one to share a camp with?"

"Hell no. It was peaceful. Just me, Gal, and the stars. That's all the friends I had and all I needed."

"Sounds like a lonely life to me, Sheriff."

"I might have been alone, but sure as hell wasn't lonely. I call it freedom."

"Didn't miss family out there?"

The sheriff paused. He wondered how to respond to James without inviting more questions. "They got their own lives. Don't need me around."

"Can't imagine that, Sheriff. You're a good man. A good protector—good with a gun."

"They'd beg to differ," the sheriff said to himself.

"Why didn't you up for another marshal role? Plenty of territories out here could use you."

The sheriff didn't respond this time. He kicked Gal into a trot rest of the way home.

They led their horses to the barn and in the stillness of the evening brushed them down, then tossed some hay in their stalls, and walked to the cabin.

James again broke the quiet as they walked. "Did ya ever kill anyone out there, Sheriff? I ain't had to do that, so just wondering…"

The sheriff's heart sank at the question. "Yeah, got my share," he said. "Not proud of a one of them."

He looked over at James to read him, to determine how safe it was to continue talking. In his mind it never was safe, but he checked anyway. He didn't want to have this conversation. He'd prefer to keep it buried than give it light. This was the point where he usually shut down, shut the other person out. James gave him pause because he was a good kid. He would never judge his boss, never use information against him, never betray him. James was simply somewhere between making small talk and looking to learn as much as he could from an experienced lawman, maybe better understand what he'd be facing in twenty years. The sheriff desperately wanted to see himself in James in that moment, some twenty-odd years earlier as a young lawman, but he couldn't. It wasn't there. James had a good upbringing and it showed in how he handled people and handled difficult situations—almost always with patience and grace. He could be rough when needed, maybe too rough, but that was the raw lawman in him. The sheriff had a different upbringing. The kind of home where no one set an example of a good relationship, how to communicate, how to handle problems. The relationships he experienced were sloshed together with a bottle, words only spoken when liquor pushed them out in anger, and problems only handled—manhandled—when drunk and out of control. To the sheriff, James was light and free; he, on the other hand, was weighed down by a lifetime of anger and guilt and shame layered thick as tar over his body. And those layers peeled off slowly at best, if ever. The sheriff could tell that James was loved; he himself was left wanting.

He stopped his look on James and turned away, peering deep into the dark of the night, and then spoke again. "Sometimes ya just wanna end it, not hassle with dragging the scum back in. Just put 'em down and let those damn bullets do what a jury would do anyway. And you want the trigger and bullet to take your anger with 'em, rip it from you and bury it deep inside the evil cuffed in front of you. But they don't. It's still there, still with you. All the bad you saw, all the bad you did. You just gotta live with it."

The sheriff looked back at James, who now showed a worried look for his boss.

"Let's get inside," James said. "It's startin' to turn cool."

Inside the cabin the sheriff walked to the kitchen and opened a cabinet. He pulled down a bottle of bourbon, only a swig or two left. He grabbed a coffee mug, the bottom stained black from a month's worth of coffee without a wash. He twisted and squeaked the cork out and emptied the last few drops into the mug, then tossed his head back and threw the shot down all in a single motion. He took the burn in and slammed the mug on the counter. He pulled down another bottle, that one near empty as well, and filled his mug half-full. He pointed the bottle at James.

"No thanks. Too much heat for me."

The sheriff pulled out a chair from the table and sat, then pointed at the other chair across from him.

James sat and crossed his arms onto the table. "Are we going to let Clay go?" he asked.

The sheriff slid back in his chair. "I don't want to, but damn... we'll have to. I'll let the cockroaches bite at him a couple more days, then... yeah, we'll let him go. We'll need him here for the trial, though, so let's keep him close by and outta trouble. The boy can't sit still for five seconds till he's jawin' it up with someone and they drag each other into the street, fightin'. He'll be like a hurt donkey to us, a damn jackass we'll have to keep watch over. Like we ain't got anything better to do. A county fulla fightin' and killin' and stealin'. Hell, Palisade had the first train robbery this far west. And now me with just two deputies—one still with his momma's breast milk leaking down his chin—workin' our tails off to keep the peace."

"Jeb's a good kid, Sheriff. Besides, he's tryin'."

"I'd put chances on that pile of horse droppings out back making a good lawman before that boy does."

James paused, wanting to defend his partner, but preferred to focus on their work. "We should be on the killing, Sheriff."

He poured what was left of his drink into his mouth, then banged the cup onto the table. "Okay, what ya got?"

James hesitated, taking in the man he hadn't seen before. He'd worked with the sheriff for nearly two years now and been by the sheriff's house, but never in it. The sheriff was a man who held his cards tight to his chest. Everyone knew he'd been a good marshal, that he could pick a gnat off a bull's ear with his rifle from the next town and could spot an outlaw just from the way he walked. But people never knew what he was thinking, or whether he was pleased or pissed at them. And everyone knew he was trying to become a good sheriff, but so far, the outlaws were winning the hand.

The sheriff could see James thinking about him—he was certainly now wondering what kind of man his boss was. James looked down and opened his notebook, then he glanced over at the coffeepot on the stove. The sheriff hesitated. With the cabin already baking in the July heat, he wasn't sure adding to it would be a good idea. But he wanted James to feel comfortable, so he walked over and tossed some kindling into the firebox, then picked up a match and ripped it against the stove. He peeked into the box and carefully lit the wood. He filled the pot with water and set it on the stove.

"Water'll take a few minutes to heat up," he said.

"Yep," James said. "I'll go over what we already know, and then anything new you'll want to hear. So Meg got just one bullet plugged through her chest. Hit her heart near square on. It come out the back, hit the cabinet door behind her, and stuck there. You found a .45 Peacemaker on the floor in the kitchen, and Doc said the hole looked like a .45 to him. He'll find out for sure once we dig it out of the cabinet. I'll go back tomorrow and look for the bullet."

"It'll be a .45," the sheriff said.

James smiled at his confidence. "Doc also said he didn't see any bruises on her face, no sign of being hurt or beat up, least the parts he could see easily. He'll strip her down tomorrow and look more closely."

The sheriff walked to the kitchen and poured himself another drink, set the bottle on the table, then checked the water. "Keep going," he said.

"When you were outside with Allie this morning, Clay asked Daniel if that was his gun that you found on the floor, kind of cocky-like."

The sheriff sat back down. "What'd Daniel say?"

"Nothin'. He just looked over at Clay like he wanted to kill him."

"That would've saved us some trouble."

James gave a small smile, then went on, "So that was Daniel's .45 on the floor. Even he ain't denying that. And it'd definitely been fired recently because of the fresh powder on it."

"That's good to hear. Should turn out to be the weapon."

"Yeah, most likely, Sheriff."

"Anything else?"

"Daniel and Meg were the only ones in the house. No one saw anyone else go in or come out. You were the first one in after Clay ran out. You saw the back door open, so maybe someone ran out the back, or could be it was her or Daniel left it open."

"Yeah, hard to say."

"The chambers in the gun were empty except for one. The box of cartridges on the table was empty, with a dozen or so on the floor around the table."

"One into Meg and one in the revolver. What do ya make of that, James?"

"Well, I guess Daniel maybe—"

The sheriff banged his cup a couple times on the table to get James's attention, then raised his eyebrows at him. "We ain't proved it's Daniel... yet."

"Oh, sorry. So... the killer maybe only had time to load two rounds, or maybe felt they just needed one or two."

"In a hurry, cocky, or too damn drunk to get more than two in. I reckon it could've happened any which way."

"I'm leaning toward too drunk," James said.

The sheriff stared into his cup, then looked up at his deputy. "But if someone else did it, not Daniel, why not use their own gun, loaded and ready to go? Leave with it, even? Seems silly and a waste of time to walk in, hunt for a gun, dump the box, chamber two cartridges, then pull the trigger, drop the gun, and run out."

"Yeah… silly," James said.

The kettle whistled softly, then quickly rose to a long scream, breaking into the conversation.

"I'll get it," James said.

He walked to the counter and grabbed two cups, looked inside them, then shook his head. He thought about rinsing his but didn't want to embarrass his boss. He filled the two cups and carried one, thick and black, to the sheriff. He added a little sugar to his to cut into the bitter. The sheriff topped his off with a good pour of the bourbon.

James stood at the counter stirring his coffee. "What if the killer knew where everything was already, like Daniel, or someone else set it out beforehand, ready to go?" he asked.

"Lots of possibilities, I suppose. It all points to Daniel, but yet it doesn't."

"And he said he didn't do it," James reminded the sheriff.

"Yeah, but he's lookin' at a hangin' if he did it, so could be just trying to save his neck."

The men finished their conversation and drinks, then James headed to the door, back to the jailhouse to relieve Jeb.

"Tell Jeb to get home and get some sleep," the sheriff said. "And if he's in the jail cell and the Lind boys are gone, well, just promise you'll come back here and shoot me."

James laughed. "You can count on me to help you out, Sheriff."

6

A PAIR OF GRAVEDIGGERS sat on the back of Eli's wagon out of earshot, hands and chins atop their shovel handles, sweat pouring from them after working the hard ground in the heat of the day, setting Meg down in, and hammering the wood marker into its place. They sipped from their canteens and waited for the order to put back what they had just dug up.

Palisade, a long spread of graying wood buildings a quarter mile back to the south, was silenced more by the distance than by its loss. Meg's coffin sat deep in the earth already, as if dropped from a good height and crashed into the ground, dirt exploding out and around and onto the edges of the hole. She lay cramped tight inside the box of fresh-cut pine, its warm scent soaking into the soil around it, nature reuniting with nature.

The preacher stood at the foot of the grave, his Bible open and resting in his hands. Gentle cries and sniffles from the gathering intruded his message. Allie stood on one side of the grave, wrapped in Rose Marten's arms; Allie's grandparents stood alongside her, but distant, far from close by, seemingly already back on the train headed out and away from their granddaughter.

Esther Jorgensen, Doc, and the sheriff also stood among the dozen or so mourners, across from Allie.

As the preacher continued with his words of comfort, Esther leaned toward the two men and whispered, "Meg's parents don't care a thing about her." She stared down the parents across the grave from her. "Maybe when she was younger, but not since she married that man."

Doc gave a small nod. "I know. It seems when your pocketbook grows, your heart shrinks. Money don't leave enough room for family."

Esther frowned. "They're burying their only child and not even taking the time for a visit with Allie, just back on their train outta town. Seems they're no better than the man that shot their daughter."

The sheriff shifted his look and thoughts away from the whispers and over to Allie. No matter what else took his attention, he always returned to her. He knew this moment would be surreal for her. She looked disconnected from the service, even from herself and the world. He wondered where her mind was—on her mother when she was alive and happy, or lying in the ground quiet and still, or maybe on her father sitting in a jail cell back in town. He watched her tears fall, light yet steady. Not enough to wipe away. He had seen her earlier, before the service, as she first approached the grave. He heard her cries and screams for her mother. That was likely her world the last few days: an uninterrupted ebb and flow of uncontrollable emotions.

A warm breeze blew in and through the gathering. The sheriff watched as the wind quietly and softly tossed women's hair and dresses about. He wondered if maybe Meg herself was walking through and touching and comforting the mourners, letting them know that she was home and safe. He looked at Allie again, hoping she had felt her mother's final touch.

"Amen and amen," the preacher said, concluding Meg Lind's service, ending her life, and beginning Allie's new one.

The mourners broke away. The sheriff watched as each person moved to the grave and one by one reached to the pile of dirt and dropped a handful onto the box below. Each handful thumped and gently burst out over the casket. The wood darkened. One by one they walked past and then away from Meg, back to town, back to life in Palisade. A few stood and gazed—in hurt, in sadness, in bewilderment—at Allie and shook their heads, then quietly walked away themselves. The diggers returned to finish what the few handfuls of dirt had barely started. They finished alone.

The sheriff started to walk over to Allie and Rose when the grandmother, Clara Franks, cut him off.

"We so much appreciate that you've taken Allie in, Rose. If we were here, we certainly would have done so ourselves."

"I'm sure you would have," Rose said, showing no attempt to conceal her doubt.

Clara seemed not to notice, or simply ignored the comment as she went on, "Walter has an important meeting in San Francisco in a couple days. We would take Allie with us, but there's really no room in the coach for her. And she would be bored on such a long ride."

Rose's anger grew. "Mrs. Franks, she's your own blood. How can you leave her behind?"

"I just said, we don't have the room. And we're busy."

No longer able to stand by and listen, the sheriff jumped into the conversation. "There must be a school Frisco you could take her to. A couple days' ride surely wouldn't be too much bother for you and your husband."

"It's just not possible," Clara countered, then reached into a small purse she carried. "Here," she said, handing some money to Rose. "Take this for your trouble."

The sheriff stared at Clara Franks, angry and grieved at the same time. Allie would be better off with anyone other than her grandparents, he decided. *Even with her father.*

"She doesn't need your money," Rose shot back. "She needs your love and attention… and a place to call home."

"Take the money," Clara demanded. "We'll send for Allie if we find a suitable place for her."

"She's Daniel's," Rose said. "Is that why you don't want her?"

Clara's eyes went dark; her lips pressed into a tight line. "He killed our daughter…. We loved her. It should be him in that box, not Meg."

"Allie is your granddaughter!" Rose said, making no attempt to control her anger. "Can't you look past him and to her needs instead of your own? Maybe see in your heart what Meg would have wanted for her?"

Clara grabbed Rose's hand and jerked it to her. She shoved in the wad of bills and curled Rose's fingers tight around it. Then, without another word, she took her husband's arm and hurried them back up the trail toward town and the train station.

The sheriff watched Rose standing there in disbelief as Allie's grandparents marched away.

"We'll find a place for her, don't worry, Rose," the sheriff said.

Rose turned to Allie, gave her a hug, then took her hand and they headed up the same path to town and home. Esther nodded good-bye to the sheriff, then worked her way up the trail to join Rose and Allie.

"Sure is a sad situation, Sheriff," Doc said, easing up from behind him.

"Yep," he said softly as Meg and Allie and Daniel twisted together in his mind. He couldn't find the words to continue the conversation. So they stood in quiet, but not at peace.

"You okay, Sheriff?" Doc finally asked.

"Okay as I can be."

"Aren't we all at times like these? Seems like Allie died right along with her momma. Poor thing."

The sheriff tried shoving the emotions of the moment away and shifting to the facts of the case, but the thought of Allie dead invited in memories of Savery Creek once again. He saw her lying there, not moving—the image fresh once again.

"You sure you're okay, Sheriff? Never seen you red-eyed before."

He didn't respond.

"Sheriff?... *Sheriff!*"

"Yeah... yeah. Sorry," he said, slowly drifting back to the conversation.

"What's on your mind? You look distracted."

"Just remembering back on something; tryin' not to at the same time."

"Thinking back on what?"

He hesitated. "What did you learn about Meg in the postmortem?" the sheriff asked, abruptly shifting the conversation. He knew most of the details already—some by observation, some by witness, others by instinct.

They headed over to the trail and toward town, breaking free from the sound and rhythm of the shoveling behind them, but never into the quiet. The stab and lift and dump of each load of dirt faded more slowly than they liked.

"The round that went through Meg was definitely a .45-caliber," Doc finally said.

"Yep," the sheriff responded flatly, looking forward, giving Doc permission to continue.

"And nothing to say it didn't come from Daniel's revolver either."

"No surprise there."

"No. Guess not."

The men went silent again as they continued their walk. Nearing Palisade, the noise of the town finally buried the digging. They stopped and stood just beyond the backside of the first line of buildings. Doc stuck his hands in his pockets and looked away, toward town. The sheriff set his hands on his hips and looked in the opposite direction, toward the cemetery, nearly hoping for the quiet that Meg now knew.

"Her arms were scraped and bruised, Sheriff. Pretty bad. Deep cuts. They were still fresh, but not fresh enough to be from that morning… so from the day before, most likely in the evening."

"Damn," the sheriff said to himself, still looking away. "Any other signs of injury or attack?"

"No, no other injuries beyond the arms. She wasn't sexually assaulted, if that's what you want to know."

"Yeah, that's it. So someone got physical with her the night before. Maybe tried something and stopped."

"Or got scared off."

"Or fell asleep drunk."

"Sheriff, it doesn't make sense that Daniel would do this. He's not a good man, no disagreement there, but a killer? I don't think he has it in him. He's a thief. A brute even—"

"But not a killer. That may be true. I need to keep that option open, though. No tellin' what a drunk man might do. Won't be the first time a drunk killed a woman, and unfortunately sure as hell won't be the last."

Doc looked back to Meg and nodded. "You're a good lawman, Sheriff. You'll piece it together and try the right man. I'll be ready to give my witness to the facts, you can count on that."

"Thanks, Doc," he said, turning his look to the ground, allowing himself to concentrate on the facts and events and timeline of the last few days. He knew he was a good lawman. *But good still lets people down, even those closest to you*—he knew that just as well. Most days "good" was enough. *But it takes just one day, one moment, one mistake, and an innocent life ends.*

"You know, Sheriff. You and I arrived about the same time a few years back. We've seen a lot of dying. Every one of them came through me, each of those bodies. I held them all. I tallied them. Noted their name and age and cause of death. Palisade's got this reputation as a wild place in the west, with a thousand ways of dying. But most succumb to disease or accident or even old age. Quite a few hit by a train, kicked by a mule, or killed themselves by the simple act of cleaning their gun a little too carelessly. But those stories don't make for lively reputations or entertaining adventure books, especially for people back east."

"You got a point, Doc?" the sheriff asked abruptly.

"Yeah. You've done good to keep so many alive in such harsh surroundings. The ones getting killed, they ain't your fault."

The sheriff looked hard at Doc. He felt the anger rise up in him and couldn't hold it back. "And what about the ones that are my fault, Doc? What the hell do you tell those families?"

He saw Doc's shocked look at his words and emotion, but instead of apologizing he simply turned and walked away.

The sheriff knew what was happening. He was losing control again. He needed to get to the jail for a drink. He kept to the back of the buildings and town as he walked— less chance of running into another unwanted conversation. He watched a man appear around the corner of a livery a block ahead from him. The man stopped and leaned casually against the building. Clay Lind. He stood expressionless. Definitely not sad. No apparent hurt for Meg or Allie. *Maybe void of emotion altogether,* the sheriff thought. *Or maybe self-satisfied.* Difficult to tell from a distance, or up close for that matter, given that he was a Lind.

Clay noticed him and called out, "Thanks for lettin' me out of jail, Sheriff. You're a good man. Got out just in time for the funeral."

"I didn't see you up there. Afraid to stand with your niece?"

"I was right here. Saw the whole thing. They all know Daniel did it, but they won't put no effort into separating me from him. So best leave them alone to their grievin'."

The sheriff tightened the distance between them to a few feet. His hands at his sides, open, relaxed, set to pull out his revolver. Clay caught the threat but kept his ground. They studied and measured each other.

"You want something from me, Sheriff?"

"You know what I want: the truth."

"I ain't got no truth, but that I didn't do it. That'll be all you get from me."

The sheriff studied him longer. Without expression he challenged Clay's words. He waited for his tell. *No different than sitting opposite a gambler at a poker table—not yet knowing whether he's bluffing, cheating, or playing it straight up.* But most every man had a weakness that gave them away—a tell. If you showed yourself patient, waited them out, played it slow, they would eventually give it up. Clay was a good player, though. His body quiet. Hands steady. Eyes sober. He gave nothing away. No movement. No tells.

"Thought maybe you was walkin' over here to take me in again, or maybe rough me up for no good reason," Clay said.

"The thought's crossin' my mind."

The two men stood and held a quiet stare, both relaxed yet braced enough to act if needed. Neither showed that the other bothered them, nor that the sun scorched their faces, nor that the sweat burned in their eyes.

"You an innocent man, huh?" the sheriff said. "And you don't know nothin' more than that."

"I saw Daniel with a gun and standin' over Meg. That enough for you?"

"Nothin' more?"

"Nope. Can I go now, or you got somethin' else you're dyin' to ask me?"

The sheriff eased his hands and stance. He could see that Clay had no intention of making a sudden move.

"You stay in Palisade, got that?" the sheriff said.

"I'll be here. But when the trial's done, I'll be headin' out and won't be back. You ain't never gonna see me again, Sheriff."

"Going straight's not your way, Clay, so I'm certain I'll see you again. You just better hope I'm in a good mood."

"When you find a good mood, let me know. In the meantime, I'll be in the Bull's Head drinking one for my brother. Stop by if you need any more help doin' your job." Clay smirked and then turned and headed up between the buildings toward the saloon.

The sheriff watched, then followed. Once he reached the center of town, he caught sight of Clay standing in the middle of Main Street, his eyes fixed on the front of the Palisade Hotel. The sheriff moved closer and saw a man standing on the steps under the crooked balcony, looking back at Clay. The man's face shrieked at the sheriff: cut up, grim, violent. Like he'd been to hell and got kicked for bad behavior. Only one man dragged around that look and disposition—Emmett

Keen. Palisade held a reasonable tang of mean and harsh and evil. This man carried it all. And then some.

The sheriff looked on as Keen pulled down his black hat and shadowed his face. Then he stuck the stub of a thin cigar into one side of his mouth and chewed it over to the other, sucked a smoke in, and puffed it out. He tipped his hat to Clay, then finished the steps down to the street, spurs clinking hard, stabbing into the noise of Palisade. Clay watched Keen. The sheriff watched them both. Keen angled himself toward Clay and crossed the street right where he stood, bumping his shoulder as he passed. Without a word or look, the cut-up man walked over and into the Iron Rail Saloon. Clay gave up on the Bull's Head and followed Keen in. The sheriff hesitated for a moment, then continued on to the jailhouse, but not giving up his senses about the two men.

*

As long as it took for the mourners to head out and back for Meg's burial, Daniel held himself on the cot of his jail cell, leaning back against the rock wall, the small window above him unable to frame the scene just north of town. He played the funeral in his head. He stood there, away from the others, but close. Moving from hymn to hymn, ending with "Amazing Grace." They quieted. The preacher spoke, his words clear and forceful: *"An eye for an eye,"* echoed in Daniel's head.

He saw himself look down into the hole and into the casket. He saw Meg pounding and screaming inside, struggling hard to take in a breath, to move her arms. Struggling for life. The air above teased her as she lay drowning deep inside the dark, airless box, the dirt piled heavy on top. Unable to free herself, to escape. Unable to reclaim her life. She surrendered. The pounding stopped, then the screams for help, then the struggle for a breath. For life. It all stopped. Daniel's mind shifted to Meg sitting on the kitchen floor. The hole still bleeding. Her eyes shot open. They gripped him. He saw her regret, for anything and everything about him. She sat there, hating her life, her choices. Him. He saw Allie kneel down beside her, praying and wishing for him to be the one shot and shoveled deep into the ground, dirt packed high and thick and heavy on him. Her mother above. Beside her. Free. Free from death and free from him.

The sheriff walked into the jailhouse. The bang of the door brought Daniel back to the present. James remained seated at his desk, but Jeb jumped up and stood innocently at attention.

"Nothin' happening, Sheriff," Jeb said. "The prisoners have all been quiet, except the drunk that James brought in last night. He can't seem to settle down."

Daniel had watched James drag in those two men the night before; they sat in the cell next to his. One was a drunk who had been unloading his revolver in the air at the center of town, and the other a passenger on the stagecoach from Salt Lake. After the stage left Carlin, he'd taken a shot at a group of Shoshone from inside the coach. "Open season!" he yelled before firing the shot. Two other men on the ride fought him down and wrestled the gun away, then bound him with rope and strapped him to the top of the coach and kept him there until they arrived in Palisade.

Without provocation the drunk now started singing a

bar song. The man who'd shot at the Shoshone kicked him. The drunk didn't stop, so the man kicked him again. The sheriff told James to get them separated and Jeb to get them some hot coffee, especially the drunk.

The sheriff caught Daniel's look. "Yeah, get the Lind boy some too."

"Sheriff," James said after getting the prisoners separated, "we got word from Frisco that there's a school for girls there. They take in young ones who got nowhere else to go. They're usually full up but have an opening."

Daniel stood and leaned into the cage door, listening.

"Good to hear," the sheriff said. "Let's see if they'll take Allie. We'll do our best begging."

"I already let them know we'd like to get her signed up," James said. "They're workin' on it and will send a message back when they know."

The sheriff paused for a moment, then said, "If she gets in, we'll need someone to ride her there, make sure she gets settled in. Let's see if Esther or Rose would be willin' to do that."

"I don't think Rose would. Her family's got enough work on their hands already with the kids and farm."

The sheriff sighed and shook his head. "Not many options past them. Talk with 'em both anyway. They'll at least be happy to know we're doin' what we can."

A mix of sadness and relief spun up in Daniel. He knew he was never a good father to Allie, but it never meant he didn't care. Her first couple of years were actually decent. He and Meg were happy. He didn't hurt her in those days. He would eventually steal that happiness, though. It hurt to think about, but he knew it was true and took it in. Allie wouldn't remember those early years, that they were good. Her memories would always reflect the bad he'd brought home every night afterward, at least the nights he cared to come home. Meg had done all of the raising, which was probably best anyway, he reasoned. No telling how Allie would have turned out if he'd done the raising. *Likely not good,* he decided. Maybe just another two-bit, wanna-be-outlaw thief like him.

His last sight of Allie had been the afternoon before Meg died. The three of them ate dinner together, and when he'd finished, he walked out the front door to go drinking with Clay, leaving Meg and Allie sitting at the table without so much as a good-bye or any sort of acknowledgement that they even existed. He knew they didn't think much of it, not after watching it happen for so many years. It was who he was and the man they knew. He tried to remember what Allie was wearing that evening but couldn't. A dress for certain, but not sure which one or even the color. Or whether she'd had her hair down or pulled back in a ponytail.

His heart weighed heavy; he felt sick. The last time he'd seen Allie he didn't even see her. And now it was too late to ever see her again. She'd be off to San Francisco starting over, doing all she could to forget him. And he'd be doing all he could to remember the color of her dress.

"Hey, Sheriff," Daniel said softly. "Is she going to get in that school?"

The sheriff turned to Daniel. It was the first time he'd spoken on his own without being prompted. He didn't deserve an answer, and Daniel certainly knew that. He didn't even deserve a response.

The sheriff walked to the cell and looked him over. Daniel showed sincerity, care for his daughter, not the mockery or selfishness the sheriff might have expected.

"Fishin' for some leniency, or just startin' to care now? A bit late for either, don't ya think?"

"Will she get in? Have a chance at a life I ain't never known? One that I couldn't give her? Give me something to live for, knowin' Allie is out of here and away from me and this town."

"Regret don't taste too good, does it, tough guy? I've swallowed my share. Never sittin' in a jail cell, though, but out where I have a lick of a chance of fixing what I did wrong."

"I ain't askin' but one favor, Sheriff—get Allie to that school. Nothing more. Just give her a life."

The sheriff studied the man in front of him. Was this his heart talking or his neck—was he trying to save Allie or himself? Daniel held his stare. The jailhouse fell quiet. Even the drunk sat back and let the sheriff work. The sheriff absorbed Daniel's words, read his face and hands and the way he was standing and the way he held his head. Then read his eyes.

Daniel swallowed hard. Not out of worry for himself but out of hope for his daughter. He breathed in deep and held it. Then out. He began to surrender. Like a mustang showing its first hint of breaking, yielding the wild bred into it, from in control of their own destiny to relinquishing that control, giving up the will they believed kept them alive. Mustangs would break because they were led there, led to a safe place by someone they learned to trust. Daniel now revealed his own hint of breaking, accepting that he was no longer in control of his own life, of Meg's, of Allie's—of anyone's. He never helped Allie, and now couldn't even repair a life he'd broken. He didn't want to trust the sheriff, but in that moment, he had no choice. His life was no longer about his own freedom and survival, but about Allie's.

"Yeah. We'll get her there, or somewhere," the sheriff said, surrendering a bit himself. "She deserves it. She needs a chance at a life. You failed at it yourself. And you failed her. I'll get her there."

The sheriff started to move back to James, then stopped. Daniel could see that he wasn't finished with their conversation. The sheriff shook his head. He lingered at the cell. He bit his lip, then let out a deep sigh. Daniel could see that he was working to fight off a thought.

"I'll make sure Allie knows you wanted this for her," he finally said to Daniel, showing his frustration at letting his human side one-up the lawman in him. "And I'll take her there myself."

7

CLAY SHOVED OPEN the doors and stepped inside the Iron Rail Saloon. His thirst wasn't for a drink anymore, but for Keen. He pulled out his side piece and checked it, full and hot. A man staggered up and into him. Whiskey and beer poured from the man's breath and spilled over the younger Lind. He grabbed the man's momentum and pushed him rest of the way onto the boardwalk. The doors banged back and forth to a stop as the man stumbled across the walk and down the stairs and hard onto the dirt street below. Without concern Clay rejoined the disorder of the saloon. He looked over the room—front to back, left to right, right to left, then front to back again. He wanted Keen out of Palisade—the man only ever brought trouble, but then that was always the case with Keen. With Meg shot dead and Daniel in jail, a man like Keen would only make the situation worse. Clay could see there was standing room only—the saloon full up of drunks, gamblers, drifters, miners, cowboys, outlaws, and at least as many wannabes of each. Some honest, most not. Men stood thick around the bar and card tables and piano, a cattle car packed tight with steer just loaded up from a muddy, smelly corral. No room for even another lit cigar. Four card tables ran the width of the back wall, each filled with players in chairs and crowded by others encircling them. The ripping and shuffling of cards and clinking of chips steadily broke into the roar of shouting and talking and laughing that soaked the saloon. Several dance hall women weaved their way through and among the crowd, keeping themselves in tips, the bar in cash, and the men in smiles. The spectacle of the Iron Rail—the epitome of every other saloon littered across the west, each as dirty and vulgar as the best of their clientele. Saturday evenings particularly hauled in the finest of the county's debauched and out-of-towners fancying to get punched in the face by the legend of Palisade.

Clay looked again up and down the line of thirsty men at the bar. He stopped his search at the far end. He forced his way through the crowd, bumping and pushing his way toward the man he eyed. He was determined and aggravated. And growing more so with each step.

He stopped behind Keen.

Clay always thought the man was the most repulsive thing he'd ever seen. His face carved up from a fight years earlier. Keen won, but his face lost, and so did anyone who had the misfortune of having to look at him. Two long knife scars were etched deep in his face. One from above his right eye down through both lips and chin; the other from above his left eye down through his left cheek. The skin of both cuts splayed open still. Only his deep-set eyes had saved his sight. His nose bent left from another fight, and his skin dark and leathered from hiding in the scorching deserts of the southwest. His bony frame matched the gaunt look of his face. A scarred skeleton of a man, with a thin layer of skin to give him the semblance of being human.

Clay pressed hard into the man. "Look, dammit. I spent a week puttin' up with that sheriff harassin' me in that smelly jail cell. I didn't kill that woman, but everybody's lookin' at me like I did. I can't leave town or he'll toss me back in. Now I gotta put up with you?"

Keen kept his lean onto the bar and ignored Clay. He pointed to his shot glass and nodded at the bartender for another.

"Just leave the bottle," Keen said. "I'll be here for a long while."

Clay pushed in again, harder and closer, his mouth nearly touching Keen's ear. "You grow deaf since I last seen you? Or did your ears get cut up like your face?"

The man slowly leaned back and turned to Clay. "Howdy, friend. Buy you a drink?" His breath steamed the already hot air around them.

Clay burned hotter.

Keen just smirked. "You got nerves eatin' at ya, don'cha, Clay? Sounds like you're feelin' awfully guilty about somethin'. Maybe that's why the sheriff's lookin' at you."

"Get the hell outta this town, outta this county, Keen. Hell, go the full way and leave Nevada too. You ain't welcome here no more."

"I'm just passin' through. Best whiskey I ever tasted right here in this saloon. Thought I'd remind myself of it."

"Finish the drink and ride out."

"I was thinkin' maybe of stayin' here a spell, pick up a

little work. You don't mind, do ya? Maybe we can team up again like all those times before."

Clay stared hard at the man. He lowered his hand onto Keen's revolver and in one motion set his thumb on the hammer, wrapped the grip, and slid his finger onto the trigger. He slowly drew the hammer back. Click… click… click… pausing a long second between each measured pull. The man didn't move. He kept one hand on the bar, the other on his drink, and his look forward. The saloon hummed on, the discreet action of the two men at the end of the bar concealed deep within its chaos.

Clay paused. His sweaty hand still gripped Keen's revolver. He'd never shot a man; that wasn't his style or nature. He understood that he and his brother lived in no-man's-land, hanging somewhere between outlaw and cowboy, but never enough of either to stick there. They had the morals to match any outlaw that ever lived, but never anything big or grand. They were two-bit thieves at best. And cowboys—real cowboys—were good and decent. They worked hard. Worked honest. They had standards and held each other accountable. A real cowboy would be insulted by the presence of the Lind brothers, no matter their ability to ride or lasso or tame a horse. They broke cowboy code by simple effort of being born, and on regular occasion after that. Clay once broke the code of taking another man's woman. And then his horse. On the same night no less. Either would get you shot. Touching a man's revolver—now that would get you slit open by a boot knife. And then shot.

Clay knew Keen was an outlaw. He passed the test. He told the brothers that he'd killed men in every state and territory west of Missouri, and in most states east. Killed women only when called for. No need to kill a child; none yet that he'd seen anyway. Keen cared about himself and his survival, nothing more. He figured that was every other man's mind-set too, so normal was normal. When he was young, before he'd seen any other death, he watched his father die a slow, painful death of cholera after returning from the war. Keen lived to not die that same slow, painful death, and that meant ensuring the other guy died—always. And fast or slow, it didn't much matter either way to him. Dead was dead.

Clay whispered into Keen's ear, "Go ahead, do it. Go for your knife. I got a round set for you already. You'll get your hand to it just long enough for me to claim you went first."

He waited. Keen didn't move.

"Now you just stay still, finish your drink, and walk out."

The man lifted his drink, tilted his head back, and slowly trickled it into his mouth and onto his tongue. His swallow was even slower, like he wanted to taste every grain of rye all the way back to the field. He shut and rested his eyes, then let out his breath from the drink. Satisfied.

"Yeah. I know," Clay said. "We done some bad things together, the three of us. But you put men in their grave, that's somethin' Daniel and I never done."

Laughing, Keen grabbed the bottle and poured another drink.

Clay jammed the revolver into Keen's hip. "You finished your drink, now—"

Before Clay could finish his sentence, Keen elbowed him hard in the chest, then pushed him to the floor. He casually leaned and stole his gun back, easing the hammer closed.

The men around them jumped back and went quiet and waited. After a few seconds, Keen rolled out a smile, even as the evil held steadfast in his eyes. Clay didn't want trouble either. He allowed himself to relax, then smiled himself and stood up. "My friend and I are just havin' some fun catchin' up," he said. They patted each other on the back, turned to the bar, and waited for the hum and chaos of the saloon to settle back in.

"You guilty, Clay, right along with me, even if I was the one always pullin' the trigger. You caught up in every one of 'em too."

"You always was slow, Keen. Slow to talk, slow to drink, and slow to leave a town. And when your time comes, I suspect you're gonna die slow too."

Keen snickered. "I'm fast at one thing, and it's kept me alive. You wanna go at it with me? Wanna see how fast I am from the front end of a bullet?"

Clay reached down and set his hand on his own gun. "I don't want you around here shootin' off your mouth about them things. I'm a free man and I aim to stay that way. Now you can leave here alive or stay here dead, don't matter much to me."

Keen didn't flinch. Confidence covered him; evil more so.

"I got the upper hand on you," Keen said. "I always have. Always will." He cocked his lip up and grinned at Clay, holding the look until Clay blinked and looked away.

"Just leave," Clay said flatly, finally taking his hand off of his gun.

The man drank the shot he'd poured earlier and again refilled his glass. He set the bottle down and pushed it away, then reached in his pocket, grabbed all of the change he had, and threw it on the bar. The coins clinked against the bottle and spun to a stop. He took hold of the final drink and threw it into Clay's face. Then Keen paused, glanced a final warning, and strolled to the door and out into the town.

Clay fisted his hands and held tight the rage he felt rising up. He wanted to shoot the man down as he walked out, square in the back. He'd never had the desire to kill another man; now the desire set in hard.

*

Back at the jailhouse Daniel sat quiet in his cell, unconcerned about what might happen to him. His thoughts drifted. The many chances he'd had to go straight wandered in and out of his mind. Deliberate decisions that kept him mean and filled with bad—bad choices and bad actions. Regrets entered. *Nothing to do about them now.* Meg did all she could for him. He did little for her or Allie. He looked down at the floor. The grain and smell of the wood pulled him back to a moment with Meg in their first year together.

The smell of the pine drifted slowly with them as they rode together on Daniel's horse into the Ruby Mountains, far east of Palisade—an oasis of green and beauty among the brown and parched earth that covered most of northern Nevada—to Liberty Lake. The only ride outside of Palisade they ever made together. A picnic she had planned, and he had rejected. Multiple times. She pushed on and he soon relented, mostly just wanting to get it done and over with and on with his life.

They were in no hurry. The first time he could remember not being in a hurry to get somewhere, anywhere, or get away from someone or a town. He used this time to plan his next trip out with Clay, thinking through the details even as Meg held tight behind him. He couldn't help but carry with him a sense that someone was tracking them—every few minutes looking left and right and behind, knowing for certain no one was there but still feeling anxious all the same.

The ride there and back would take from sunup to sundown. Most of the way would be across desert with its acres of low sage and bitterbrush. In the Rubies they would be among a mix of pines and junipers and golden aspens. He felt Meg holding tight to him the full way there and back, resting her head against him much of the time. He felt her comfort in him, even her trust, something he'd never known. No one had ever dared venture this close to Daniel Lind. He knew she desired to escape her parents, and that forced her to push hard into him. She had told him he was more than just an escape, though. He was handsome, when clean and shaven, and he had a heart of gold, when he allowed it to show. "Let the world see your heart, Daniel," she would tell him in those early years. But over time he buried the good in him deeper and deeper.

He'd ridden among the mountain peaks and trees of the Rubies many times but had never seen any of it. They were there, but he didn't notice. The place was functional to him— not a place to enjoy, but a place to hide. Meg brought them to life.

The shoes of the horse steeled and clicked on the rocks and pebbles, twigs snapped, and the sand and dirt crunched— a rhythm of sound that broke the tedium of quiet between Daniel and Meg. Once they arrived at the lake, Daniel stopped and helped Meg down. He knelt and filled the canteen with cool water, and she drank.

Daniel sat on the bank and watched Meg walk along the lake and in and out of the trees that lined the edge. The sun's rays flowed down and across the water and glistened around her. Everything seemed soft and gentle and bright, unlike the desert they'd just ridden through, hardened and raw and dark. Untamable. One out of place with the other, but yet entangled as one.

They sat for a while together and stared at the glassy stillness of the water. Before long, trout began hitting the surface, rippling the glass. Robins and juncos swooped in, chasing bugs and playing at the lake's edge.

After their meal Meg took an apple from the saddlebag and washed it in the water. He couldn't remember the last time he'd eaten an apple, at least couldn't remember the taste. It felt cool and sweet in his mouth. Meg smiled as he wiped the juice from his lips. That feeling returned—he was sick in his stomach again, but happy about it.

Daniel filled the canteen one last time, then stood and helped Meg up and onto the saddle. He walked them back to the trail for the ride home.

"Daniel," Meg said.

He looked up and she was patting the saddle. He'd already had his fill of closeness. Maybe enough to get him through rest of the year, maybe even a lifetime. But he relented and stepped up to sit in front of her. Meg happily wrapped her arms around Daniel once again.

"I like it when I can feel your skin," she said, reaching her hands up to his face. "You smell kinda good too."

Daniel felt his body warm at her touch. He smiled and let the feeling melt through him. He wished for more of this closeness with Meg, but just as quickly knew he would give it up for the next adventure out with Clay. The man inside desired freedom and would tear away from anything holding him back in relentlessly pursuing it, as if freedom was a physical thing he would eventually catch and hold and own.

They rode on.

"How much farther?" she asked.

"Not much, Meg. Just a few miles."

He knew she liked hearing him say her name. Each time he said "Meg," she would softly pull him in tighter. And he also knew that she knew exactly where they were; Meg simply wanted more conversation, her way of connecting with her husband. He didn't want more conversation. Daniel was now focused on other things. Those final few words would need to keep her until they reached home. And likely longer.

Clang! Clang! Clang!

"Daniel... Daniel!" The sheriff rapped his coffee cup on the jail cell bars to get his attention.

The noise and words broke into Daniel's memories. With his head still down, he gave the sheriff his attention. "Yeah," he responded.

Only the sheriff and Daniel were in the jailhouse. The other prisoners had been released, and James and Jeb were out riding their rounds across the county.

The sheriff pulled his chair over to the cell, sat, and leaned forward with his elbows on his knees and hands clasped. "You keep saying you're innocent. I've looked at the facts up one side of the hog and down the other, from tail to snout and back again. It's smellin' like a pig, Daniel. I think you did it. You ready to tell the truth?"

The sheriff waited, hoping he could coax Daniel into talking.

"You don't have to say anything, you know that," the sheriff said, trying again to reel him into a conversation—or better yet, a confession.

"I know what I can say 'n' not say," Daniel responded, ending the exchange. He looked at the sheriff and waited for him to give up.

"You'll get an attorney and he'll do his best for you, but you'll sure get something. Not clear enough if it'll be a hangin', but there's a chance of that, you know."

Daniel looked away and quit the conversation.

"I can't make you talk," the sheriff said, shaking his head, then standing up. "Your attorney and the judge will be here in a couple days."

Daniel glanced back and watched the sheriff drag his chair back to his desk, scraping and bouncing it across the wood floor. He banged it down and sat again. He took a sip of coffee and immediately spit it back into the cup. He pulled open a drawer and looked inside, then slammed it shut and grabbed his cup again and hammered it onto the desk. Coffee jumped and splattered across papers stacked neatly in front of him. Without hesitation he stood up and bumped his chair backward and stormed out of the jailhouse.

Daniel clenched his jaw. "It's my damn life," he said out loud. "I can talk or not talk, die or not die. I'll decide my own punishment. Ain't no one else gonna do it for me."

8

A S THE SHERIFF stormed out of the jailhouse, he had no idea what to do next. He was too angry to think straight. As he stepped onto Main Street, he decided to visit Henry and check on the school in Frisco for Allie. "At least I'll feel of some damn use," he muttered to himself. As he walked to the telegraph office, he kept his frustration on Meg's killing. The facts pointed to Daniel, but his eyes read honest. Not typical for a thief. Clay was running wild in town, likely both his antics and his mouth. The sheriff passed Jeb in the street and, without stopping, told him he'd be at the depot and to get to the jailhouse and watch Daniel.

The sheriff walked the couple streets over to the depot and into the telegraph office. Henry had on the same gray pants, white shirt, and black vest he'd worn every day for the nearly ten years he'd sat in that office. His spectacles hung halfway down his nose, with no itch to push them back up. The sheriff always had the itch, though, and would scratch the top of his nose to give Henry the hint. Low spectacles and all, Henry was in that office night and day. The job fit him. And he possessed an eerie ability to transcribe messages a few words ahead of the tapping.

"Howdy, Sheriff," Henry said.

"Hey, Henry. Got anything for me?"

"Not good news, I'm afraid. The girls' school in Frisco can't take her in. They're full up. Without her grandparents' help it's not gonna happen."

"Damn," the sheriff responded. He pulled his hat off and scratched his head. "Well, thanks, Henry. Thanks for the effort." He set his hat back in place and shifted his look out the window, to the empty tracks and hills beyond. *Sheriff turned babysitter,* he thought. The teletype ticked on. Henry didn't stop his look at the sheriff, though.

"They did recommend Mount Josephine, an orphanage nearby. Not ideal, but the best they've been able to come by. That's all I got back."

"Can you message Mount Josephine and see if they can take her in? Give 'em the story. Make it sad and pull on their good nature, if they got any. Schedule a visit for a few days out if you can. Hell, maybe more than just a visit; maybe to drop her off."

The telegraph had stopped. Henry turned and jotted down the last message that came in while he and the sheriff were talking, as if he were as much machine as the telegraph itself.

"I'll get your message out today. You gonna be the one goin'?"

The sheriff didn't answer. He was already halfway out the door.

He knew that his presence on the streets didn't much

affect anyone's behavior. They respected him as a lawman, but he seemed invisible. Travelers would point his way. A minor legend in the east, but in town just another shell of a man drowning in a sea of debauchery and bad. He was tempted at least once a week to pull out his revolver and empty it loud into the air and watch the cockroaches scramble every which way. Establish some authority and send a warning that the law still existed, that it had a role to play and demanded respect. He stopped himself in the middle of Main Street as his mind shifted from the town back to Allie. The town rolled on around him. "Dammit," he murmured to himself. "I need to get this right for Allie. I need to get this right for my own sanity as well."

The words came out of his mouth and brought odd looks from those strolling nearby and around him. He immediately picked up his walk to the jailhouse. He stepped inside, noting that Jeb hadn't made it back yet, and immediately headed over to Daniel, who was lying on the bed with his arms over his eyes.

"Don't feel you deserve to know, but I see it more like it's my duty to tell you. Seems the only option for Allie will be an orphanage in San Francisco. No promise yet, but we're gonna try to get her there. Not the best option, but it's looking like there ain't a better one."

Daniel sat up in his bed and looked out to acknowledge he heard the sheriff's words. "Thanks for what you're doin' for her, findin' a safe place for her to go."

He lay down again; the sheriff turned to leave.

"Hey," Daniel said. "Do you think I can see her one last time before she goes? Might be the last chance I ever get."

Daniel sounded sincere, but the sheriff wasn't convinced.

"I'll ask her," he said, and left the jailhouse with no intention of asking.

*

The thought of never seeing Allie again struck hard in Daniel. He took the pain in, owned it for the first time. He admitted that no one took her from him; he'd done it himself. He'd rejected her and left her an orphan long ago. He'd once left Meg and Allie at the house while wondering himself if he'd even return home. Heading out into the rain with Clay, they chased a man clear down to the Arizona Territory. That man had taken $200 from them, a few weeks' worth of work. Thinking back on that chase, it now seemed wrong to get revenge on a man for stealing something they'd stolen themselves. It seemed right at the time, though, being the nature of a thief. He and Clay weren't off to kill the man, just take back what was theirs. They stayed low the full way, no mistakes, not wanting to lose him by getting themselves locked up in some small-town desert jail. They'd never been so long straight before. The man they chased rode alone ahead of them and out of their reach. But not out of their sight.

He remembered Meg and Allie being more trusting and hopeful about him then, less so after those two months out with Clay. He came home after that trip and into the house as if he'd simply gone to town to buy a new pair of boots—or steal a pair, more to character. And nothing to talk about with Meg, not even boots.

When they finally caught up with the man they were chasing, they found him chained to a mesquite tree in the center of Wickenburg, Arizona, along with two other prisoners. It seemed scandalous even for the brutish west to chain prisoners to a tree, but the town had no jail to hold its criminals. They did have three saloons, though, which quickly demanded more than a tree. Some towns didn't even have a tree, just a hole no prisoner could climb out of. Daniel and Clay entered the town just as dusk set in, light enough to see, but not so much to be seen. They laughed at the man sitting cuffed around a thick branch growing up and out from the base of the tree, his hands above his head and arms pulled near tight. The face was the same ugly, cut-up one that had held them at gunpoint a month earlier outside Palisade and taken their money, but now it was burnt red from the sun, his scars striped white across his face. They knew he wouldn't bring more than a few of their dollars into a town, so they'd need him alive. They moved on innocently past the men and tree and headed for the nearest saloon. They would return in the middle of the night to free him, wrestling the key from a deputy marshal on night watch, who would likely be asleep himself.

When they returned and freed the man and started their ride out of Wickenburg, he told them of a large stash of bills he knew about. Always cautious but hopeful at the same time, the brothers listened. They agreed to a three-way split, not a fifty-fifty, and the man would have to return their stolen cash as well. He'd stay baking in the hot sun a few more days without them otherwise, so he took the deal. The man had learned where one of the saloon owners kept his daily take before sending it off to Phoenix and to a secure bank. He told them that the owner slept with it under his mattress, in a saddlebag right beneath his head.

They easily broke the latch of the back door and headed into the saloon and up the stairs. The wood creaked with each step they took. Daniel knew that sound. The stairs at home would make the same noise when he stole into the house and into bed. The men slowed their ascent in order to quiet each step. They finished climbing the stairs, then crept to the bedroom door. Closed. They tried the knob. Locked. The man slipped his gun out, making sure the brothers didn't see or hear. Clay nodded to Daniel, then the door. They each took a step back and Daniel set himself to kick the door in. He raised his foot, but the man pointed his revolver where the latch held and fired a shot. Bang! Daniel and Clay looked at the man, shocked at his action. The noise. The unplanned act. The man kicked the door himself and broke the latch the full way, and the three men busted in.

The owner started to stand but fell back into the bed; his wife curled herself up tight and hid under the sheet.

The man pointed his gun at the owner. "Get out," he said.

The couple froze.

The man clicked the hammer back. "Get out," he said louder, flipping the end of the gun away from the bed and toward the hallway.

The owner rolled to one side and out of the bed. His wife rolled out the other side. They both moved to the opposite corner of the room, next to the window. The man kept the gun and his stare straight at them, daring them, almost wishing them to move. Daniel and Clay lifted the mattress off the bed. The saddlebag lay right where it was supposed to. Daniel grabbed it, then he and Clay ran out the bedroom door and into the hallway.

Voices picked up in the street below.

The man closed in and pointed the gun at the wife and spoke to the owner. "Yell down and tell 'em everything's okay."

The owner stuck his head out the window. "It's okay. We're okay." He smiled and waved, then quickly ducked back in to stand next to his wife.

The man with the gun moved in closer to the couple. He lifted his revolver and aim at the owner, square on his forehead. He closed his right eye, then began slowly stepping backward toward the door. The husband and wife stood numb and terrified, holding tight to each other. The brothers waited impatiently in the hallway. The man stopped at the door, in no hurry to run. Click... click... click. He pulled the hammer back.

Daniel shouted at the man. "No! Let's go. Dammit, let's go!"

Bang!

The shot plunged square into the owner's forehead and slammed him back against the wall and down. The bullet exited his head and pierced the wall where he'd stood. Blood stamped the hole red and trailed down the wall with the owner. His wife screamed and dropped to her husband. The man soaked in the scene, then turned and strolled past the brothers and down the stairs, out the back door. The brothers ran past the man and beat him to their horses.

The three rode hard a few miles north to their meeting place. After they stopped, Clay pulled his revolver and pointed it at the man. "Git down," he yelled.

The man smiled and leaned forward in his saddle. "Go ahead. Pull the trigger. It'll make you just like me."

"Take us to our money," Daniel said, more to prevent Clay from killing the man than to get their money.

The man didn't move. "Ain't got it in ya, huh? I knew it." He sat up in his saddle and shook his head.

Clay lowered his gun.

"You ain't no outlaw," the man said, and leaned to his right and spit.

"We better ride on," Daniel said. "They'll be coming after us any minute."

"Is this worth it, Daniel?" Clay asked.

"Money always is," Daniel responded.

"Listen to your friend here," the man said to Clay. "Don't think nothin' about me. Let's get this money split up—that's what matters."

"He ain't my friend," Clay said. "He's my brother." He leaned and spit in the man's direction.

"I'm Daniel, and this is Clay. We're from Wyoming originally, now Nevada—Elko County... Palisade to be exact."

"I don't give a damn if you're from Paris, France," the man said. He squinted a look at the brothers, finally getting the chance to size them up. "You did okay back there, boys."

"You didn't need to hell kill that man," Clay shouted. "We just wanted the money. Now we'll have the law after us for a killin'."

"The name's Keen."

"Don't give a damn what your name is," Clay said, still angry at the man.

"Clay, let's go," Daniel said. "Keen, show us where our money is or you don't get your share of this take."

Keen kicked his horse into a sprint and the brothers quickly followed.

After they got their money back and split up the saloon loot, the brothers rode back to Palisade. News and bounties traveled slow. They'd be safer back home and far from Keen. But a month later he showed up again in Palisade, with another score planned. They'd do a job together and then he'd be gone for months, only to show up unannounced once again. The brothers talked and plotted to kill Keen but never could follow through. His scores set them up for months at a time, not just the few days or weeks they were able to manage on their own. Several more years of stealing followed, in and out of towns across Nevada, Arizona, Idaho, and Utah. Keen pulled acts of his own at times, and only occasionally found himself in a jail cell. The brothers always seemed to stay free themselves, caught only a few times, but always out just as quick as they went in.

As the years went by Daniel continued to slide closer to outlaw and further from Meg and Allie.

9

I T TOOK UNTIL mid-August for the judge and attorneys to arrive in Palisade, nearly three weeks after Daniel's arrest. The sun burned mercilessly across northern Nevada, even late into the evening, leaving the cell where Daniel sat sweltering, and him soaking in his own sweat. The days languished in the heat, as if time withered and melted them to a crawl. Daniel didn't bother to count them. Cell mates came and went too. He didn't count them either. Most were drunks; some were outlaws wanted in other counties, even other states and territories. The smell of the jailhouse from early on carried forward without letup, but now hung thick in the air from the heat and sweat of men. Daniel didn't notice the odor anymore, except when a new drunk got thrown in with him. He could usually tell what they'd been drinking, down to the make. Clay didn't visit, and Daniel didn't expect him to.

Daniel watched as the sheriff welcomed William Flowers into the jailhouse. He would be the public defender representing Daniel. The two men spoke in whispers at the front door. After a few minutes Flowers walked over and sat next to Daniel's cell.

"Hi, Daniel. I'm William Flowers, and I'll be—"

"I want to plead guilty," Daniel interrupted.

Flowers frowned. "Well… I urge you to reconsider. If you plead guilty, there won't be a trial, only a sentence from the judge. Based on what I know so far, you'd likely be hanged."

"Don't care," Daniel replied.

"Think about pleading innocent. No doubt in new states like Nevada, juries tend to start with guilty and usually end there too, regardless of the facts. But I have a good track record of moving a jury from a death sentence to a prison term. Let me take this to a jury for you."

Daniel eyed the attorney. Hard. He wasn't swayed.

Flowers shook his head in disappointment. "Okay, this is your decision. Let's at least go the plea route. I'm confident I can get the charge dropped from capital murder to something less. You'd have a chance to be free in twenty years, maybe earlier."

"I'll never be free. I'm guilty and deserve to be punished. Leave it alone and leave me alone."

The attorney dropped his head and looked at the floor, then back at Daniel. "I don't know if you killed her or not, but that doesn't mean you have to take the punishment. Let me plead it down for you. Give me a chance to help you."

"I don't want your help. Meg never had a chance with me. Allie neither. Why should you get a chance? We can go to trial or straight to a judge, I don't care which. Just let 'em hang me."

Flowers kept on him. "I can't let you do this, Daniel. I know the judge. There are ways—"

"I've been stealin' and cheatin' my whole life. I know there are ways. There are always ways. And from where I'm sittin', those are coward's ways and I'm done with that. I'm goin' straight through this. No lyin'. No hidin'. No stealin' a lesser charge than guilty. I'll take what's comin' to me. Now you can help me plead guilty or I'll do it myself."

Daniel stopped the conversation and lay down on his bed, hands behind his head, face up and eyes open.

Flowers gave up. He sighed in disbelief, then left Daniel in the jail cell, holding tight to his death sentence. Flowers stepped out onto the front porch and closed the door. The low murmur of the attorney talking with the sheriff carried to Daniel's cell. It didn't bother nor distract him. And he wasn't going to care what they decided.

After several minutes the voices from the porch ended. The door opened and the sheriff stepped in and over to Daniel. He pushed his hat back and rubbed his forehead. "Is this what you want for Allie? Seems your death wish is all about you. Maybe it's time you put Allie in your thoughts."

Daniel didn't answer. He knew it wasn't the right thing for Allie, though. As much as she had the right to hate him and wish him dead, he knew both parents dead wasn't the best for her.

He abruptly sat up. "You tell me what Allie would want," he demanded.

"Well, I'm pretty sure she doesn't care any which way about you, whether you're dead or in prison or rotting in this hellhole of a jail cell. Her mother's gone and she'll be gone too, headed for a place where she don't know anyone, but away from you. Can't get any worse, I don't think."

Daniel sat silent.

"She's seven, Daniel. She doesn't understand all that's happened to her. Somebody needs to be the grown-up here. Maybe even a parent."

Daniel felt the anger and anguish of the sheriff's words. Of his failures as a father. Daniel reached down for his coffee cup that sat on the floor. He gripped it tight in his hand and squeezed hard with all of his might, wanting desperately to crush the metal cup until it collapsed and crumpled into a useless piece of tin. His anger poured into his hand as he continued to squeeze. He was unsure of what to do. Of how to be a father. Of how to help Allie. He reached back and threw the cup as hard as he could against the wall. The metal clinked against the rocks, hit the floor, and clanked a few times more before it tumbled to a stop at his feet.

He closed his eyes. "I've ruined three lives. Meg's dead and I'm as good as dead. Maybe I can somehow save Allie. Maybe I have a purpose yet."

"Choose life for yourself, Daniel. It may not matter now, but someday it might. Someday she may need you, maybe even want you. If you're dead, well, then you just abandoned her one more time."

Daniel didn't respond. He continued wrestling with the anger and anguish. He wished to be free of the pain and hurt he felt for Allie, and a hanging would do just that. Ten, twenty, thirty years in prison would be punishment too, but it might also give a chance for Allie to learn to forgive him.

"I'll let you sleep on it. I'll send Flowers back in tomorrow morning."

*

The sheriff walked to his desk and fell into his chair, his hat still tilted back. He picked up the stack of wanted posters and pretended to study the faces, but instead stared right through each one. His mind was fixed on Allie.

Atonement. Restoration. Redemption. He was looking for the right word. No—the right *feeling*, how this moment felt to him personally as he worked to save Allie.

He never took a case personally. Not a single time in all of his career. It was a job, but one he took seriously. If you did it right, you blinded yourself to the victims just as much as to the perpetrators and to justice. Riding as a freshly badged marshal outside Reno fifteen years earlier, he came upon a covered wagon stopped in the trail. A man on a horse behind the wagon stood out. Black shirt and jeans and hat and sitting on a chestnut horse with a blond mane against the light brown of the hills and grass beyond gave an appearance of the rider floating in the air. He watched the man stroll up on his horse and stick his arm and handgun into the canvas slit of the wagon cover. He yelled and pointed them to climb out. The driver of the wagon sat slumped over on the seat up front, half fallen to the ground. A woman stepped out the back and then lifted her children safely to the ground with her.

The marshal rode slowly up behind the rider, who abruptly turned with his gun aim at him. The marshal expected that movement and shot the rider before he was fully set to fire. He hit the man with a single bullet to the chest and watched him fall backward from his horse and hang from one boot caught in a stirrup. The marshal laid the two dead men in the back of the wagon, set the woman and her children on the bench seat, and led the family back to Reno, a full day's journey. Without a word. Just a job. He'd thought of their difficult road ahead, likely now headed back east or to wherever they came from. Without a husband. Without a father. That was the closest he ever got to caring. He dropped them off at the jailhouse in Reno and was back out on the trail in thirty minutes doing his job.

The sheriff looked over at Daniel, who had drifted off to sleep. He needed to give Flowers an update, so he headed for the door and the walk over to the Palisade Hotel. As the sheriff grabbed the door handle, he stopped. Without a doubt he wanted the best for Allie, which meant he now wanted the best for Daniel as well.

"Damn odd feeling," he whispered to himself. "Normally I'd want you dead, out of my hair and trouble. Now… well, now I don't know. What the hell you doin' to me, Daniel Lind? Makin' me care and I ain't used to that." He yanked the door open and walked out of the jailhouse.

*

The next morning Daniel woke early. He had James bring him a bowl of clean water to wash himself. The eggs, hash, and coffee tasted better than any he'd had since he'd been locked up the past few weeks. As he finished the last of his coffee, the door opened, and Flowers walked in.

Daniel had barely slept. He'd spent the night reflecting

on his life and choices, from his days growing up in western Wyoming, to all those years of lawlessness with Clay, then to Meg and Allie, and to this very moment when he would choose life or death. Most of his thoughts during the night, though, went to Allie. Where she might end up over the next few days and months and years, what kind of young woman she would become, what he now missed about her, and how he might be able to someday be a part of her life. He weighed the chances of that happening. They weren't good, but what else was there for him and his life? He also ran through the day before Meg's death in his mind, wanting desperately to remember the last time he saw Allie and the color dress she wore. He missed her that day, like he'd missed her every other day of her life. He didn't even see his own daughter; she was right there, but she wasn't. She was like a wisp of air to him. In his cell, in the middle of the night, with the moon high and bright in the August sky and offering the only light in the jailhouse, Daniel cried. He longed for his daughter. He wondered if Allie was looking at the moon at that same moment. The light gave him hope, though, the only real hope he'd known outside of himself.

"Good morning, Daniel," Flowers said.

"Mornin'."

"Did you sleep well?"

"What would it take to plead to something less?" Daniel asked, ignoring the attorney's attempt at small talk. "If I were to plead guilty, what would I get—how much time?"

"I don't know, Daniel. I can talk to the prosecutor and get an idea. I'd certainly work out the best deal I could for you."

Hope filled Daniel again, just as it had the night before

with the moonlight flooding into his cell. It was a feeling he'd not known in a long time. When he was six years old, his father told him that for his eighth birthday that he would buy him a long gun of his own. Daniel leaned on that hope for those next two years. He could almost feel the weight of it in his hands. He could see it leaning against the wall next to his bed. He could hear the loud POP! and trailing smoke with each trigger pull. And he knew that it wouldn't just be about having his own gun, but about being with his pa in the woods hunting squirrel and rabbit and deer together, each carrying their own weapon. He remembered that feeling of hope, and he liked it. His eighth birthday came and went, though—and still no gun. Another birthday passed by, and another, and still another. He gradually let go of the hope he'd held of the gift of his own gun. At fifteen he decided to acquire one himself. He'd heard his father talk about a family nearby that had recently purchased several newly released Henry Model 1860 repeating rifles. Not the slow-loading, short-range muzzleloader that his father used, but a genuine repeating rifle. He rode to their ranch with no plan. He hid out in the woods and waited. After a couple hours he heard gun shots. He followed the sounds and watched as two young boys began loading and firing their Henry rifles. Daniel resolved to not go home until he had one. The young boys left before he could make his move, so he spent the night in the woods. He loved the freedom, the adventure, and the anticipation of owning something new. His father would certainly beat him for being gone overnight, but the punishment would be worth the Henry rifle. The opportunity came early the next morning as the boys returned to the woods. They had both leaned their rifles against a fallen tree and walked a hundred yards across a pasture to set up targets. Daniel crept in, grabbed one of the rifles and two full boxes of ammunition, and snuck out, going deep into the woods and back to his horse, then rode home—his heart racing with excitement the full way.

He loved owning that rifle, loved holding and firing it, but loved that taste of independence even more—of being away and free and self-reliant. He made the decision to pursue that freedom, and to not trust or rely on another human being ever again. If he wanted something, he'd damn well get it himself.

Daniel looked at Flowers. What he needed now was punishment for what he'd done to Meg and Allie. But he also wanted to see Allie again, apologize to her, and maybe even receive her forgiveness—he certainly wouldn't get that lying dead in a box next to Meg.

"I need to trust you," Daniel said to Flowers, "trust that you can keep me from a rope. I desperately need that now."

He resolved to take the prison sentence, whatever would be given him, and let that serve as his punishment, let that relieve him of his guilt. He would be a model prisoner. Not much for a daughter to be proud of, but it was the best he could do. He would write to her and pursue her. He chose to not only hope for a relationship with his daughter, but he dug deeper and desired it. Hope had always failed him before, hoping in someone else, but this time desire and his own pursuit and effort wouldn't. It would be something to live for. To focus on. To strive for. He would redeem himself in his daughter's eyes and win her back.

Flowers nodded and promised to do what he could. He walked out of the jailhouse and left Daniel alone.

"Damn you, Pa. Just damn you," Daniel said to himself.

*

The courtroom was small, barely enough room for a judge, jurors, and attorneys. Towns and counties of the west could barely afford their lawmen, so a full-out courthouse was unheard of for territories recently birthed into statehood. The jury box to the side, normally filled with men, sat empty. Three locals watched from a bench in the back—regulars, regardless of who was being tried or why or what might unfold before them.

"We've reached an agreement, is that right?" the judge asked the opposing attorneys.

"Yes, Your Honor. The state accepts the plea."

"And my client accepts it as well," Flowers said.

The judge turned his look on the defendant. Daniel could see that the judge was reading him, studying him as he would any defendant in his court. Daniel sat there, surrendered. There was no fight in him. He was broken and sincere.

The judge smiled his approval at Daniel and banged his gavel down. "Ten years it is," he declared.

The judge filled out the sentencing report and signed it. The prosecuting attorney signed, then Flowers. Daniel took the pen. His hand trembled; the pen shook.

Flowers set his hand on Daniel's shoulder. "You did well. Just your mark, if you prefer."

Daniel looked at Flowers, then slowly etched a jagged "Daniel Lind" on the paper.

Embarrassment and shame filled him, but just as quickly hope replaced them. He was ten years from seeing Allie again. He stood as the judge motioned to the sheriff, who took Daniel's arm and walked him to the door.

Even in handcuffs Daniel somehow felt free. And he now had a purpose: live out the harsh punishment due him, then find Allie.

They left the courtroom for the short walk back to the jailhouse. Daniel kept his head down the full way, but something forced his attention up. Clay was there, watching him, from the steps of the Palisade Hotel. Daniel managed a near smile and nod at his brother. A sense of care, then sadness, shot back and forth between them. Daniel glimpsed the little boy in his brother's face, in his eyes. He remembered that same sad, boyish look the time Clay shot his first deer. Daniel had smiled at his little brother's win that day. The soft crunch of hooves in the snow steadily approached and then stopped within a hundred feet of where they knelt behind some brush. The young buck raised its head and turned its eyes on them, then perked and twisted its ears. It waited. It listened. Bang! The buck took a few steps, wobbled, then fell. The boys cheered and hollered. Their father calmly walked to where the deer lay and looked it over. "If you'd hit him where I taught ya, a little lower, he woulda fallen on the spot. Take your aim better next time." Daniel watched as Clay's joy fell away. He saw the hurt and sadness well up in his brother's eyes. Their father was a tough man, hard on them most days. That day, in the field, after the harsh words, Clay's father looked at him and nodded once. When you did something that he figured made a man, well, you got his slight nod of approval. Nothing more.

The brothers kept their look on each other as Daniel continued his walk to the jail. Boot spurs clinked from the balcony above Clay. Daniel looked up. It was Keen. He stood there—arms resting on the railing—steadier and stronger than the balcony itself. Even under the shadow of Keen's hat Daniel could see the man's cuts. Keen grinned, then flicked his cigar butt in Daniel's direction. Daniel quickly dropped his gaze from the balcony down to his brother below, catching Clay's attention. Then he slid his eyes up toward Keen. Clay stood there, unflinchingly, until Daniel was inside the jailhouse and the door closed behind him.

The sheriff led Daniel back into his cell, then removed the handcuffs. Daniel rubbed his hands and wrists, which were scratched from the cuffs. He sat and began his wait for the prison carriage to take him to the state penitentiary in Carson City on its cycle through Palisade in a couple days. He shifted his worry from the uncertain future he'd known the past several weeks to a different anxiety: life inside a prison, his punishment, and his hope of one day seeing his daughter again.

10

A s soon as the jailhouse door closed Clay ran into the street and looked up and scanned the width of the balcony. Empty. He didn't need to see anyone, though, to know who'd been there. Clay sprinted into the hotel and up the stairs. Eight rooms lined the second floor— four to the back of the hotel, and four to the front, each of those with a door out onto the balcony. He carefully moved along the railing to the first door at the front of the hotel. He stepped to the side of the door and listened. Too many men had been gunned down standing square in front of a closed door. And Clay knew that Keen was the type of man who would fire a shot in that situation, unconcerned about who might be on the other side. The first room was quiet. He moved to the edge of the next door and listened again. Then the third. And the fourth.

"Clay," came Keen's voice from the third room.

Clay moved back a door and stood to the side once again.

"Sorry about your brother," Keen called through the

closed door. "The price ya pay for gettin' caught. Sad thing, it is."

Clay could feel the man's mocking even through the door.

"I guess killin's free," Keen went on. "It's gettin' caught that'll cost ya."

Clay stilled himself.

"You out there, Clay, or maybe you run off scared already?"

"I'm still here. Just waitin' for the invite to come in."

"We ain't got no more business, you and me," Keen said. "I just came back to collect some money a fella owes me. Ain't nothin' to do with you or your brother."

"I told you to leave and not come back. You were still breathin' last time you left town. I ain't got no more patience for you now."

"I got no business with you, Clay. Let me take care of what I came for and I'll be on my way. You can trust me on that."

"I don't trust you worth shit."

Clay reached across the door and softly turned the knob. Locked. He stepped to the front of the door and lifted his leg up against his gut and booted the door. It half busted at the latch but didn't open. He jumped left just as two gunshots blasted and splintered through the middle of the door. High-pitch screams erupted from across the hall. He faced the door and booted hard once more, then flipped away again. A third shot ripped through the frame and splintered as the door flung open and banged hard against the wall inside. Clay peeked into the room and then stepped in. Keen stood by the open door that led onto the balcony, his revolver leveled at his waist and aimed on Clay.

With bare hands raised, Clay nodded down to his gun belt, showing Keen that he wasn't carrying. In the hallway behind him, he could hear people scurrying from other rooms and down the stairs.

Cries for help came from the lobby: "Run and get the sheriff! Get the sheriff!"

The hotel quieted. Clay breathed hard. Keen gritted and squinted, then pulled back on the trigger slowly.

Click.

Nothing. The misfire didn't rattle Keen. Without hesitation he pulled the trigger again and ripped the shot into Clay's right shoulder. Clay groaned and covered the hole with his left hand, keeping his eyes on Keen.

"Sheriff, upstairs!" yelled a voice from below the balcony.

Clay heard the sheriff's words: "Get everyone away."

Keen took a step onto the balcony and looked to the street below; at that move, Clay turned and ran out and into the room across the hall. The woman inside was crouched and crying in the corner between the bed and a dresser. Clay closed the door then stuck his head out the back window and looked down. *Dirt. Nowhere soft to land.* He heard the sheriff's steps. With no other option, Clay stretched one leg out the window, then the other. He sat, then slipped himself down, falling to the ground, feet first. His legs jarred hard and stung up his entire body and into his shoulder. He winced at the pain for several seconds, then stood and began to hobble down behind the next building and back up to Main Street.

He pulled his hat down to cover his eyes and face, walked over to Molly, took her reins, mounted, and rode off north.

*

The Sheriff ran into Keen's room out of breath but gun up and ready to shoot. Keen still stood by the balcony door, his own gun now on a table next to him. The sheriff looked around. He expected to find someone in addition to Keen but saw no one. They held silent for a moment. Each studied the other.

"What the hell you doin' in Palisade, Keen?"

"Just meetin' up with some old friends, Sheriff."

"All I see is you causin' trouble. Again."

"Ain't so. I was just layin' on my bed restin', that's all. Honest. Someone kicked on my door to break it open, so I took a couple shots. They kicked again, so I took another shot. The door come open and I shot again. Hit him in the shoulder. He turned and ran."

"And I'm guessin' you didn't get a look at him."

Keen shook his head. "Nope, didn't. Not good enough anyway."

"And you wouldn't tell me if you did."

"I can take care of myself, Sheriff. Don't need no one else… especially child-killin' scum posin' as a lawman."

BANG!

The sheriff let his anger pull the trigger.

Keen didn't move. He barely managed a flinch. His eyes locked on the sheriff, then he tensed his hands and started to reach for his revolver on the table—but stopped.

The bullet had screamed past Keen and torn through the

wall, ricocheting to the street below, and finally burying itself in the dirt.

The sheriff kept his aim and anger on Keen. "I'm taken you in. You're a wanted man in more places than I care to count. Turn around."

Keen squinted, then licked his lips and shook his head.

The sheriff pulled the hammer back again. Click... click... click. The cylinder turned as slow as the clicks rolled. Both men stood quiet. Keen looked hard at the sheriff, then eyed the revolver aimed at him.

"You're thinkin' right," the sheriff said. "The next one's got your name on it. I promise not to miss. And all I gotta do is say you went for yours first. There ain't a soul in all of creation gonna question the law against the likes of you."

The sheriff pulled out his cuffs and stepped closer to Keen, who hesitated, then turned. As soon as the sheriff set his revolver in his holster, Keen spun around and tackled him to the floor, then took the revolver and stood up. Keen kept the gun aimed on the sheriff as he picked up his saddlebag and weapons and backed his way to the door.

"If you yell for help or say a word, Sheriff, I'll shoot the first woman I see. And if you come down after me, I'll shoot the first kid I see."

Keen pushed opened the cylinder of the sheriff's revolver and dumped the cartridges, then tossed the gun onto the bed. The sheriff could only watch as Keen walked out of the room.

*

After Keen left, the sheriff sat up against the bed frame, set his face in his hands, and screamed—angry that he'd let Keen get away, but more that he'd pulled the trigger and sent a bullet into the street, showing himself no different than Keen. He kept his face buried in his hands and worked to calm himself. After a couple minutes, the hotel manager appeared at the door and asked if he was okay, if he needed anything. The sheriff didn't respond. He stood up, grabbed his empty revolver, stormed past the manager, and headed to the jailhouse.

"Jeb! Jeb!" he yelled as he opened the jailhouse door. "Get a wire relay going across the state. Include Salt Lake and anyplace within a two-day ride. Let 'em know Emmett Keen just rode out of Palisade."

The deputy hesitated, but as the sheriff gritted his teeth and stabbed his eyes into Jeb, he sprinted out and ran to the telegraph office.

"Damn Emmett Keen," the sheriff grumbled to himself. "Right here in Palisade."

"Can I help, Sheriff?" James asked.

He glanced at James. "Yeah, sure. Find Clay Lind. Especially check the saloons. Then try out to Daniel's place. I wanna know that he's stayin' out of trouble. If he's hurt or bleedin', bring him in. Keen was tusslin' with someone at the hotel and I'm certain it was Clay."

James nodded and hurried out.

The sheriff looked over and pointed hard at Daniel. "Once you're off to prison, I can't help you. You better talk now."

Daniel stood and looked at the sheriff through the bars. "I ain't ridden with Keen in six months. Ain't seen him till earlier today neither. My brother and him get along good, so that couldn't have been Clay."

The sheriff kicked his desk and shouted, "Dammit, it don't add up! You're going to prison for somethin' you say you didn't do. Keen's in town causin' trouble. And I'll bet a year of my pay that Clay was the one he just shot and wounded. Something's going on and you better damn well talk. I ain't stupid and didn't get this job for bein' stupid. *Talk dammit!*"

Daniel lay back down. "I'm guilty, Sheriff. Let it be. Let Clay be too. He's innocent in all this."

The sheriff grabbed a piece of wood from the woodpile next to the stove and charged the cell. Without hesitating he threw it into the bars. "Dammit, Daniel Lind!" he said, grunting in anger. *"Dammit!"* His antics didn't sway Daniel, who just lay there.

Not knowing the full story ate at the sheriff—partly out of needing to know everything, partly out of duty to the truth. He couldn't leave anything in the gray. Everything had a place—black or white, didn't matter, it had a place. That's why the law fit him. He was relentless when he got locked on to something he didn't understand or couldn't explain. He looked at the piece of wood on the floor, picked it up, and threw it again, this time into the jailhouse door. Ignoring the wood, he walked to a cabinet that stood along a side wall, opened a drawer, and lifted out a whiskey bottle. He bit the cork, spit it onto the floor, and drank down three long swallows. The dribbles rolled down his chin, and without bother he drank down two more swallows. He winced as the drinks burned his mouth and throat, but the hurt felt good, like it matched his anger, like he deserved it. He felt its warmth. It felt like home. It comforted him. But it also pushed his anger out, beyond what he cared for. He walked to his desk and slammed the bottled down.

"Damn! Damn! Damn!" he yelled to himself.

The sweetness of the whiskey in the open bottle called to him. He wanted more. He looked over at Daniel, who'd kept his stare on the sheriff the whole time. The sheriff walked to where the cork lay on the floor next to the cabinet, picked it up, and shoved it back in the bottle. He set the bottle in the drawer, slamming it closed, and wiping his mouth of the lingering whiskey.

"Three crooked bastards," he said to himself, then immediately looked at Daniel again and stepped to his cell. "So that's it?" he shouted. "You're not talkin'? You're gonna make me figure this out the hard way, is that it? Force me to hunt for the truth until it kills me. You playin' martyr? Savior? Protector? Just plain ignorant? Or tryin' to be a man for once in your life?"

Daniel didn't move or speak. He stayed calm and kept his look on the sheriff. And the sheriff saw it—saw it in Daniel's eyes: that for once in his waste of a life he was the bigger man... bigger and more sober and clearheaded in that moment than the sheriff.

With no response from Daniel, the sheriff turned and stormed out of the jailhouse and into the street.

*

Still heading north out of town, Clay had slowed and finally stopped riding after he'd run out of the hotel away from

Keen and the sheriff. He was free to leave the county now but felt a betrayal to his brother doing so. Daniel would soon be off to Carson City for ten years. Their parents long gone. Meg gone too. And Allie likely gone for good. Nothing left. Nothing left worth fighting for. Certainly nothing left worth dying for.

Clay turned his mind to Keen. A sting pierced his shoulder. He reached up and felt the entry hole. He reached behind and searched for the exit. "Damn Keen," he said, feeling where the bullet left the back of his shoulder. The sharp pierce fell to a dull pain and throbbing. He saw the bloodstains on the front of his shirt and knew they'd be down the back as well.

"Taking care of Keen would be worth dying for," he said to himself. Not much else would, though.

Keen would likely head south, all the way to Arizona, where he'd always run when he wanted to hide for a spell. Clay wasn't ready to tangle with him just yet. He decided to ride back into town, to Daniel's house. There he could clean up and take on supplies, including all of the ammunition he could find. He winced again and grabbed his shoulder, then lightly pulled his horse to the left and rode her back to town. He didn't see sight of Keen on his ride back, but also didn't let up his senses about him either. They'd meet again, he was certain of that. He just didn't know when or where or which of the two would surprise the other.

*

James made his rounds through the saloons looking for Clay, keeping his eye out for him in the streets and shops as well.

After a good sweep of the town he made his way to Daniel's house. Nearing the edge of town James watched as Clay rode to the side of the house from the opposite direction and slipped to the back. James stopped his ride and waited for a minute to see if Clay would ride back out. He waited another couple of minutes, weighing whether to fetch the sheriff or take on Clay himself. He chose to handle this situation himself and started slow-walking Sky to the house and then around to the back.

Clay had tied Molly to the post behind the house, near where he and Daniel had sat on the ground that Sunday morning a few weeks earlier. The pigs were gone. The smell wasn't. James could hear banging from inside the house, then the light whistle of a coffee kettle. James dismounted and tied Sky next to Molly, then walked to the back door. He could hear the kettle scream louder.

"Clay?... Clay! You in there?" James asked, knocking on the door.

"Who's there?" Clay responded.

"Deputy James. Open the door. I need to talk with you."

"You here to take me back to jail already? I ain't done nothin'. Been keepin' to myself."

"No. Sheriff just wanted to know where you've been."

James could hear the wood latch of the door being raised and then saw the door crack open a couple inches.

"Ain't you done watchin' me yet?" Clay asked, peeking through the opening. "Daniel's done confessed and sentenced. And you ain't got no evidence says I had a hand in it. Figure I'm free to go."

James took a step closer and roamed his eyes around the house, as much as Clay would allow.

"Sheriff ain't said you're free to leave Elko County. Though I reckon not much reason to keep you around. Got even less reason to want you around."

Clay opened the door another couple inches, giving James more of a look inside.

"You wanna come on in and catch up a spell?" Clay said. "Just fixin' some coffee."

"No thanks. Got better things to do. Just checkin' on ya."

James looked left and right and around the house as much as he could see. A bloodied shirt was laid across the table. James studied Clay. He kept his innocent look about him.

"So Deputy, I'll be leavin' town here soon. I got your address. I'll be sure'n send you a letter from time to time. Wouldn't want to lose touch with those I care about."

"How long you been here?" James asked, still thinking about the bloodied shirt and the shooting at the Palisade Hotel earlier.

"Well, guess near an hour, maybe more. I was in town to see Daniel get walked back to the jail. A sad day for me. We was close. I tipped my hat at him and then rode right back here."

"You ain't hurt, are you?"

"No, sir. Perfect as the day I was born." Clay swung the door open to let James look at him. He had a shirt on, though unbuttoned. James eyed the bloody shirt on the table again, then saw the gun belt around Clay's waist. Clay pulled his shirt back, revealing a revolver.

"Shirt's kinda big on you, ain't it?" James said. "Looks more like something your brother would wear."

"I told you. I've been here at least an hour. Now, if you got somethin' to ask me, then ask it. Otherwise get off the property."

James looked hard at Clay. These were the moments he felt the true weight of the badge. He needed to make a decision. He could trust Clay and let him go, or he could pull his revolver and drag him to jail like the sheriff asked. Letting a man like Clay go could get someone else shot; pulling his own revolver on a man like Clay could get himself shot.

James was bred to be a lawman. The honest and caring kind. He was cut straight and narrow. Hair neat. Face shaved close every day. He was twenty-eight, but his baby skin showed him barely out of his teens. He was a straight-up lawman just as much as Daniel and Clay were straight-up crooked.

James held still. Clay matched him.

Then James flinched quick for his gun, with no attempt to draw it. Clay dropped his hand to his revolver, wincing in pain at the move.

"You been shot, Clay. You're comin' with me to—"

Clay slammed the door shut in James's face. "I ain't done nothin' wrong! Keen threatened me, then shot me."

"Open the door, Clay. Sheriff wants to talk with you. You best come with me."

"Go to hell. And take that drunken killer of a sheriff with you."

James was taken aback by Clay's words. He lost his purpose in the moment at the thought of his boss being called a killer. It certainly didn't make sense. Maybe Clay was just trying to distract him. Either way he didn't wish for a shootout. It wasn't worth it. But he knew if he left to get the sheriff, Clay would run. He let up on the situation.

"You still there, Deputy?"

He didn't respond.

"Didn't know that about your boss, did you? Yeah, he's too drunk to protect a little girl or this county or a territory—hell, even his own family. You should ask him about Savery Creek sometime."

"Where you headed now?" James asked, still holding on to Clay's words about the sheriff.

"I'm gonna head out and take care of Keen myself."

"Don't do it, Clay. That'd be murder. You'll end up splittin' rocks and sweatin' down to skin and bones alongside your brother."

"Hell, I'll probably get a reward for doin' somethin' the law ain't been able to do. You wanna thank me now, or at Keen's funeral?"

"Have it your way. Do what you gotta do, but just don't come back to Elko County ever again. Deal?"

"We're square on that one, Deputy. And no need to bring the sheriff back. I'll be gone."

"I know. I know…" James said. He stood at the door, not ready to leave. "Clay."

"Yeah?"

"Who shot Meg?"

It felt like a question the sheriff would ask, James thought. The type of question where he would try catching someone off their guard, maybe have them give up something they didn't want to. James felt good asking it, proud even, like a real lawman. He knew the sheriff never assumed the obvious. He always dug deeper into the facts, and James better understood that mind-set now. He waited for Clay's answer.

"What the hell kinda question is that? You know who shot her. Daniel. He even confessed. Goin' to Carson City for it."

"And you didn't have nothin' to do with it?"

"You know I didn't. Got that old lady across the road supportin' my story. Why you askin' me this?"

"Just tyin' up loose ends. Makin' sure we got all the guilty ones."

"You know I was outside when she got shot. And I seen my brother with the gun in his hand standin' over Meg."

Something clicked with James. "Where was Keen?"

"What the hell you talkin' about?" Clay asked, swinging the door open again. "Ain't you got nothin' better to do than chase wild ideas?"

"Like I said, we're just tyin' up loose ends. You three did a lot of bad things together, maybe worked on this together too."

James could see Clay's impatience at the questions.

"You got anything else to say I should know about?" James asked.

"Yeah. Get off the property."

James paused, then walked back a few steps and turned to his horse and mounted. When he looked back, Clay was still staring at him.

"I'll be gone in five minutes," Clay said. "You ain't never gonna see me again. Count yourself lucky."

James turned Sky and rode hard back to the jailhouse and gave his report to the sheriff, with Jeb listening in, and Daniel asleep in his cell.

When James had finished his report, the sheriff shook his head. "I don't know whether to be relieved that Clay's leaving town or frustrated that he was in a shootout with Keen and both got away."

James could tell that he chose frustrated.

"Did he say anything else?" the sheriff asked while reaching for a bottle in his drawer.

"Yeah," James said, then paused. "Clay called you a drunken killer."

The sheriff stopped, then slid the bottle back into the drawer and closed it.

"It's Clay Lind," the sheriff said. "He's just jawin' his mouth, tryin' to stir up trouble and take the focus off him. Don't mind anything he says."

"He said you couldn't protect a little girl, or even your own family. And something about Savery Creek. Is that where—"

"*Dammit!* Can't either of you do a damn thing right?" The sheriff exploded and slammed his fist on the desk. "You shoulda dragged Clay's ass back here. Do your job, James. *Just do your damn job!*"

James worked to remain emotionless. He watched Jeb stand, his eyes awash in fear. And he felt the sheriff's anger burn on them, his face now unrecognizable, like he was half-possessed. Both deputies froze, unsure of what was happening. James braced himself for what might come next.

"You two ride out and find both Clay and Keen!" the sheriff yelled.

James looked at the sheriff like he'd just ordered them to ride to China and be back by morning.

"Now!" the sheriff yelled.

The men quietly headed to the cabinet for their shot-guns, but the sheriff interrupted, "Never mind. Just never mind. I'll do it my damn self. If you two were any slower, it'd be Christmas by the time you left."

Without another word, the sheriff stormed out of the jailhouse and slammed the door behind him.

James stared at the door and waited for it to swing back open and for the real sheriff—the one he knew—to walk back in and set all right with the world again.

*

The sheriff rode to his cabin before heading out to chase the men. He pulled a new whiskey bottle from the shelf and banged it onto the table next to his dirty shot glass. He opened and slammed closed a cupboard door, then another, and another, cussing each as they banged shut.

"Damn jerky hiding again," he said out loud. He shoved a holster hard off of a side table, sending his bag of jerky to the floor with it. He kicked the holster against a wall, picked it up, and threw it onto the table, then grabbed the jerky and sat down.

Out of control and he knew it. And he knew where he was headed. The last time had been a few months earlier, when three innocent men were shot dead in Palisade on the same day. He wanted to choose the sober path, but damn if Meg, Allie, Daniel, and now Clay and Keen wouldn't let him. He was the one doing the pursuing, but he couldn't help but feel pursued himself. He never knew if it was the bad in him or the good that drove him hard. He seemed to feel one, then the other, and then both mixing together a bit too often. Either way he despised himself when he used drink to calm down.

He teethed the cork of the bottle, then twisted it and pulled hard until it squeaked free. His teeth hurt but he didn't care. He spit the cork onto the table and poured his first. After drinking it down, he bit off a chunk of dried beef and chewed while pouring another. He soon took a third and fourth before pushing the bottle away, but only a couple inches. He wasn't near full. The whiskey mixed and burned with the spice of the beef as it flowed over and around his tongue and down the back of this throat. He pinched his eyes closed and held his breath, waiting for the pain to ease. His body warmed. He pulled the bottle back in and took another drink.

Liquor on top of spiced beef never sat well with him. He knew this. But it was just one of those things you knew for certain how it would go and you did it anyway. He poured another drink just as the room started to twist and turn. He held still, but the room spun on. He set the shot glass aside and reached across the table to grab a near-stale half loaf of bread, tearing off a chunk. It would sop up the whiskey inside and soften the spice of the beef. He returned to the shots and continued with the mix of whiskey and jerky and bread for another half hour. The sheriff's frustration gave way to the numb of the whiskey. He sucked in a deep breath and cussed Daniel, Clay, and Keen as he breathed out again. He knew it was too late to head off to chase those men, and they'd be long gone by now anyway.

"Sure glad I didn't send James and Jeb out there to hunt those men," he whispered to himself. "They wouldn't stand a chance if they ran into 'em. And I'd be feelin' guilty about now."

He remembered his anger at James and Jeb and wondered how he could face them again, how he would explain his behavior. He hoped he wouldn't have to, hoped that they wouldn't ask about it, or about his past again, that they would just stick to doing their jobs and being lawmen. He realized at those thoughts that he was hiding once more, running away, and that he was far from being a lawman in that moment.

Dusk fell to dark; the bottle fell to dry. He closed his eyes and felt the warmth of the whiskey and the spin of the room. He laid his arms on the table and his head on his arms and fell asleep.

11

"MORNIN', SHERIFF," JEB said as he walked into the jailhouse.

The sheriff didn't look up from staring at the papers on his desk. He'd already stuffed the bottle he'd opened that morning into his drawer. He didn't want to give the deputies any reason or cause to ask about his behavior yesterday. The night was short, but he'd been handling morning headaches and limited sleep for twenty years. The pain was expected. A couple drinks down and he'd be set for the day. He took a sip from his coffee cup and welcomed the heat of the bitter coffee with a pour of whiskey.

"Jeb," was all he could muster in response to his deputy.

"Um… Sheriff. Henry got all of the messages out to the other authorities in the area. You know, about Keen bein' here yesterday."

"Lotta damn good that'll do now."

The sheriff glanced up at Jeb. He saw the fear and nervousness in his deputy. He wasn't there to babysit so decided to say nothing to put him at ease.

"So are you goin' after them or should James and me go?" Jeb asked.

"Does it look like I'm headed out?" he said, his focus back on the papers on his desk.

"Well, okay. And…"

"What, Jeb? Spit it out."

"Henry said the orphanage can take in Allie, but only if she's there by Friday. They can't leave a place open or they'll have another sad story weighin' on 'em."

"Finally, some damn good news." He glanced over to see if Daniel showed any sign of hearing them, but he just lay there on his cot staring at the ceiling.

"Who do you want takin' her?"

The sheriff ran his hands into his hair, then grabbed and squeezed and pulled tight. He didn't want to, but knew he needed to see this through, to help save that little girl.

"I'll do it," the sheriff said. "It's gotta be me. Be gone for a few days."

He gathered his things, rose, and started to walk out. At the door he said, "Can you and James manage to keep the town in one piece till I return? Daniel may get picked up for Carson City in a day or two, so don't screw that up. Send a message to Sheriff Waggoner over in Eureka County if you need help with anything."

"Yessir, Sheriff," Jeb responded, his arms tight to his sides.

"And keep your gun in your holster."

"Sheriff," came Daniel's voice.

The sheriff looked over and saw Daniel standing at the door of his cell.

"Can I talk with you before you go?"

The sheriff pursed his lips, his thoughts running wild. He wanted to have a heart for Daniel and put in effort to that end, but Daniel had created this mess on his own. He was the reason for the sheriff's trip to Frisco and away from Palisade for several days to take *his* daughter to an orphanage. He worked for a reason to let Daniel speak. He kept his gaze on the man in the cell for a few seconds more as his thoughts settled, then he turned and walked out of the jailhouse and slammed the door behind him.

"Maybe another day and another mood," he said to himself.

*

Daniel rested back onto his cot. He knew Allie would be leaving that afternoon, leaving Palisade and leaving his life. For good. The brute and father mixed and tangled inside him. The brute still strong and overpowering and all he'd ever known; the father fighting for breath and life and a voice.

As he sat there by himself, Daniel hardened his heart. It was a deliberate act. A choice. A decision. He froze everyone out. Easier to not care so he didn't feel the hurt. He thought back to all of those times he left them, Meg and Allie, not knowing where he'd be or when he'd return. Not really caring much either. He now felt the sting of those decisions, what they'd now led to, what they resulted in. He always put himself first. Selfishness layered atop brutishness layered atop mean. Like freezing rain layered thick and hard over a heavy snowfall atop the Grand Tetons, the mountain range that towered over the land where Daniel grew up. Cold. Hard. Immovable. Impenetrable. He knew there was no way to fix it, to apologize, to reset his life. And regret proved good only for remembering and wrenching tighter the pain and hurt. His vow to see Allie again and apologize seemed distant now, maybe too distant—an impossible reach, an impossible journey.

*

The sheriff led Allie to the train station to catch the 2:35 west to San Francisco. He held her hand; he knew she didn't much hold his. Her grip was light, already letting go of the only place she'd ever known. There was nothing there to remember—nothing good anyway. Allie showed herself an orphan already. She wore the same wrinkled, tattered, dirty blue dress she'd worn that Sunday morning. Her eyes were tired and heavy; her hair straggled over her face and to her shoulders. He noticed her slow pace to the station, not so much due to her small steps, but more of her hesitation to a future and place unknown and uncertain. He knew Allie wasn't thinking of what she was leaving behind, only fearing what lay ahead.

They walked up to the train car. Allie stopped. The sheriff touched and lifted her elbow and guided her onto the first step. She gripped the handle and turned back to him. He knew that look. He'd lifted Jed "JT" Treeman up those train steps two years earlier before cuffing him to a federal marshal. JT had shot a man in the back for a small bag of silver. This trip would take him to his hanging back in Arizona Territory three days from then. The sheriff's gut hurt the same now as it did then. *An outlaw's still a human, even more so when they turn and look you in the eye one last time knowing they'll be dead in a matter of days. They look you deep and leave a mark.* "Remember me," JT had said. And the sheriff had always remembered.

Now Allie had turned and looked him deep, just like JT had, and notched another mark in him. They both finished the stairs, slowing as they ascended. Wishing, hoping, for a different way out.

They boarded for the almost three-day ride west to San Francisco and the orphanage. He'd already come to hate that word. It reminded him of his failure as a lawman. Nothing she did to end up there; that burden lay with her father... and him. Dozens of young girls, all losers in society's eyes, unwanted and unwelcomed somewhere, seemingly everywhere. But society didn't have to look them in the eyes. They just put them in a large building with walls around it out in the middle of nowhere. Then washed their hands of the situation.

In a matter of days the Lind family would be spread across disparate locations. Mother dead and in the ground in Palisade. Father in prison in western Nevada. Allie alone in San Francisco. Without her having any say in the matter, this was the best that life had to offer Allie Lind.

She took a few steps into the train car. The sheriff pushed her through the tight doorway to the right and into the aisle. The narrow way and tall seats on either side squeezed her. She moved down the aisle, gazing at each passenger to the left and right, as a death-row inmate might on their final walk past the cells to the gallows, eyeing each and every inmate he passed, as if seeking clemency, forgiveness, or a saving hand.

"To the back, Allie. Let's sit there."

She walked to the last row and up and onto the bench seat, then slid into the corner and stared out the window. She didn't stop her stare until they hit the plains far west of town.

The sheriff sat opposite her. He kept his own gaze on Allie for a few minutes, then his nature took over and he began sizing up the passengers. A lawman didn't miss much, but you still had to look. He could spot a criminal on the loose, though he wasn't in a position to do much about it on this ride. He wished he could let down his guard a bit, stop being a lawman for a few days until he returned to Palisade. Each time he attempted this, though, it felt like he was shirking his responsibility, letting the public down. He'd raise his guard up again and keep it up. Mercilessly so. Long periods would go by where he'd be studying passengers and forget about Allie, then find himself jerking his head back at her in fear she wasn't there. A few seconds on Allie, then back to the other passengers, then to Meg, to Daniel, Clay, Keen. To this whole damn mess.

The train made its stops in Battle Mountain, Rye Patch, and eventually Reno the next day. A few hours later they were in California at the Truckee station. It would be another day before they arrived in Sacramento, then Stockton, then Alameda, and though a short distance as the crow flies, another several hours to make the trip around the bay to arrive at South San Francisco Station, their final stop.

More and more passengers boarded as they moved farther west. The cars filled to near capacity. At nearly every station, passengers would stop and look at the open seats around the sheriff and Allie. One look from the sheriff and they always moved on.

At the stop in Reno two men walked up and one of them sat down without looking. The other man grabbed his arm and pulled him up and whispered in his ear. They quickly walked through the doors to the next car. The sheriff didn't recognize them but knew they didn't want to be seen or found. He let them go.

Allie slept almost the full time through to the California border. The sheriff tried to sleep but couldn't keep his eyes shut for more than a few seconds. Duty would always wake him. He wished for a drink to help him rest but knew it would be wrong on a trip like this. He pushed his desire aside and focused on his job. Not easy to do, but necessary.

Tired fell hard on him. He knew he'd need some sleep over the three-day ride and was happy when a young couple stopped and stared at the open seats next to them. The lady looked at Allie, then him. The young man with her was busy storing their luggage.

The sheriff motioned them in and moved across to sit next to Allie.

"She's with me," the sheriff said softly, not wanting to wake Allie. "We're headed to San Francisco." He stopped his words. "We're going to visit family."

The young lady smiled. "We're moving to San Francisco. Started in DC. We've been on trains for ten days. We're desperately anxious to sleep in a bed that isn't constantly rocking."

"Not a lot of comfort on a train, that's for certain," the sheriff said.

"A bit out of your territory, aren't you, Sheriff?" the young man asked with some bravado as he sat down.

The sheriff looked him up and down head to toe. He

knew the man. Not the particular man, but the easterner who attempted to play the role of westerner—poorly, that is. It never worked. The cowboy hat alone contradicted the three-piece suit. Like trying to shove a gentleman's suit on a cowboy and drop him in the middle of a big city expecting him to fit in without a fuss. A wild pig would fit in better. He ended his search and curiosity of the man at that thought.

"Did you buy that hat as soon as you crossed the Mississippi?" the sheriff asked, showing no attempt to hide his mocking tone.

The man looked away from the sheriff to his wife. "Are you comfortable, dear?"

The sheriff slid back until his neck rested on the top of the seat. His eyes fell closed, and he immediately jumped himself awake. He slid back once more and again jolted himself awake.

"How long has it been since you slept?" the woman asked.

"A few hours."

"More like a day, I'm sure," she said. "Why don't you lie down and rest? We'll happily watch your daughter. What's her name?"

The sheriff hesitated. Going to sleep on the job didn't seem like a good idea. He feared waking up and Allie would be gone. He needed rest, though. He looked the couple over again and judged them trustworthy.

"Thank you, that would be nice," he said. "Allie. Her name's Allie."

"I'm Genevieve, and this is my husband, Robert. And you are?"

"Sheriff... just 'Sheriff' is good enough."

"You still make people call you that even when you're out of range?" the husband asked.

The wife lightly smacked him with the back of her hand. "Robert. Behave. We should feel safe with him here."

"Yep, I sure do," the sheriff responded to him. "It makes me feel tough."

"I'll protect you, Ginny. You don't need to worry about that."

She smiled at her husband; the sheriff could only grin at him. Then he lay down and set his hat over his eyes for a rest.

*

The steam whistle screamed loud and abruptly woke the sheriff. His first look was to Allie—who was no longer there. He quickly sat up and looked around, and then at the young attorney across from him.

The attorney sat there, glaring at the sheriff. No words.

"Where is she?" the sheriff asked.

"Did you lose track of her?"

The sheriff started to stand and grab the man hard when he saw Genevieve and Allie walking up the aisle.

He burned at the man's game, but with the women back he relaxed. His mind moved to badly needing a drink.

The sheriff helped Allie onto the seat. He watched as she lay down and immediately closed her eyes and fell asleep.

The husband continued his stare on the sheriff. "Where did you say you and your, umm… daughter, is it… are headed?"

The sheriff looked at the young man and snickered. "DC, huh? You a politician?"

"Oh, goodness no. Robert W. Guilford, attorney at law." The man reached into his suit coat pocket and pulled out a business card, hesitated, and then put it back.

"It's our first time west," the wife said.

"Ya don't say," the sheriff responded. "By the looks of your husband's sombrero there, I'd a guessed he was a right regular out here."

The man took off his hat and set it away from him. "Ginny likes adventure. I like business and law. Figured we'd head to Frisco and set up a law office. She gets adventure; I get to expand my business."

"Start a family..." the wife added with a smile.

The sheriff returned her smile.

"She's not your daughter," the man said.

"Robert!" Genevieve said, politely smacking her husband again.

"I know people, and you don't have a daughter. You don't treat her like one anyway."

The sheriff stared at the attorney. Hard. He bit his lip and imagined himself jumping up and punching the man in the face.

"You're right," the sheriff said. "She's not my daughter. Her mother was killed, and her father is in prison. I'm taking her to an orphanage where she'll not know a single person. You satisfied now?"

"That's awful," the wife responded.

"He killed her, then?" the husband asked flatly.

"Well, he's in prison."

"He was convicted?"

"Confessed."

The man squinted. "You don't seem convinced that he did it."

"He denied guilt at first pretty convincingly, then confessed. I'm goin' with guilty until evidence says otherwise."

"Why do you care one way or the other?"

"I'm a lawman. I care about justice. I care about gettin' things right."

The engine's whistle blew, and the train slowly screeched to a stop. Passengers stood and grabbed their suitcases and moved to the exits. The men allowed Allie and the young woman to exit first, then they grabbed their bags.

"I'm curious," the sheriff said, stopping the young man before he stepped into the aisle. "From your experience, why would a man admit to a killin' if he didn't do it?"

"Most likely to keep from being executed. Or maybe protect someone else."

"Yeah, sure. Maybe."

The men stepped into the aisle and headed for the steps and onto the platform of the South San Francisco Station.

"Or maybe out of guilt?" the young man added as they hit the platform.

"How's that?" the sheriff asked.

"Maybe he didn't do it, but he's still guilty. I've seen it before. Remorse and guilt set in and someone feels the need to be punished."

"You mean like he didn't do it, but he did?"

"Yep. Maybe he didn't pull the trigger but may as well have."

The sheriff took in the attorney's words, though still unmoved from the fact that Daniel had ultimately confessed… and Clay had found him standing over Meg, revolver in hand. Yet, as a good lawman, he couldn't dismiss the fact that maybe Daniel hadn't pulled that trigger. But the best he could do was hold on to this notion and wait for new information to prove or disprove it.

Once on the station platform, he and the attorney looked over the crowd and found Allie and Genevieve.

"You might wanna think about a bowler versus that thing you got on," the sheriff said, pointing to the man's hat. "Not a good look for a big-city attorney, even here in Frisco."

"Well, at least I'll have something to wear if I give up the city life and become a ranch hand."

The sheriff laughed. It felt good. The first time he'd remembered laughing with such innocence in months, probably longer. The man stuck out his hand for the sheriff, who hesitated.

"Sorry," the man said. "I didn't mean to insult you. Just trying to fit in a bit out here."

"No need to apologize," the sheriff said. "The west has a way of trying to turn a man into something he ain't meant to be. Maybe something to remember."

The sheriff reached and shook the man's hand. "Stick with law books and courtrooms, young man, and leave the lassos and ranches to us men."

The man smiled and nodded. "Will do, Sheriff."

*

The carriage ride out to the orphanage was cold and wet from several days of light rain and winds. "We don't get many dreary days like this in Palisade, do we, Allie?"

She didn't respond, just inched closer to the sheriff. He put his arm around her and pulled her in tight and rubbed her arm. Without a proper winter coat, the sheriff had layered Allie in a couple dresses and long-sleeve shirts. Even with the extra clothing and tucked up against him, he still felt Allie shake in the cold of the carriage.

In the distance he saw the dark structure emerge. It sat on a small hill in the midst of a broad expanse of barren land, giving it an ominous presence even from a mile out. The structure grew more ominous with each turn of the carriage wheels. Darkened brick covered the building, stained near-black in spots from a lack of upkeep and the smoke and soot of the several chimneys that rose up at distances along each side. The orphanage stood four stories high, with some ten or twelve windows running across the front and down the sides at each level. Corner towers gave it the feel of a military compound; a wrought iron fence, tall and black and half-rusted, fully surrounded the building and added to the feel of a compound.

The carriage rolled to a stop at the front gate. The sheriff sat and soaked in the sight, wondering if maybe he should be dropping Daniel off to prison instead. He opened the carriage door and stepped out. His boots sank an inch into the mud. He took the bags from the driver and thanked him, then picked up Allie and walked to the iron gate, flipped the latch, and pushed it open. It squeaked loud and eventually clanged to a stop against the fence. The sheriff stepped through and set Allie down on the walk, then swung the gate closed. He watched as she looked up at the structure—its size bearing down on her. The sheriff hesitated. Then, feeling in a hurry to get Allie inside and himself back home, walked to the portico and banged the metal knocker onto its plate. He turned and looked back. Allie hadn't moved. She'd kept her stare up at the building, her mouth hanging open.

The sheriff allowed regret in. He wished he'd come up with another plan, a more reassuring way to save Allie. But they were at the orphanage, and he was going to follow through on his promise to give her a life, any life outside of Palisade.

He knocked a second time, and in a few seconds the door opened. "Hi. I'm Sister Abigail. How may I help you?"

"Hi, Sister. I'm Sheriff Taggart from Elko County, Nevada. I'm here to drop off Allie Lind. We telegraphed a few days ago."

"Oh, yes, we're expecting you. Please, come in."

The sister was polite yet firm in her words and posture. She pulled the door open, and the sheriff stepped in. He looked around the entryway and to the grand staircase in front of him, leading up the four flights.

"And the young girl? Did she make the trip with you?" the sister asked.

"Allie. Yes, she did."

The sheriff looked behind him and then out the door. Allie still hadn't moved. She remained standing just inside the iron gate. He stepped to the porch and gestured. "Allie, inside. C'mon."

Allie didn't move, even after the sheriff's invitation.

"Allie. It's okay," he said, moving back to where she stood.

He gave her a few more seconds to take in the sight and then placed his hand on her back and gently pushed her. Slowly she began her steps to the porch and then up and inside.

The sheriff looked from Allie to the sister. "Allie, this is Sister Abigail."

As he introduced her, the sheriff recalled a detail from their telegraph communication, and added, "Sister Abigail is the head mistress of the orphanage."

"School. We prefer 'school.'" The sister smiled at him, then returned to her polite but firm posture as she looked down at Allie. "Welcome to Mount Josephine's School for Girls, Allie. There are many young ladies here your age. We have a lot to study and learn. And we have other regular activities as well."

The sheriff could see that Allie was overwhelmed. And not just overwhelmed by the loss of her mother, her home, and her town, but by this trip and the monstrous building that would be her home.

Another sister walked in and greeted Allie and the sheriff.

"Sister Mary," Abigail said, "will you take Allie to her room? The sheriff and I will finish up the paperwork."

As Sister Mary led Allie up the stairs, a young girl appeared at the top of the first landing. The sheriff could see that she was about Allie's age but smaller and thinner. Her face hadn't been cleaned in a few days, her white dress in weeks. Her hair was tattered and cinched together with a yellow bow that now appeared more brown than yellow.

"Angel, you best be back in your room," Sister Mary said. "We'll get everyone introduced to the new student later."

The young girl turned and sprinted up the stairs.

"All of our girls are here because there's nowhere else

for them to go," Sister Abigail said. "No family to turn to. No funds for a proper girls' school. We don't charge for our services. We are funded by the church and the donations of the good people of San Francisco."

"I understand," the sheriff responded.

"Having said that, we live, survive really, day to day. We don't have money to buy the girls fancy clothes, or even clean their clothes on a daily basis. They are bathed twice each week. They don't go hungry—there's plenty of food… but only the necessities."

The sheriff stared at the sister, disappointed but understanding.

"And we teach the basics—reading, writing, arithmetic, English, and history. Allie is seven. In a couple years she'll start learning a trade. Cooking, cleaning, washing, sewing, or basic nursing. She'll pick up the trade by working jobs around the school."

He continued staring at the sister. His hurt for Allie grew. For her future. He thought now that maybe her prospects would have been better in Palisade, something he never imagined possible until now. He was supposed to save her; this didn't feel like a saving.

"If you are her closest relative…" She looked at the sheriff with apology. "Pardon—caregiver. Please write down your name and mailing address. We'll provide a report for you once each year. You can visit anytime outside of school hours. She can write to you as often as she'd like, and you may as well."

She slid the paper across the desk and handed him a pen. The sheriff hesitated, then quickly ran through his mind how he might be able to give her a life in Palisade, who she might live with. How she would be educated. Given a chance at life and kept safe. He knew it was wrong, though, cruel even, to drag her back to that town. He thought of other options. Her grandparents. Another school somewhere. Then Savery Creek. But at that thought he grabbed the pen, filled in the information, and signed his name.

"Thank you, Sister. I'm not sure anyone will be visiting. I'll inform her grandparents of her location, but don't expect them."

She nodded. "Very few of our girls receive visitors. But they are cared for and loved to the best of our ability."

"How long will Allie be allowed to stay here?"

"They must leave at eighteen. We do everything we can to place them with a family sooner, but there is never a guarantee of that happening. Very few are adopted."

The sheriff contemplated these girls' prospects. *Not adopted. Leave the school at eighteen. Homeless. No place to go. No job. Minimal skills. Out on the street.* He closed his eyes as unwanted images seeped in.

"It's unfortunate," Sister Abigail said, "but we just don't have the funds or space to continue care past the age of eighteen. We have to focus on those who cannot care for themselves."

"Of course. I understand," the sheriff said, wishing he didn't.

The images continued their assault in his mind, regret followed. The future he just handed Allie didn't feel like a future at all, but a death sentence. He shook the thought from his mind and forced the lawman back in. This was just a job after all—nothing more.

As the sheriff left Sister Abigail's office and stepped into the hallway, he saw two teenage girls standing nearby, their heads lowered. They seemed healthy, but unkempt. He tried to catch their attention and smile, but they kept their looks down.

He walked to the entranceway, where Sister Mary met him once again.

"Allie is getting settled into her room, Sheriff," she said with a smile.

"How is she handling all of this?"

Before Sister Mary could answer, a line of about a dozen girls marched through, separating her and the sheriff. The girls didn't speak. No giggles. Just the same look that Angel and the two teenagers held. Dirt-worn dresses and faces. Eyes looking down. The sheriff expected a smile from the sister, maybe even a "Good afternoon, ladies." Some form of acknowledgement of their existence. But nothing.

"She's sad and hurt, Sheriff," Sister Mary replied. "Like every other girl who enters our home, Allie will experience sadness, hurt, and confusion. She'll feel lost. She'll show her anger in a couple days, and then for a few days more. After that she'll talk about how evil this place is. If she has any fortitude at all, she'll attempt to run away a couple times within the month. Don't worry, she won't get far. That's when she'll begin to convince herself that this place isn't bad after all. That this is probably the best place for her. She'll begin to make friends, and enemies, and settle in to her new life. She'll never truly believe or accept that this is the best place for her, but she'll be convincing enough."

The flood of regret that the sheriff had just shaken off returned in full force. The responsibility of saving Allie pushed the lawman away.

"Will she survive, Sister? Is this truly the best place for her? I've seen the worst that life can deal in this world, so give me the truth."

"She will survive physically. Emotionally is a different matter, though. This is a hard life, Sheriff. She needs a mother and father and the unique love and nurture only they can give. We can't take the place of that. We do what we can with what we have. That's all I can promise."

He shook his head and told himself he'd done his job, and then some. Besides, he had a full county to look after.

"Thank you, Sister. I'm sure she'll be fine."

Sister Mary shook her head. "No... no she won't, Sheriff. I'm sorry, but you wanted the truth, and this is it. She won't be fine. This isn't her family. It's not supposed to be like this. She won't have a normal childhood. Allie will be denied that. So she—all of these girls—have every right to be sad, hurt, confused, angry. Wouldn't you be? Would you want to be denied those feelings? She's already been denied her mother and father and her freedom. We need to allow her the one thing she has left that's her very own: her true feelings."

"I'll grant you she's being denied her mother, but her father—"

"I know the story, Sheriff. She was denied her father. He was there, but he wasn't. That wasn't her choice. She needed him, but he chose not to show up in her life. He chose to be absent. He wasn't there. *He* denied her a father. That makes him a coward. And now she's denied a mother as well. It doesn't matter what took them away from her. The fact is they're gone. Let her have her feelings. Those are the only real things in her life now, and frankly, the only things she can trust."

Reality hit the sheriff like a coldcock punch in the gut. Not his own reality, but Allie's. His throat tightened. He didn't want to say any more. He wasn't sure he could get the words out anyway, words that would still leave a little girl without a future.

"Thank you, Sister, for all you'll do for her. I need to get home."

With that he allowed the lawman to win, fully aware that the man in him had just failed seven-year-old Allie Lind.

The sheriff turned and stepped onto the porch and without hesitation headed to the road. He looked up for Gal, but she wasn't there. In that moment he felt lost himself. Homeless. Standing there, in the cold and mist of the early evening, the sheriff felt the gloom—of this place, Allie's new life, his own life. He paused, then glanced back at the school building, which now stood even darker with the sun fading to the west behind it. His eyes moved up to the rows of windows above the first story. He scanned the full breadth of the building to the left, and then to the right, expecting to catch Allie staring at him—rain pelting and dripping down the window to mask her tears—and asking him how it felt to be lost and homeless. He looked over the windows a moment longer, then turned away and fastened his coat to the top button, adjusted his hat down and tight, opened the gate, and stepped onto the muddy road for the walk back to the train station.

12

DANIEL LIND WALKED into the Nevada State Prison on August 30, 1878. The cold, hard stone of the floors and walls cooled him from the heat of the cage ride from Palisade to Carson City. Prisoners always wanted to get out, escape. Be free. But Daniel wanted to be there. In prison. For him, he was on a journey to seeing Allie again and prison was his path to freedom.

The ride to Carson City was about the worst experience of Daniel's life. A caged wagon full of murderers and thieves. These were the kind of men he'd hung around; they were his equals. But he'd always had the freedom to leave, to walk away when the wrong kind of trouble brewed. Or when the smell was unbearable. He did all he could to shut out the sounds and words and smells of that ride. And their empty cries of innocence and revenge smelled the worst. He was of it before, but not now; now he felt outside of it. He saw the lies for what they were, the brutish behavior, the selfishness, and that meant he now saw it in himself. He was buried among his kind in that wagon and would be for the next ten years.

The prison itself was only partially finished; two of the four sides remained to be built. Inmates would finish the work. Daniel would certainly be there long enough to break and chip and set in place the last stone. He welcomed the work, the sweat, the punishment intended in the labor. Each swing of a hammer, each drop of sweat, drop of blood, would take away another ounce of hurt that he had caused others, and bring him closer to seeing Allie again.

The deeper he walked into the prison, the hotter it got. The coolness he initially felt faded, replaced by air weighed heavy with the breath of a hundred men packed into a space meant for fifty. There were no cells. Just a large room with beds stacked two high jutting out the length of the side walls and a third row of bunks down the middle. The men barely had standing room between the beds. A man could have rolled either way and instead of falling to the floor would simply roll onto the next cot over. Aside from the beds, there was no other furniture in the bunkhouse. Each man had two sets of prison clothes, one to wear for a week, the other to be washed. The boots they wore were meant to last a year, but it took a year to get a new pair, so most lasted two. There were small, square windows with bars every few feet along the side walls, each no more than a foot high and wide. There were no showers, only a handful of tubs that were filled once on Saturdays and took in all of the prisoners without a refresh. The men knew the order of bathing—those who had been there the longest and those who fought their way to the front went first, followed by the newest arrivals, and then the weakest. Daniel didn't care much. He would just quietly stand in line and wait his turn. Another sign that he knew his days of selfishness, fighting, and cheating were over.

As Daniel walked into the bunk room for the first time, the guard ordered him to strip. A few men lingered about nearby but none showed care or concern for him. The guard tossed two sets of striped prison clothes and a pair of boots onto the bed, then folded his arms and waited. Daniel hesitated. The guard pulled a baton from his belt with his right hand and began tapping it into his left. Daniel slowly turned his back to the guard, stripped fully, and put on the prison clothes.

"Pick 'em up—your old clothes," the guard ordered. "We'll set 'em in the storage room. Somebody'll get out in the next few days and they'll be their first set of freedom clothes."

Daniel again hesitated. The guard whipped his baton into Daniel's side. He grimaced and bent over in pain.

The guard grabbed his hair and pushed him to the floor. "Pick 'em up, I said."

Daniel looked at his pile of clothes just inches from his face. He felt humiliated. Like the time he got caught red-handed stealing a box of ammo from a gunsmith shop when he was seventeen. He'd walked out of that shop and the door didn't even have a chance to close behind him before the owner grabbed his wrist, twisting it hard until he fell to his knees and cried. The box fell from his hand and the ammo spilled across the ground. "Pick 'em up!" the owner had yelled at him.

Daniel pulled his pile of clothes together and stood.

"The men that listen, survive," the guard said to him.

"The ones that don't listen leave in a wooden box. Your choice. We get paid the same."

"You in the Nevada State Prison now, big fella," a man lying on a bed across from him said. "You best listen and do as they say."

"Yep," said another. "Grab a hammer 'n' pickaxe 'n' shovel. No tellin' what you'll need out there today. You a prison worker now."

The guard pushed Daniel toward a door. "Let's get you some tools, big man. We got two more sections to build and a new load of rocks just arrived."

Most of the hundred prisoners were in the yard hammering, chiseling, shoveling, and dragging stones to the unfinished sections of the prison. A guard yelled at Daniel: "Over here! You see these seven boulders here? They need broke down to this size." He pointed to a pile of rocks that were all about two feet long and a foot or so high.

Daniel again hesitated, but less so this time. Holding onto the sledgehammer, he dropped the pickaxe and shovel and walked over to one of the boulders and began swinging. The head of the sledgehammer weighed several pounds. It took an effort to set the hammer behind him and then swing it up and over his head and hard onto the boulder. He was tired in five minutes. *Ten years of this will kill a man.* But the thought of dying in prison would also mean dying without seeing Allie again. He chose to live, to survive, no matter what the guards or work did to him.

Daniel was a big man the day he stepped into the prison. Not fat, just tall and broad. He would lose a quarter of his weight inside those walls, leaving ten years later thin and gaunt. The strength and meanness he had would be stripped from him. Most prisoners quickly lost their striving to be tough and mean. It never left them, but the energy to act it out got lost along the way. Many prisoners died within three years. A few died from fights, most from disease or malnourishment, many from the loss of will to carry on. Daniel would survive his ten, but the years would take a toll on him.

He knew the hope of seeing Allie again would pull him forward. Braving the torture and punishment of prison was necessary in order to see her once again and have the chance of apologizing and maybe even hearing her words of forgiveness. A life of thirty-three years full of mean and bad, and then ten years of prison, all to spend a few minutes with his daughter and be forgiven. *Seems like a waste of a life from beginning to end,* he thought. But no choice now to go back and redo things. He was there. He'd saddled this horse, no matter how poorly, and now he needed to ride it the full way home.

Daniel did his best to be obedient and well-behaved in prison, to stay out of fights and gangs, keep to himself. He kept his head down and his hands busy with work. He despised the guards, the warden, and every other man inside those walls. But he never showed it or voiced it. For the first time in his life he knew what it was like to be on a mission for good. Every other pursuit in his life meant someone else lost something for his benefit, and always having it stolen from them.

Rather than taking, he was choosing to lose. Choosing to give up. Choosing to surrender. His life. His time. His desires. His will. All for his daughter's gain. And if along the way he could achieve forgiveness, that would be welcomed.

The strength it took to stay out of trouble, though, to swallow his pride and put Allie first, surprised him. He'd never fought so hard in his life. And it wasn't a physical fight but a mental one—one that exhausted him more than hammering those boulders into rocks. All of his efforts to this point in his life had been to create trouble; he now fought within himself to prevent it.

Inside the prison there were gangs, mostly of whites, but multiple other races and nationalities as well, and pretty much any distinction a man felt like creating. As the remaining sections of the prison were completed, more men entered, and more groups formed. Everyone fit somewhere. Except Daniel. Each group took their run at him—an attempt to either recruit him or harm him. He'd been beaten and near-killed by most every group. He took the beatings and went back to being by himself. He'd been stabbed by picks and homemade knives. He'd had bones crushed by sledgehammers and his body pelted with stones from head to toe. Daniel didn't fight back; he simply worked to keep Allie in the forefront of his mind and purpose.

Group by group they surrendered. He became a loner and liked it that way.

Daniel might not have thrived in prison, but he survived.

It took two years to complete the prison and two years for Daniel to set himself apart from everyone else. Work became easier as well. From hammering and picking and dragging rocks to cleaning and washing the prison.

Daniel wrote a letter to Allie every month for ten years.

Never much. His written vocabulary was limited. Each letter he wrote was short and simple. He didn't know where she was, so he had the letters sent to Sheriff Taggart in Palisade. None were answered, not even a note from the sheriff. His hope of seeing Allie again ebbed and flowed. He realized over time that he became more ill when he lost hope. He worked at holding tight to the hope of seeing her again, of apologizing, and hearing her words of forgiveness.

As he chipped away at the stones, he expected to also chip away at his guilt. He worked harder and harder at working off his sin and mistakes in the labor yard. But the guilt remained thick and heavy on him—a rock that couldn't be broken. Time watered down the memories, but not the guilt. The guilt only weakened and sickened him.

The years ran by. His letters went out. As new prisoners entered, he would ask them where they were from, who they knew. A few knew of his brother or Keen or the sheriff, but he learned nothing of note. And none knew of a little girl named Allie Lind. After these conversations he would have no more use for the men. He simply returned to his life of punishment and hope.

13

THE MORNING AFTER the sheriff left Allie at the orphanage, he sat on the train departing from South San Francisco Station, heading east and back home to Palisade. It didn't feel right leaving Allie at that school, but she wasn't his responsibility. He wasn't the one who had abandoned her. Though now it felt like he'd done just that. He dropped his head and closed his eyes. A sickness fell in his stomach. *No. Don't do it, Jim. Dammit, please don't.* He leaned forward, elbows on his knees, biting his lips, twisting his hat in his hands. He tried shaking Allie from his mind, but she continued to weigh on him, as did Angel and the two teenage girls outside Sister Abigail's office, and the young girls who'd marched through the entranceway. Their dirty, tattered dresses. Their faces. Ratty hair. Heads and eyes always down. Allie wasn't much better off the day she walked in, but he'd hoped it was her chance at a better life. That chance now looked like a losing bet. She'd maybe learn to cook or clean, but he knew how certain the odds looked of her ending up on the streets, selling herself for food and shelter, or with a man just like her father.

He sat back and pulled his hat over his face and started cussing himself. Not for the situation, but for leaving Allie behind, and especially for his next move. Already gone three days, he was about to add a few more days to his time away from the county. But he wasn't going to make another fatal choice. He was sober and this was a sober decision.

As a porter passed by, the sheriff stopped him. "How long until the next stop?"

"Well, we just left Millbrae, so not long... fifteen minutes or so."

He fleshed his plan out in his head. What he'd say to her. Why he'd been gone so long. And once again, he'd apologize.

As the train pulled into San Jose, he was already at the bottom step. He jumped before it made its complete stop and headed to the ticket agent.

"One for South San Francisco," he said.

"Return ticket?"

"No."

"Arrives in one hour, leaves in two."

"Where can I get a bath and meal?"

"Best place is Satterbury Inn. Three blocks up, then a block to your left. Look for a white stallion on the signage."

San Jose was nicer than Palisade. Cleaner. Streets and buildings were straight. People dressed proper and showed good manners. Palisade seemed thrown together in a flurry by a band of miners after a full night of drinking. Dirty. Ruthless. Crooked. *Nothing crooked about this town,* he thought. A town planned and architected—perfectly lined streets, perfectly constructed buildings, perfectly formed townspeople. *Wonder if they need another lawman?* He laughed to himself, knowing he'd be bored in a place like this, and would miss the open space of Nevada.

He listened to the quiet. No saloon noise pouring into the streets, gunshots, shouting, or riders racing through town. Only the hum of the train station stood out among the stillness. San Jose was vibrant, healthy, and full of life. Palisade stood dying.

The sheriff took his time with the bath. It had been a long while since he'd stepped into a tub of hot water and still able to see the bottom. He was used to murky water from the previous bather at Bertie's. Along with his bath he was offered a shot or a beer. He took two shots and then took the offer of a beer. He lingered longer, even as the water cooled. He turned down the offer of a cigar.

A train whistle blew in the distance and the sheriff knew it was time to finish his bath and get some dinner. He stepped out of the water, dried himself, put on his dirty clothes, and headed down the stairs.

He was back at the station with five minutes to spare. He'd given himself a couple hours to change his mind. Rethink his plan. As foolish as he knew it was, it was the only thing a man could do. Foolish, yet righteous at the same time. She might just reject him and his request outright. He hoped she knew it was his only option.

The mud still lay thick on the path to the orphanage. The gate screeched loud again as he pushed it open and then swung it closed. He walked to the door and knocked.

Sister Abigail opened the door. "Sheriff? Did you forget something?"

"No, ma'am. I mean, no, Sister. I forgot some*one*."

Her look understood. "Please, come in."

She moved back and pulled the door open. The sheriff stepped in and stood where he had just a day before. He felt the same nervousness, the same uncertainty for Allie, and for himself.

"Wait here. I'll gather her and her things."

He heard small steps descending the stairs one at a time. Whispers weaved with the taps of hard soles on wood. Allie turned and stood on the first landing, holding onto her bag with both hands. Two other girls her age stood guard on either side. Tears trickled down her cheeks, begging to understand this torture he was putting her through. A yearling too young yet to be broken but forced without permission or want.

The sheriff walked to the stairs and up to the landing where she stood. He took the bag from her and took her hand.

"C'mon, Allie. Let's go. This isn't the place for you."

Without another word to the sisters, Allie and the sheriff walked out the door and to the waiting carriage. The sheriff continued to wrestle with his decision as the driver turned the team back toward the train station, leaving the option of Mount Josephine in their wake. He loved the hero feeling that filled him walking out of that orphanage with Allie in hand, like he'd just reached into her tragic soul and pulled her back to life. It felt good. And while he knew the decision to rescue Allie was the right one, he wasn't so sure about the decision to take her to Wyoming.

*

Allie sat quietly in the carriage, lost again. No home and no comprehension of where they were headed or why. She wondered where the sheriff was taking her, and even began to wonder what kind of man he was to treat her like this. She hadn't done anything to him, to anyone. She felt unwanted, and it seemed that he was stuck with her and mad about it. She was overwhelmed by the moment, by being unwanted, and by her life of the last few weeks. It was too much for her. Allie gasped for a breath and cried. She searched for feelings and questions and words. It wasn't until they were back on the train that she finally spoke.

"Are we going home? Am I going to live with you?"

"No, Allie, we're not going back to Palisade. There's no one there able to take you in. Besides, that's no life for you."

She sniffed and brushed the tears away, one side, then the other.

"It's just not safe, Allie. It's not a place for a young girl."

"Another school for girls who aren't wanted?"

The sheriff smiled at Allie. "No. No. A place where you'll be free and happy. And you'll be wanted. You need a happy life, Allie. Let's see if we can't give you that, okay?"

"Okay," Allie said softly. Then she lifted her legs onto the bench seat, laid her head on the sheriff's lap, and fell asleep.

14

THE TRAIN RIDE east into the Wyoming Territory took four days. They had traveled through Palisade and made the stop there, but the sheriff chose to lay low and not venture off. He spoke with incoming passengers about the town to learn if there had been any happenings or killings in the last couple of days. Nothing that alarmed the sheriff. James and Jeb were holding their own.

After departing Palisade, they continued their trip east, with their final stop in Rawlins, Wyoming. The sheriff knew they'd need a ride down to Savery Creek, which was situated a bit north of Medicine Bow, easily a four-hour ride from Rawlins. Thankfully, people in the area looked out for each other. They found a farmer at a feed store in town willing to take them along on his trip home to Savery Creek.

Even with the heavy jostling of the farm wagon the full way, Allie slept. The sheriff couldn't relax, though. He felt anxious and tortured. The farther away from the station they rode, the more he regretted his decision. As the wagon neared the homestead, the scenery grew familiar. He'd ridden this road hundreds of times, but not once in the last twelve years. This would be the end of the line for Allie. Her new home. At least that was his hope.

The cabin appeared in the distance. The sheriff's heart beat fast and hard. His breathing fell deep and heavy, his gut wrenched tight. Regret quickened. He thought of jumping off the wagon and running all the way back to Palisade. A selfish thought, no doubt, but an honest one. He simply did not want to face her. He took a deep breath and exhaled, then ran his story through his mind again and again, working to perfect it so he didn't forget any of the details that might tug on her heart. But he knew that he'd just blurt out the truth, forgetting all of the thinking and planning and storytelling he'd worked hard to compose.

Allie sat tight against him. The sheriff didn't feel her, though. He was lost in worry. They hadn't spoken much at all on the ride from Mount Josephine. The sheriff didn't have children, so he struggled relating to Allie. And this trip home was ripping him apart—tearing Allie away from the only life she'd known by taking her into the deepest pain he'd ever known.

*

Allie had cocooned herself in a world she fabricated after her mother's death. Better a world of your own making than what others thrust you into. In her new world she was a quiet heroine. Strength she had once expected in others she now carried in herself. Stories she'd heard her full life of seven years growing up in Palisade would be nothing compared to the stories she would survive herself. She was now a fighter, a role bequeathed to her not by her mother, who lacked the strength to stand up to her father, nor certainly by her father, who lacked the strength to be a husband, a father, or a man. She stole her fight. Took it without asking. It seemed the only way one could survive in this world when life was ripped from you. Take. Don't ask. So she did.

In her one day at the school, she never saw fight in any of the girls. Only surrender. In those instances when the sisters seemed overbearing and harsh, she expected pushback and fight, but only saw submission, appeasement. Even against wrong. Those girls weren't taking, they were given what others had taken and didn't want. Leftovers. Now they were leftovers themselves and would be for the remainder of their lives, short of some miracle or grace of God. Walking out the door of that school, Allie chose fight. She chose to be a taker. She decided not to be a leftover.

The wagon finally rolled to a stop. The wind blew light and cool from the north. Allie's hair twisted into her face. She shook it back and gazed at the log cabin. The dark brown of the logs stood out from the light brown of the dirt surrounding it and the burned-out grass of the hills behind. Lush green forest stood beyond, farther down the road, seemingly out of reach.

A large garden stood to the right of the cabin—the corn stalks browned and crisp from a summer of heat and little rain. Rows of other plantings stood at varying heights and colors, a mixture of green and brown and splotches of red and orange and yellow. End of the harvest. Winter was closing in.

A small barn stood to the back and left of the cabin. It

leaned eastward, in the direction the wind chose to push it. Short of the house and barn and garden, the land lay barren and wanting.

Muffled cries and bleats of animals broke the silence, but none were in sight.

"Sheep," the farmer who drove the wagon said as he jumped off to help Allie down. "They're out back. Only about twenty of 'em, maybe less." He paused. "Probably less. Hard to tell, though. One or twenty, they smell just as bad."

The sheriff, still seated and staring at the cabin, let out a soft, slow "Yep." It was all he could muster. He knew. The only life and livelihood within miles.

He took in a deep breath and let it go. Home. But to him it no longer felt like home. Weathered by a dozen years of harsh summers and harsher winters. A hard kicking of sun and drought in the summer, only to be relieved by snow and ice in the winter and pounding rain in the spring. Repeated year after year without an ounce of mercy or forgiveness. The land and buildings and animals survived, the homesteaders did too, but at the same time they didn't. A tough life that no one would choose.

Smoke rose up from behind the cabin. The smokehouse. The sheriff could smell the mix of smoke and meat and salt.

The cabin door opened and a woman stepped out onto the covered porch. Her arms to her sides, a knife in one hand, blood covering her arms and apron. Her brown hair fell straight and just past her shoulders. A thick smudge of blood ran across her left cheek. A few strands of hair danced across her face. She let them go. The sheriff sat, not moving.

He looked at the woman. The wind picked up and blew and whistled and broke the silence between them.

The woman wiped the knife on her apron, turned, walked back into the cabin, and shut the door.

"Maybe the wrong place?" the farmer asked as he jumped back onto the wagon.

The sheriff handed the man a dollar. "Thank you for the ride. We can walk rest of the way in."

"No need, happy to help. It's what we do out here. Besides, Becky could use the company."

"I'm not sure I'm the kinda company she wants," the sheriff responded.

He jumped off and reached for their bags. The farmer turned his team back the way they came and rode off.

The sheriff stared at the house, waiting for the woman to return and wave him in. She didn't.

You sure about this? he asked himself, heart pounding, memories racing. He set the bags down, then wiped the sweat from his palms onto his pants and swallowed a mouthful of dry air.

"Where are we?" Allie asked.

"Home, Allie. Well, hopefully home for you…. Hell for me."

"Do you know that lady?"

He didn't respond.

"Maybe she doesn't want us here… just like everybody else."

"Maybe?" he responded. "You might wanna try being a bit more certain about these things, Allie."

They strolled slowly toward the house and stopped

short of the porch and waited. He could hear voices coming from inside.

A young boy slowly cracked the door open and peeked out. "Mommy, that man and little girl are here."

The woman didn't respond.

The sheriff could feel her on the other side. Standing. Angry. Not wanting this. He imagined her jabbing that knife into a chicken or sheep carcass, ripping it apart, blood splattering everywhere, wishing it was him.

The door opened halfway, but no one approached.

The sheriff and Allie stood waiting.

"It's open," the woman said.

He stepped up onto the porch and lightly pushed the door fully open. Becky stood in the kitchen. A butchered lamb lay scattered on burlap across the table.

"You practicin' up for me?" the sheriff asked, nodding at the bloodied body on the table.

"You been dead to me for twelve years, Jim, so no point in even practicin'."

"It's good to see you, Becky."

She stabbed the knife into the wood table, put her hands on her hips, and stared at the sheriff. He could see the anger in her face. He knew she truly did not want him there. She kept her anger but went quiet as if waiting for him to take the hint and leave.

He expected the cold welcome and the anger. Seeing it and feeling it, though, was difficult to take in. He reminded himself that he was there for Allie, not himself.

"What are you doin' here?" she asked.

Becky looked at Allie, who was standing beside the sheriff. Quiet. Still. Unwanted.

"I see you're causin' more trouble." Becky nodded toward Allie, then looked at the sheriff. "Need me to bail you outta this one, too?"

"I'm not here for me, Becky. Honest, I'm not. Please hear me out."

She shook her head and grabbed the knife, then stabbed it into the animal's side. "What ya got for me here? This one looks alive. The last one you brought to me was dead. Remember, Jim?"

"Becky, you know I remember. Every waking moment I remember."

He wanted to say that he was sorry. He knew it would come across pointless and empty, even heartless, but…

"I'm sorry, Becky. You know that. You know—"

Becky's voice cracked. "Damn you, Jim! Damn you for always apologizing. Every time it's like you resurrect her and then she's dead again. Just stop it, okay? Just stop it."

"Yeah, sure," he said. He took off his hat and took a step closer to her. "Becky, this is Allie. Allie, this is Becky. My sister."

Allie looked at Becky and set herself to say hi, but Becky kept her look and anger on her brother. He lowered his head, knowing now that she wasn't going to be open to taking Allie on.

"Becky, no… Allie's not mine."

"My daddy killed my momma and now I got nowhere to go," Allie said.

Becky's face steeled on her brother.

The sheriff set the bags down and pulled Allie to himself.

Becky looked at the little girl wrapped in her brother's arm.

"Davey," she said, "why don't you and Jacob take Allie out back and show her the chickens? Might be more eggs ready to gather."

"Okay," Davey said. "C'mon, Jacob. C'mon, Allie. We got some new baby chicks. You can hold one if you like." He opened the back door and led them out.

The sheriff watched as Becky turned away from him. She stepped to a window at the back of the cabin and crossed her arms and looked out. The sheriff started to walk to her but stopped. Becky squeezed her arms tight to herself. She wiped tears from her eyes and shook her head slowly. She turned, arms still crossed, jaw clenched. He braced himself.

"*Here?!* You bring her here?"

He looked down, now certain he'd made the wrong decision.

"What the hell is wrong with you, Jim?"

"I took her to an orphanage but just couldn't leave her there. Her mom's gone. Her dad's in prison. No other kin wants her. Palisade ain't a town for a little girl. I need to give her a chance at a life. She needs a place—"

"This is supposed to make up for it? Is that what this is about? Ruin a few lives, but here—here's a good deed. That should even things out."

"Becky…"

"Feelin' better already, are you? Ready to head back to your hideout in Nevada? To some damn county no one cares about?"

"I made a mistake, Becky. And I paid for it."

"Paid for it? How? By running off?"

"With guilt. I ain't had a good night's sleep—"

"Wow, Jim. You never grew up, did you? You know what you left me here with? Do you?"

He didn't answer.

"Have you put the bottle down yet?"

The sheriff bit his lip and ignored her question. "Can you help me or not? Can you help Allie? Will you help her?"

"I been the only one helping. That's all I do is help. And all you do is run."

"I'm sorry, Becky. I'm sorry for leaving when I did. For leaving you with Mom gone, Dad sick. And I'm sorry for showin' up now without you knowing I was coming. It's not right, I know."

"Mom died because of *you*, Jim. Out in that cold and snow huntin' you down. Dragging your drunk body back into the house that night."

"Stop, Becky. I need you to stop. What am I supposed to do now? I've apologized. What else?"

"You can leave."

The sheriff let her harsh words sink in. The two of them stood in the quiet for a moment, in the thick of Becky's anger, in his regret of showing up after twelve long years. He waited to see if she would settle down, give in to the moment, to show a hint of joy at his arrival. She didn't. He knew it would be a difficult reunion, but not this difficult. Time had not healed this wound; the cut lay open and deep and painful. The sheriff looked over to the table. Blood slowly dripped and tapped onto the wood floor and splattered. He kept his look on the falling blood and waited for her to speak.

"Is this you playing savior?" she finally asked. "You kill my little girl and now you bring me another? Redemption? Is that what this is?"

"No…"

"Do you feel better now? Whole again? Justified?"

"Becky, please stop."

"You think this will bring her back? All is forgiven now?"

"Becky, please, hear me out."

She looked at the ceiling, then the carcass on the table, then the knife. She closed her eyes tight and threw her hands into her hair and squeezed and pulled hard.

"What are you doing to me, Jim?" she yelled.

He didn't answer. She squeezed and pulled again and screamed, then slowly let her hands fall from her hair and down her face. She opened her eyes and looked at her brother. He saw her pain—resurrected pain that had long been buried, until he arrived.

"Why, Jim? Why? Why should I hear you out? You go away, free to live your life. I stay back tendin' this damn farm by myself. Daughter dead. No man to help. Two boys to raise. Now you bring me another burden?"

The sheriff kept his eyes on Becky. He let her talk.

"Damn you, Jim. Just damn you!"

"I know, I know," he said, nodding in agreement.

"Here, sis!" she said mockingly. "Here's another problem for you to take on. See you in another twelve years!"

He turned from her and looked back toward the road in front of the house. It now felt like a wasted trip. The little hope he'd had for Allie was gone. The pain of not being able to save her, on top of what he'd done to his sister and her life, welled up in him. He set his head in his hands and pushed the emotion and tears back. Then he gave up on Becky as an option. And gave up on ever being forgiven. He started to envision his life as Allie's guardian back in Palisade. He shook his head. It wasn't him. He'd be as bad a father as Daniel. Maybe worse.

He dropped his hands and walked to the back door and opened it.

"Allie, let's go."

Allie carefully set down the baby chick she'd been holding and walked to the door. He could see it on her face. The hurt. The confusion. They were leaving again.

"I'm sorry, Allie. I'm just sorry."

The sheriff watched his sister take in Allie's emotions as she stepped into the house. He could see Becky's own hurt for the little girl. He placed his hand on Allie's back and began to guide her to the front door.

"No... wait," Becky said.

The sheriff and Allie stopped.

Becky looked away, took a deep breath, and let it out. "Just wait," she said, now looking at them.

They waited for Becky to continue.

A moment passed before she spoke again. "Allie, go ahead and play out back with the boys. I'll get you something to eat."

Allie looked at the sheriff, unsure of what to do.

He paused and thought. "It's okay. Go out with the boys," he said softly.

After Allie went back out, the sheriff and Becky stood in silence for a long minute, trying to make sense of this moment twelve years in the making.

"Set me aside, Becky. Set *us* aside. Allie needs someone. She needs a home. I'm simply asking if you can help."

Becky moved to the table and leaned into it and closed her eyes. "My life is already complicated and hard enough, Jim. I got two mouths to feed and Del gone, gone for good."

She picked up the knife and jammed it into the table again and looked at her brother. "Damn you for doing this, for putting me in this position."

He looked away. "I know, I know. But I got nowhere else to go."

"That's your fault. Stop dumping your problems at my feet and runnin' off."

The sheriff picked up their bags and turned to leave.

"Okay," Becky said. "I'll do it. But not for you. I'll do it for Allie. She needs a home. Something stable and predictable, even if we're rock-bottom poor."

The sheriff held the bags and stared at the door. He felt relieved, yet also felt the full weight of shame and guilt for what he'd done to his sister's life. And no way to repair it.

"I'm mad at you, Jim," Becky said softly. "I had to set my life aside because of you. Run this farm myself. Married a guy I didn't love. And here you are, dumpin' and runnin' again."

"You have every right to be angry, Becky. I'll take all you want to give me. Go ahead, pile it on as high and deep as you want. I just want to save Allie and give her a life. That's all I'm after."

"I said okay, Jim."

"I've got money to leave with you, and I'll send more every couple of months."

Becky looked down and set her hand on her forehead. "Everybody gets a damn life but me," she said to herself.

The sheriff started to move toward his sister, to hold her, but he stopped himself. "I hear you, Becky. I hear you. I really do. What else can I do to help? To fix things? To repay you for what I've done?"

She didn't move. The sheriff waited.

"Spend a week here," she said, still looking down.

"What? I can't do that! I have a county to—"

Becky looked up and hard on him.

He stopped. Not just his words, but his dumping and running. His selfishness.

"What do you need done?" he asked.

"Everything. There's a leak in the roof. Barn door's broke. Garden needs tilled over. Woodpile's down to splinters. Smokehouse is near empty. And..." She fell into a chair and buried her head in her arms and cried.

"I'm sorry, Becky," he said, lightly placing his hand on her shoulder.

Davey came in the back door. "Mom, you okay?" he asked.

"We're okay," the sheriff said. "Can you hitch up the wagon? I need to make a run into town."

The sheriff looked at his sister, her head still buried. Then he nodded for Davey to go ahead and do it.

Davey ran out and Becky said, "This is hard... just too damn hard for me."

He leaned in and kissed the top of her head.

"Thank you, sis. I'll do all I can to help get Allie settled and fix what's broken. Teach the boys all I can while I'm at it."

*

The week flew by. He didn't mind the work—manual labor proved good for his spirit. Allie settled in quickly. Becky struggled, though, and fought the new burden, but at the same time appreciated time with her brother and his help.

Each day of the week he tackled another project for his sister. He fixed the leaky roof, though it took him two days and two trips into Savery Creek. The top hinge of the barn door had rusted and broken off. He replaced both hinges and rehung the door. He butchered two more sheep and set them in the smokehouse, then traded a third for some beef and set that meat in the smokehouse as well.

The kids followed him around and joined him on some of his trips to town. Becky welcomed the break from having to work all day and evening on the farm and watch her boys at the same time. The sheriff allowed Davey to help with fixing the roof and door, and in the smokehouse. All that Davey learned would give Becky additional support once the sheriff left.

The sheriff worked from sunup to sundown each day. He was drenched in sweat by midmorning and ready to quit by noon. But he was working for Becky, so he worked in earnest for her and desperately for her forgiveness at the same time.

Later in the week he gave Davey his first shooting lessons, and even took him hunting. Allie showed interest in the revolver and rifle. The sheriff let her hold them but told her that she was too young yet to use them. She made him promise to teach her how to shoot when she was big enough.

He snuck some whiskey back to the farm, keeping it hidden from Becky, and keeping himself to just a swig or two at a time. As the week went on, he found less need for a drink.

The following Saturday morning, with more work accomplished than Becky had asked for or expected, the sheriff hitched up the wagon and they made the trip into Rawlins for the 12:35 west to Nevada. Allie and the boys joined them, sitting in the back, laughing and giggling the full way. It was a quiet ride for the sheriff and Becky, though.

As much as he wished for more time with his sister, the sheriff was anxious to get back to Palisade and Elko County and his job. He also knew James and Jeb would be needing him. It was a rough town and a big county, too much for two young deputies to manage on their own. A week of hard work on the farm, though, had proved restful for him. He was leaving the farm in good shape and proud of that. And he was pleased that he was able to get Allie to a safe place where she would be loved and cared for. She would now have a life. What he'd done to his sister, though, weighed heavy on him. He'd reopened that wound in Becky and added to it. He was also leaving without the forgiveness from his sister that he'd hoped for. Nearing Rawlins, his heart raced as he anticipated those words from her. She certainly wouldn't let him leave continuing to carry that burden, he thought.

At the train station, the sheriff jumped off the wagon and grabbed his bag. Becky took the reins and leaned forward as if ready to leave without another word. He stood to the side of the wagon looking at her, waiting for her to speak. He felt the next words, maybe the final words, should be hers.

"Come back anytime, Jim," she said, finally looking at him.

"I will, Becky. Thank you."

"There's always work to be done," she said with a pinch of anger.

He swallowed hard.

"Best be gettin' to the train," she said. "I'm sure you don't wanna get caught here any longer and miss your life back in Nevada."

"Becky..."

"Don't say it, Jim. I heard you the first ten thousand times you said it. I know. You're sorry. I am too."

She pulled the reins to the right and turned the wagon toward home. The sheriff's heart sank. "It seems I'm better at hurting people than I am at helping," he mumbled.

As the wagon rolled on, Allie leaned to the edge and looked back at him. Becky stopped to let a group of riders move past, allowing Allie and the sheriff to hold their look for a moment longer. Allie smiled and waved. He smiled in return, then lifted his hand as a final good-bye to her. She kept her gaze on him until they were finally out of sight of each other. He kept his stare on her for another minute, certain that Allie did as well. Sadness crept into him. He missed her already, and wondered when, or if, he'd ever see her again.

The clock above the station entrance showed 12:15. The

sheriff turned and walked toward the town. "Just enough time to grab a bottle for the trip," he said to himself.

On the train he walked the cars, working to sense which seat would give him the most undisturbed ride. He knew wherever he sat, though, the seats around him would fill in soon after and with the noisiest bunch.

A thirty-six hour ride and more than twenty stops, he reminded himself. *I'd rather take the extra time and ride with Gal, sleep out in the open, away from people. Sure could use a good dose of that solitude about now.*

He chose a bench with just two other passengers, an older couple who sat across from each other. They seemed proper and quiet, likely knowing how to keep to themselves and not nose in on someone else's business. He sat next to the gentleman, who then stood and moved next to the woman. He studied them. Nothing spoke bad or evil or outlaw about them, but he'd known that right when he'd laid eyes on them.

After ending his study of the couple, his mind immediately jumped to Allie and Becky. He laughed to himself, then at himself, and shook his head. Studying people wasn't so much his job, he realized, but a way of distracting himself from his own life, from studying himself.

He reached for the bottle in his bag, then let it go. Thoughts of regret for how he'd treated his sister crept in, as if a sickness was falling on him. He made no attempt to push them away. He thought of her tough life, for which he was at least partly responsible. Now he'd dumped Allie on her and run off once again. No matter how much that was about Allie and saving her life, he had selfishly made it

Becky's responsibility. *Maybe she didn't forgive me because I simply don't deserve it.*

The sheriff thought of Allie and her dad. He hoped they would find forgiveness and reconciliation someday. He knew it wouldn't be easy, and likely would never happen.

He reached again for the bottle and pulled out the cork.

15

TWO YEARS AFTER Meg Lind's death, Daniel was settling into his new life in the Nevada State Prison. Despair and loneliness ate at most men in prison; Daniel welcomed it. They served as punishment, sentences deserved. He lived resolute in his journey to survive his ten-year term, see Allie, apologize, and seek forgiveness.

In the yard, among the noise and clamor of work and shouting and fighting and cussing of men, he found peace from his demons. It amazed him that the demons wouldn't come out among those men in the yard. As if the demons were afraid of something. The only fear that weighed on him was never being released; never having the chance to see Allie again. He would never be able to forgive himself, that much he admitted, but receiving Allie's forgiveness would be enough for him to rest in peace.

Daniel was down to 170 pounds in just the six months after entering the prison at 225 pounds. His tall build now gave him a wiry look, something he hadn't known since a teenager. The work added muscle and strength, but to him they were of no use, a waste of both. Breaking boulders into rocks was pointless, not his purpose.

Allie lived foremost in his mind; the torture of prison life secondary. In the middle of breaking rocks, with rock chips constantly flying into his face and eyes, he wished he had lived the reverse. He wished he'd kept his focus on Meg and Allie, put his work second—that is, his bad ways.

As he was swinging his hammer, and lost in his thoughts, a shadow moved in and covered the boulder he was working to split.

"Howdy. My name's Shuler. Shuler Cole."

Daniel looked up. A tall, dark man set his hammer on the ground, leaning the handle against his thigh, and held his hand out for Daniel.

"Been here just two days. How long you been in?" the man asked.

Daniel ignored him and continued striking his sledge-hammer against the top of the boulder. Shuler watched and timed the swings, then began driving his hammer onto the rock a second after Daniel. They swung their hammers onto the boulder in rhythm for several minutes.

Craaaaack!

Shuler's swing hit just right and the boulder cracked in two. "Glory be," he said, laughing. "Never saw nothin' like that."

Daniel looked at Shuler, a black man, the blackest he'd ever seen. And near the same age but taller. And Shuler's voice was deep and jarring. Seemed like God Himself speaking. His eyes were kind and welcoming, though, contradicting his size and voice, and the fact that he was in prison.

He held out his hand again for Daniel. "Name's Shuler, but everyone calls me Sugar."

"Daniel," he responded, but he didn't shake Sugar's hand.

"Have it your way, Daniel. Nothin' hurt by it."

Needing a quick breather, Daniel turned and sat on the ground, setting his back against the split boulder. Sugar joined him.

"They call me 'Sugar' 'cuz my little sister, when she was learnin' to speak—we lived way down in Georgia—well, she couldn't say 'Shuler.' She kept sayin' 'Sugar.'"

Sugar laughed again, only louder. He sounded as if thunder rolled from him. "Sugar don't much fit a black man, does it?" he said.

Daniel continued to ignore him.

"It's okay, Daniel, you can laugh or not. No one ain't never hurt my feelings either way."

Daniel half smiled.

"There ya go, Danny boy. We may be in prison, but we can still be happy and free."

"What are you talkin' to this garbage for?" came a voice from above them.

Daniel and Sugar looked up at the man in front of them. Levi Brockton. He led a mixed gang of prisoners, outcasts of every other group. Brockton was short and thin and carried a hardened nature about him, as if acting tough all the time might make him taller. He held a pickaxe slung over his shoulder. A few other men gathered behind him, each carrying a tool of their own. None were smiling.

Daniel stood and faced Brockton, who was at least four

inches shorter than Daniel. Size didn't deter him, though. He looked past Daniel and down to Sugar.

"I see, I see," Sugar said, still smiling. "We a bit far from the south for this, ain't we, fellas?"

With no response coming from the men, Sugar put his head down and lost his smile.

"He needs a lesson," Brockton said to Daniel. "He shouldn't be here. You gonna teach him or do I get the pleasure?"

Daniel looked at Sugar, then back to Brockton. "I'll teach the lesson," Daniel said.

The man smiled and nodded. "I knew you were one of us."

As Daniel shifted his look back to Sugar, he noticed the two guards that stood nearby. They showed no sign of intervening. They simply tipped their hats back and watched.

"Pay attention, then," Daniel said to Brockton, returning his smile. "I'm only gonna show you this one time."

Sugar kept his look down and waited for the lesson he'd been learning his whole life, but never understood.

"Stand up, Sugar," Daniel said. Then he reached down and held out his hand and pulled Sugar to his feet. "My name's Daniel Lind. It's good to meet you. And just so you know, I coulda broke that rock myself. Didn't need your help."

Sugar smiled, then laughed, and squeezed Daniel's hand.

"Oh, you took the wrong side," Brockton said to Daniel. "You as good as dead."

Sugar leaned over and picked up a large rock that had broken off when the boulder split. He stepped in front of Brockton, shoving his chest into the man's face, and glared down at him. "Anyone touch my friend here," he said, his voice echoing deep across the yard, "and I'll beat the devil out of you with this rock, then I'll use what's left of your body as a sledgehammer until this here boulder splits again."

Daniel grabbed his own sledgehammer and set it over his shoulder. He and Sugar stood staring at the men until they eventually backed away.

Sugar smiled once again. "Always makes me sad when they show themselves coward and run. Takes all the fun out of a beatin'."

Both men laughed.

"I'm done fightin'," Daniel said. "You're on your own next time."

"No problem there, Danny. Thank you for the helpin' hand this time."

Daniel returned to his spot and set himself to swinging his hammer again.

Sugar hesitated and studied his new friend. "How long?" he finally asked.

"How long what? Have I been in or till I get out?"

Sugar shrugged. "Whichever."

"Got ten. Two done."

"I got just two. Pretty lucky at that."

"*Break!* Take five, men," yelled one of the guards who'd just watched the confrontation.

Daniel dropped his hammer and sat back down. Sugar followed.

"Is there drinkin' water around?" Sugar asked.

"Yeah. I'll show you. Follow me."

The two men walked to the center of the yard to a trough. Each grabbed a metal cup, dipped, and drank.

"This sure is cool water for a desert," Sugar said.

"They pump it up fresh a coupla times a day."

"I was ridin' down around Pioche in southern Nevada," Sugar said. "Biggest silver mines in Nevada down there. Thought we could whip up some quick wins at the tables with all that silver money in town. Had another man with me. Meanest sumbitch I ever seen or rode with."

Daniel dropped his cup in the trough and walked back and sat again.

Sugar followed and continued his story. "Now I ain't never killed no one—hope to never, neither. But I almost got this one pinned on me."

Daniel leaned his head back and raised his shirt up over his eyes to help shield the sun that was scorching his face.

Sugar didn't seem to care whether Daniel was listening to his story or not as he went on, "We walked into this bar for a drink. Damn, if there weren't a hundred men in there squeezed tight as hell. Every color in there 'cept mine."

After wiping his forehead with his shirt sleeves, Sugar leaned closer to Daniel. "We started pushin' ourselves up to the bar. Got the nasty looks and all. But when they seen my friend's face, it's like they forgot I was black. They just turned scared like. If they'd had tails, they'd a tucked 'em between their legs."

Sugar leaned in more. Daniel stuck to his quiet. Sugar stuck to his story.

"'A bottle,' I said to the bartender. 'And two glasses.'"

Daniel lowered his shirt and closed his eyes.

"And then my friend yells, 'Clean ones! They better be clean.' Like the bartender had some bad habit of handin' out dirty shot glasses. Well the bartender didn't like that one bit, so he turned and walked away, just ignored us. My friend got real agitated. I tried to calm him down: 'Keen,' I says to him—"

Daniel jerked his head to Sugar. "Keen? The man you were with—his name was Keen?"

"Yep, it was."

"I sure as hell hoped he'd be dead by now," Daniel said.

"You know him?"

"I rode with him awhile. All over Nevada and into Arizona and Utah."

"Damn. You in here 'cuz a him? He sure as hell got me in here."

"Where was this?" Daniel asked.

"Like I said, down around Pioche."

"You ever come across a guy named Clay?"

Sugar paused, then shook his head. "No, I ain't. Like I said, I got two years, right? Well, I should still be ridin' if not for that sumbitch. That Keen just up and shot the bartender, killed him quick-like. Didn't hesitate. Reached for his piece, pulled the trigger, and set his gun back. Did it like you and me would reach around and scratch our backside."

"And you got caught and Keen's still runnin' free," Daniel said.

"Yeah. How'd you know?"

"That's the way it works with him. Like he owns every damn place he walks into. He does whatever he pleases. Ain't no one gonna stop him or catch him, and he knows it."

"Lucky sumbitch, I say."

"Evil don't need no luck. Just a gun and no care for anyone else."

"Did he get you in here?"

Daniel eyed the ground and saw Meg on the kitchen floor. He missed her now. Every day even more so. He wanted out of prison and back home with her and Allie. It was the first time in years he could remember having that strong of a feeling for Meg. It surprised him that missing her this badly took two years to show up, but there it was. He thought of Allie and knew she would be missing her mother just as much. He missed his family. The hurt and regret for what he'd done matched his longing for Meg and Allie.

"Pick 'em up!" the guard shouted, interrupting Daniel's thoughts. "C'mon, you lazy bastards. Pick 'em up and get at it."

"Did Keen ever talk about the killin' of a woman in Palisade? In northern Nevada?" Daniel asked Sugar.

"Mmm... no, can't recall nothin' like that."

"Didn't figure," Daniel said as he picked up his hammer and readied himself for more swinging.

"Why you in here?" Sugar asked flatly.

Daniel didn't answer.

Sugar continued his swings in rhythm after Daniel, and not one to settle for quiet, he continued talking as well.

"When you get out, where you goin'?" Sugar asked.

"Back home, to Palisade. No place else to go. You?"

"Suppose I'll head down to Texas. Ain't been that way yet."

"Not goin' after Keen? For what he done to you?"

"No. Don't wanna end up dead or back here for somethin' else he done. I'll just let it go. Ain't no good ever come of revenge."

Daniel quit the conversation. Sugar took the hint and without hesitation began singing:

> "When Israel was in Egypt's land,
> Let my people go,
> Oppressed so hard they could not stand,
> Let my people go.
> Go down, Moses, way down in Egypt's land,
> Tell old Pharaoh: Let my people go.
> The Lord told Moses what to do,
> Let my people go,
> To lead the—"

WHACK!

A guard had stepped behind Sugar and slammed the stock of his shotgun hard into Sugar's side. "This ain't no Sunday mornin' meetin'. Get to work and stop your singin'!" he yelled.

Sugar fell to his knees and crossed his arms over his side in an attempt to cradle the pain. Daniel moved to help, but the guard raised his shotgun at him.

"You want what he got?" the guard asked.

Daniel looked at the guard, then at Sugar, and returned to his work.

Clang! Clang! Clang! Clang! Clang!

"Lunch!" multiple guards yelled across the yard. "You got thirty minutes to get in and out. Let's go!"

Most prisoners dropped their tools and ran toward the mess hall, setting themselves into two lines as they ran. A few strolled in, as if in no hurry at all.

Sugar still lay in pain on the ground. Daniel knelt down to him. "I don't see no blood. I think you'll live. And, hell, I'd a hit you too; you don't exactly sing like an angel."

Sugar looked at Daniel and smiled and laughed. "Help me up, old man, just help me up."

Daniel gripped his hand and pulled him to his feet, and they headed to the mess hall together.

"What was that you was singin'?" Daniel asked Sugar.

"Just somethin' we sung in the fields. Passed the time. Kept us strong and close to the Lord. Songs like that made us one. You gonna join me singin' when we get done eatin'?" he said, laughing.

"No way. Can't sing. Don't wanna lose a rib neither. And don't know the words or the story."

"The words is easy. And you may not know it, but you livin' that story, Daniel."

"I may be in prison, but I ain't no slave."

"Daniel, we all slaves. The Isra'lites in Egypt, black folk down south, you and me in here. And I don't mean 'cuz we're locked inside."

The two men made their way to the mess hall. Sugar kept a hand to his right side and groaned every few steps. The quiet hum of the line of men was drowned out by the loud chatter and clanging inside the hall.

"We're slave to sin, Daniel. The Isra'lites weren't just Isra'lites. They represent a people oppressed by sin, not just by Pharaoh. That's my story, my people's story, and that's your story, whether you like it or not. And that's truth, Daniel. Truth like you never known before."

As the two men reached the door of the mess hall, Sugar stopped Daniel and pulled him back.

"When you get out of this place, you still gonna be locked up, you still gonna be a prisoner. You ain't gonna be free. Not until you surrender to Him." Sugar kept his look on Daniel and pointed straight up.

Daniel didn't say a word. He just turned and stepped inside the doorway. Sugar grabbed Daniel's arm and pulled him back again, closer.

"Most folks think songs like that, and the Bible, even God Himself, is out to condemn us and want nothin' but to send us to hell. We're already condemned, born that way every one of us. Those words don't condemn us, they save us."

Daniel held onto Sugar's look this time.

"Let me know when you're really hungry—I got somethin' that'll fill you full up."

Daniel held a few seconds longer, then turned away as they walked into the hall.

"You ain't never gonna get much outta him," said a man in line behind Sugar, nodding at Daniel.

"We tried talkin' to him and got nothin'," another said. "Bull here tried to pick a fight with him awhile back."

"I did," said Bull, a man about five foot tall, and near as wide. "Called him all sorts a names. He didn't even look up. Just kept swingin' that hammer."

"Killed his wife. Did you know that?" the first man said.

"No, I didn't," Sugar responded. "Don't know nothin' about him. He don't seem that mean a man, to kill his wife."

"Best to leave him alone anyway," Bull said.

"Know anything else about him?" Sugar asked as they picked up their food trays.

"I know he works hard and don't cause no trouble," Bull said. "Can't say the same about others in here. Do just like Daniel and you'll be fine. Act up and cause trouble and you'll get your fair share of bruises and cold nights chained to the pole in the middle of the yard."

Across the hall, Daniel had set his tray on a table. Before he sat, he looked back and caught Sugar's eyes. They held for a moment. Daniel nodded. Without hesitating, Sugar smiled and started singing that song again right there in the prison mess hall.

Daniel smiled as well. In that moment he tasted freedom for the first time—real freedom. Hope surged in him for the only thing he wanted out of life: to see Allie again. He only needed to survive his prison sentence and the journey home to Palisade.

16

I N THE YEAR she turned fourteen, Allie had been with Becky for seven years and her father was seven years into his ten-year sentence. Allie became a quiet, yet tough and focused young girl. She did work around the house to help out, but she hadn't let go of the anger for her father. Instead of dissipating, the anger grew for what he'd done to her mother and to her life. Her determination to do something about it, about him, grew stronger.

Becky was pleased with and blessed by Allie's helping hand. Allie loved tending the animals most—the sheep, chickens, and especially the horses. Soon after Allie's fourteenth birthday, a man rode up to their farm and asked Becky if they had any horses that needed to be destroyed. He had three horses in tow with him. A pony lay dead in his wagon and two were tethered to the back of the wagon and trailed along behind. The two that trailed were bony and appeared near death themselves.

"Not this time, but I appreciate you checking with us," Becky said.

The man tipped his hat and rode on.

Allie stared in shock at the sickly horses. "Becky, what did he mean about destroying horses?"

"When a horse is lame or ill beyond saving, they need to be put down. Most farmers destroy them on their own, but some allow them to be collected and processed humanely."

Allie went from shock to dread and tears. She had seen so much human life destroyed growing up, and more animal life on the farm. Those ponies looked beautiful and strong to her. It seemed senseless to destroy them, to not give them a chance at life. All they needed was a place to live and some care; they needed to be rescued and loved. She knew in her heart she could do that for them.

"Those were beautiful horses," she said to Becky.

"Yes, they were, but a lame or sickly horse is of no use. They only consume a farmer's precious time and money. So they need to be put down."

"They didn't look lame," Allie responded. "Maybe they just need some food and proper care."

Becky looked at Allie. "I suppose it's possible that those two trailing ponies are in good condition, that maybe the owners just couldn't afford to feed and care for them any longer. These are difficult times. We're all short of extras around here."

"So maybe they just need someone to feed and care for them and love them?"

Becky gave Allie a hesitant smile. "Yes, that could be all they need."

Allie's face lit up. She smiled and jumped to her feet and put her hands together and began begging. She wanted to rescue those horses, give them a life, just as Sheriff Taggart had done for her.

"Please, can we keep them?"

"Oh, Allie. We're one of those families that can't afford another mouth, especially one that won't stop eating."

Allie kept her excited expression fixed on Becky. She leaned into her, anticipating the yes.

Becky looked up to the sky as if this was an agonizing decision. Then she smiled. "Okay, okay. Just one of them, though. And only if it needs nothing but food and love."

"*Yay!*" Allie shouted, then fell into Becky and hugged her.

"It's yours, so it'll be your responsibility to feed and care for it, not mine. And you can't take food out of our mouths for it either."

"Yes, of course. I promise!" Allie exclaimed.

She sprinted toward the man, who was nearly a mile away already, yelling at him the full time she ran. She didn't slow down or quit until she'd caught his attention. Chasing after him, after a life she could save, filled her with joy and purpose. Although it meant money out of his pocket, the man allowed her to rescue one of the horses.

"I could never say no to that smile or enthusiasm," he said to her. "You saved his life. Take good care of him, little lady."

Allie beamed as she walked the horse back to the farm. Her very own pony. Never had she owned anything so big or beautiful or meaningful. She imagined him following her wherever she went, as well as herself riding him like the cowboys around Palisade did. Allie felt happy and full of life.

"I think you picked the best of the two," Becky said. "Do you have a name for him yet?"

"Yes. It will be 'Sheriff Jim Taggart,' but I'll call him 'Tag' for short."

Becky's demeanor dropped.

"You don't like that name?" Allie asked.

"Oh… yes, the name is fine."

"It will remind us of your brother. I wouldn't be here if it wasn't for him. He saved me, and now I saved Tag."

Becky brushed away tears in both eyes before they had a chance to fall. "No, no… you wouldn't be here if it wasn't for my brother. He did a good thing."

Allie smiled.

Tears still hung in Becky's eyes. She wiped them again. "I would be really sad if you weren't here with us, Allie, if you weren't part of our family… really, really sad."

Becky pulled Allie to her and hugged her, then kissed her head.

"And now Tag is part of our family too," Allie said.

*

It wasn't long after that conversation that Allie began a habit of riding off on Tag, initially for an hour or two, then a few hours at a time, and eventually for full days. Tag gave her reason and ability to take these adventures. She loved the freedom of being gone for hours at a time. And on one particular ride some several miles east, she found more reason to keep up her adventures.

Arriving home after dark one evening, Becky's patience with Allie gave out.

"*Where have you been?!* It's late and you've been gone all day. I need you here, not running off!"

Allie was taken aback. She stared at Becky as if she was a ghost. A memory flashed in her. She was back in Palisade, at home. It was her mother's voice, not Becky's, that she heard yelling—one of the few times her mother had found the courage to confront her father. Only in this moment it felt like her mother was yelling at *her*, not her father. Was she becoming like him? The thought scared her, but she resolved to continue the rides—they gave her freedom and a purpose she'd never known.

Becky tried talking with Allie about her behavior, but she refused to talk. In her anger Allie reminded Becky that she wasn't her mother and didn't own her. She would do what she pleased with her time and with her life.

Becky worried about Allie. She wrote to her brother, but he simply sent additional money and promised to visit soon. She needed to know that Allie was safe, so she had Davey follow her one day.

As had been her habit for weeks now, Allie got out of bed before sunrise and slipped on a pair of jeans, a pullover rag-shirt, and her boots, then quietly snuck out of the house. She saddled Tag and rode west, away from Savery Creek. Davey snuck out behind her, saddled his horse, and followed a good distance behind. After a couple miles in the quiet of the morning, Allie knew someone was there, following her. She looked back with a quick jerk of her body. No one. She rode on for another couple minutes and jerked around again. Davey quickly pulled off the trail and into the trees, but not before Allie saw him. She kicked Tag into a full gallop. Her anger grew as Tag hit his full stride. She'd never sat so low on him as she raced on. Her anger fell away as she breathed in the wind and speed and freedom.

When Davey heard Tag and Allie ride off hard, he popped out and rode to catch up.

The forested terrain soon gave way to an open grassland. A large herd of cattle grazed in the far distance. After a couple miles of racing, Allie pulled off the trail and hid just inside a line of trees along the open range. She dismounted and walked Tag farther from the trail, then tied him to a tree branch. She moved back to the trail, laid low, and waited.

When Davey was upon her, she jumped out and yelled, "What are you doing? Why are you following me?"

His horse bucked up on two legs and spun them around and then back down hard. Davey held tight to the reins and settled the horse.

Allie wasn't rattled by the bucking. She yelled again and pointed toward their home. "Why are you following me? Get out! Go!"

"What are you doing?" he asked her.

"None of your business! Now go!"

"I ain't gonna leave. Ma said to keep up with you, make sure you're safe."

"She better worry about you!" Allie pulled a revolver from the back of her pants and pointed it at Davey.

"Go! Git!" she said.

Davey laughed. "You ain't gonna shoot me," he said.

Allie pulled the hammer back two clicks.

"Silly girl. It ain't fully cocked. You got two more to go on that Colt."

"I know," she said, looking at the gun and pulling on the hammer again.

Click! Click!

"Holy cow, Allie! You gone crazy?"

"No, I ain't. I'm as normal as you. Though I guess that ain't sayin' much, come to think of it. Now go. Git home. Leave me alone."

Davey eyed the cylinder. Empty.

With the horse fully settled, Davey tossed the reins forward, spread his arms wide, closed his eyes, and looked up. "Go ahead. Shoot me. I dare ya."

"Your momma's gonna wish she hadn't sent you. You're goin' back dead. And I won't shed a tear for you."

Allie kept her aim on Davey. Anger rose up from her gut. She didn't try to stop it, she let it boil over. The freedom she'd felt on that ride was gone, taken from her. And so was the freedom she'd always had on these rides. She was determined to take it back.

"I'm waitin'," Davey said, arms still wide and head back.

Allie clenched her jaw, took a breath, and held it.

Bang!

The gun went off. Davey's horse bucked again and sprinted away, tossing Davey backward and onto the ground.

Allie gasped. Her eyes went wide and she dropped the gun and ran to him. "Davey!" she yelled.

He lay sprawled out, flat on the ground, not moving. She dropped to his side and placed her hand on his shoulder and nudged him.

"Davey?" she whispered. "Davey."

She nudged him again.

He still didn't move. Fear pierced her gut and ran up through her chest and into her throat. She placed her hand on his cheek, then as she leaned in to see if he was still breathing, Davey jumped to his feet, shoving Allie backward onto her butt.

"You coulda killed me! I thought that thing was empty! You *are* crazy!"

"I didn't know it was loaded, Davey, honest! I'm afraid of keepin' it loaded. I guess one didn't fall out when I dumped it last night."

"Damn you! I hate you! Just go. Go ahead and do whatever it is you do. I'm goin' home. You can die out here for all I care."

He walked to where his horse had run, about a hundred yards up the trail, then mounted and trotted back toward Allie. She watched him the full way. He slowed and stopped alongside her, giving one last look to kill, then rode on.

He didn't get far when Allie finally spoke: "I got a job."

He stopped but didn't turn.

"Did you hear me?" she asked.

"Yeah, I ain't deaf."

He rode on.

"Don't you wanna know why?"

"To make money for somethin' I reckon."

Davey kept riding. Allie stood up and watched him until he was out of sight. Then she dropped to her butt again and laid her head on the ground, staring straight up at the sky. The morning was clear and bright as the sun rose above the eastern horizon. She relaxed. Her secret was out. It felt good. The weight and burden of carrying it fell from her, as if giving the secret freedom set her free as well.

*

Allie arrived at the ranch late. She was to start every weekday morning by eight o'clock. This would be her first time being late in the three weeks she had worked there. She worried what Elsa would say.

Elsa Worthington ran the kitchen for Tuck and Dena Keller's five hundred-acre cattle ranch near Savery Creek. Elsa had worked at the cattle ranch for several years. She kept the ranch hands well-fed and nourished when they weren't out on the range or on a drive. She was pleasant and spirited, and Allie never knew her to lean toward strict.

Allie tied Tag outside the livery and ran to the kitchen. "I'm so sorry for being late, Elsa. It won't happen again."

"Not to worry, girl. That just means you get to clean the breakfast table *and* do the dishes. I'll get the dinner bread started. Now put your apron on and get to it."

Allie smiled. "Yes, ma'am."

She ran to the dining room and gathered as many dishes as she could carry, clanging them on top of each other, then returned to the kitchen. She set the stack down and scraped the leftovers into a slop bucket, then returned to the dining room for another load. Each trip meant a round of conversation with Elsa.

"Anything special for lunch today?" Allie asked.

Elsa gave her the look she'd given most every other day. "If by 'special' you mean the same thing we had yesterday and the day before that and the week before that, then, yes.

Havin' food provided by the good Lord is *always* special, even if it's the same ol' pickins: rice, beans with bacon, and bread."

Allie smiled. She loved Elsa's warm and easy demeanor.

"Gotta keep energy in those men handlin' all that cattle and keepin' this ranch singin' like a song," Elsa said. "The Keller's have enough cattle for every man, woman, and child in this Wyoming territory to start their own ranch. And that means long days and hard work and big appetites."

Allie listened even as she continued to scrape and then dunk plates into the washbasin. "We should surprise them one day—a special stew, or at least a dessert."

Elsa shook her head. "The money Mrs. Keller gives me for food don't allow for no more than rice, beans, and bread for lunch. They get chicken at night, steak on Saturday, and a ham on Sunday. Just like clockwork."

Satisfied with Elsa's answer, Allie headed out for another round of dishes. She managed to carry rest of the plates and much of the silverware, pressing everything against her body to keep the forks and spoons and knives from sliding off.

"Why you always wearing jeans, girl?" Elsa asked as Allie returned to the kitchen.

"Because I feel funny ridin' Tag in a dress."

"Why don't you keep a dress here, change before you start?"

"I don't have one that ain't dirty or torn."

"You've about made enough money to buy a new one."

"No, I can't."

"Can't, girl? *Can't* is a dangerous word. *Can't* settles things. Maybe you don't *want* to."

Allie shrugged. "You're right. I don't. Just not important to me, I guess. I'm okay with jeans."

Allie didn't like the questions Elsa was asking. They were too nosy. But she respected Elsa, so she didn't say anything.

"Hmm," Elsa said. "You ain't gonna catch a boy by wearin' jeans with a rope belt and a floppy rag-shirt."

Allie felt her face turn red even as her jaw hung open. "Elsa! No!"

"Allie! Yes! I see how the younger ones look at you."

"No, they don't. I'm just some ugly girl that feeds 'em and cleans up after 'em. They like those pretty town girls."

Elsa stopped her work kneading the bread dough and looked at Allie. "I know you been runnin' off with that Miller boy after lunch."

Feeling too upset at Elsa's words to stay there another second, Allie dropped the last dish into the water and ran out to the dining room for the coffee cups. She took her time collecting what she could carry, hoping Elsa would be ready to move on to another topic. Allie had her plans and just wanted to be left alone to pursue them. She didn't want anyone in the way; the more others knew, the more they would try to stop her. Elsa had always been nice and pleasant to her, but she now felt like an antagonist.

Allie slipped back into the kitchen, head down, and went straight to the washbasin.

Elsa cracked a smile for Allie. "Did you get lost in there?"

Allie ignored her.

"I'll keep on you, girl, until you talk. I can work and wait, or work and talk, whichever."

"It's not what you think, Elsa. He's... He's..."

"Yes?"

"He's just helping me with somethin', that's all. Nothin' else. There ain't nothin' to it. He doesn't want me like that."

"Okay. Suit yourself. Now finish up the dishes and get the bucket out to the pen."

"Yes, ma'am."

Allie rushed through washing the dishes and headed to the back door with the bucket.

"While you're out there, you wanna get the chickens set for dinner? Need five. Heads cut, blood drained, full plucked. Can you do that?"

"Sure. I've helped Becky do it lots of times."

"The killin' don't bother you?"

"No. Some animals are for dyin' anyway. Almost like they deserve it."

"Girl, you best soften your edges."

"Sorry. Just got my head on somethin' else."

"Besides the Miller boy?" Elsa asked, smirking a bit.

"Elsa! Stop. He doesn't care about me. Just wants the money I pay him."

"*Money?* What? Say that again!"

Elsa reached and stopped Allie as she pushed open the back door.

"You okay, girl? Are you in trouble?"

"No, I'm fine. Just… Just let me be," Allie said, desperate to keep her reasons to herself.

Elsa was working hard to pull it out of her, though, and getting close to doing just that.

"Well, that's one way of gettin' a man—pay him!" Elsa said, laughing. "I never thought of that!"

"No, it's not like that. Besides, I ain't ready. And even if I was, that Miller boy's too skinny. I'd have to peek around his rifle just to see if he was there."

Elsa laughed again. "You're funny, sweet one. Okay. So it ain't love, it's just money."

Allie was torn. She didn't want to talk about her plans, but Elsa was pushing so hard. She also didn't want to upset Elsa and maybe lose her job at the ranch. She decided to tell Elsa what the Miller boy was helping her with, but nothing more.

"He's teachin' me to shoot," Allie said, looking away from Elsa.

"He's what?"

"Teachin' me to shoot."

Allie lifted up her rag-shirt and pulled out a .38-caliber revolver tied around the back of her waist. "I wanna learn."

"Whatever for? Let the men do the huntin' and killin' and protectin'. We'll make meals, clean the clothes, and steam their bathwater."

"I'm fourteen and think I should know how to protect myself."

"So all this money you been makin' is going from me to you to the skinny Miller boy?"

"Not all of it. Just twenty cents a lesson."

"Tsk, tsk, tsk." Elsa shook her head. "I ain't never known nothin' like this before."

Allie felt hurt by Elsa pushing hard to get her to share what she was up to. She was embarrassed to have to reveal something so personal. But giving up that part of the secret did stop Elsa from pushing on, keeping Allie's full plans safely hidden.

Elsa walked back to the table and to her kneading, leaving Allie at the door.

"You any good shootin' that thing?" Elsa asked.

"Not yet. Besides, I don't need to be the best, just good enough."

"Good enough? That sounds like trouble."

"No… no trouble. I'm gonna get to the chickens."

"You be careful with them guns. And you listen to that boy."

"I grew up around guns. I ain't afraid of them. But anyone better be afraid of me if I'm aimed at 'em."

"I think either way, whether you're a good aim or not, people gonna be afraid of you, Allie Lind. Now go. Git to those chickens."

Allie dumped the breakfast slop into the trough by the pen, then headed to the chicken coop. She breathed a sigh of relief after escaping Elsa's prying questions. She resolved to be more guarded around people. She had her plans and they would stay her plans. No one else had a right or reason to know what they were.

Inside the chicken yard she worked to catch the first bird, chasing several for a couple minutes before finally cornering and grabbing one by its feet. She carried it to the chopping block, the bird flapping and thrashing its wings the whole time. Allie held tight to it as best she could. An older ranch hand saw her struggling to manage the chicken in one hand and reach for the hatchet with the other. He ran to her rescue.

"Looks like you need about four hands, miss."

Allie looked up and saw an older, stocky man standing in front of her. He wore a white cowboy hat tipped back, his gray hair curling out from under it.

"I'm Jack," he said.

Allie didn't respond. She gave up on the hatchet and let it drop to the ground. She held the chicken tight with both hands and pushed far away from her face.

"You wanna hold it or cut?" Jack asked her.

"I'll cut. You take this thing," she said, shoving the chicken at the man.

Without much fuss he gripped the bird by the feet and head and laid it across the stump, its neck pulled taut.

"Swing hard all the way through the neck. Pretend you're cuttin' this stump clean in half."

Allie held the hatchet with two hands. She eyed the neck and swung. The blade hit and then bounced off the chicken and into the man's hand.

"I'd like to keep that if you don't mind," he said with a smile.

"Sorry, sir."

"Not even a nick. I'm fine. I'll hold the neck tighter. You think of someone you might want layin' across this here stump. That might help ya."

She took a look at Jack, his hand, and then the chicken as it fought and struggled to free itself. Allie breathed in deep as she lifted the hatchet high over her head, held the breath, and tensed her lips. She let her life flash through her mind. From Palisade to Savery Creek to the ranch. She was definitely upset with Elsa now, but that would pass. Becky had sent Davey to follow her, and that felt like she wasn't trusted. She ran her mind back to Palisade. To home. That Sunday morning. Allie grunted and plunged the hatchet down hard into the bird's neck.

Thump!

Blood shot out in every direction. The man quickly raised the chicken up by its feet and tied it to the side of the coop to let its blood drain.

"I pity whoever you was thinkin' of, miss!"

Allie didn't respond. Her mind was still on that Sunday morning.

"Those are chicken clothes now," the man said, laughing.

Allie looked at the blood splattered over her clothes. She'd heard that her mother's apron had blood splattered all over it when she was shot. Allie showed no emotion at the thought, nor any for the dead bird. She felt strong, empowered, emboldened.

"I need four more chickens. Go catch another one," Allie ordered Jack, as if she owned him and the ranch.

*

After the men ate their lunch and Allie finished cleaning up, she took her own lunch break—shooting lessons with Rueben Miller at the edge of the tree line near where she and Davey had fought earlier that day, a couple miles from the ranch house.

"Hey, Rue."

"Hey yourself, Allie. I got the target set up for you. Hung on that dead cottonwood across the field."

Rue was seventeen, thin, baby-faced, and stood only a

couple inches taller than Allie. He had the voice of an older man, though, which didn't fit him any more than a baby that comes out with a full head of hair. Allie hoped he would grow into his voice, as a baby eventually would grow into its hair. He was strong, though, she thought, and kind.

"Thanks. Here's your money before I forget."

She laid the dimes in his hand and he slipped them into his pants pocket.

"I've been carryin' the handgun you gave me all week. Even slept with it," Allie said.

"Hell, Allie. You're serious about this, ain't ya? Just be sure it's not loaded when you're ridin', or sleepin' now. I don't wanna see you get hurt."

Allie smiled nervously, thinking back on nearly killing Davey just that morning.

"And don't ever—" Rue started before Allie broke in: "—point it at anyone or anything unless I want it dead. I know, I know," she said.

"All this practicin' because you're scared of snakes? Don't make sense to me."

"Just wanna be able to protect myself. Snakes, cougars, bears. Whatever might be out to get me."

Rueben laughed. "You gotta be pretty good to hit a snake, especially one settin' to strike at ya. And this Colt might help ya with a cougar if you know what you're doin', but ain't gonna do you no good with a bear. You best get a long gun for that. If they want you, they'll get you, and if they don't want you, they won't. No way around it."

"Well, I'll feel better with something," she said.

"Okay, but like I said last time, at best this will be good at fifty yards. And that's on a calm day and your aim is straight. So you best be dancin' with whatever you're aimin' to kill or you'll be in a licka trouble."

"I know," Allie said, a bit overwhelmed by all of the information, but resolute in her desire to learn how to shoot and handle a revolver.

"Okay, let's get on with it, Allie. Here's a few cartridges for you. Load up and set your feet and aim to the red cloth on the cottonwood."

Allie pushed open the cylinder and, one by one, picked six cartridges from the box and dropped them in. She peered into the back of the cylinder, spun it, and clicked it closed. Before Rueben could say anything else or stop her, she pulled the hammer back, lifted the gun, and pulled the trigger.

Bang!

Dirt kicked up several yards in front of the tree.

"Whoa there, anxious Alice!" Rueben exclaimed. "You sure can move fast. But if you wanna actually hit what you're aimin' at, you're gonna have to slow down."

"What if I need to go fast? Snakes ain't slow, ya know."

"Fast don't matter until the aim is right. Get that into your head, okay? You're better off bein' slow and straight than too fast and dead."

"I missed, didn't I?"

"Nope. When you pull a trigger you never miss; you always hit somethin'. This time you hit the dirt about twenty feet short of the tree."

Allie wrinkled her face. "Why was I so short?"

"Because you're still fearin' the kick and pushing the gun down to stop it. That's why you hit low. Don't worry about what'll happen after you pull the trigger; just focus on a smooth pull. Let the gun do what it wants after."

Allie took her stance, cocked the hammer, and carefully aimed at the center of the cloth. She steadied herself, then sucked in a deep breath and held it. The cloth jumped and rippled from a light wind, causing Allie to lose her focus. She lowered the gun.

"Dammit," she said.

She quickly raised the gun again and pulled the trigger at the target without aiming.

Bang!

"Dammit is right, Allie! This ain't no war. No one to be angry at. Settle yourself down now."

Allie glared at him. Yes, she *was* angry—and she wished others would just leave her alone to her feelings. "We all got plenty to be angry at," she said. "And I didn't hire you to be my preacher. I paid twenty cents for shootin' lessons, nothing more."

"Okay, okay. But you take another quick shot like that today or any day and I'm done with you. You hear me?"

Allie held onto her anger. Not at Rueben, though—he just happened to be the one standing there, so he was taking the brunt of it. She knew he was right, but her anger was consuming every other emotion and she couldn't stop it.

"Just do what I'm payin' you to do, Rueben. Teach me to hit that old, worthless rag."

"Okay, okay," he said, raising his hands to calm her down. "There's no need to rush your shot. Just take your time. The target will be there for you, I promise. It ain't goin' nowhere."

Allie took her stance again and set herself proper at the target. Rueben stepped behind and to her side.

"This time don't hold your breath. Just breathe in deep and slow, then let it out easy. When you still have a little breath in you and you feel calm, pull smooth on the trigger."

Allie's mind was reeling. It had been an emotional day. Tears started to build. She shook her head and squeezed her eyes. The tears blurred her vision. She lowered the gun and ran her sleeve across both eyes to dry them. She set herself again at the target and worked to remember all that Rueben had taught her. *This is for you, Mom.*

Allie clicked the hammer back, breathed in, let it out slowly, stilled herself, then pulled the trigger.

Bang!

Bark splintered and flew out from the tree.

"Better," Rueben said. "Much better. You're still a little low and to the right."

Allie took her time and finished the remaining three shots, each one inching closer to the cloth. She filled the cylinder again and took six more shots, hitting the cloth twice.

"Don't ever rush your shot, Allie. Don't get in a hurry about shootin'. That leads to regrets."

Allie didn't say a word. She ripped the box from his hand to reload. It was empty.

"I only got one more," Rueben said, opening his other hand to reveal a single cartridge resting in his palm.

Allie stared at him, glanced at the cartridge, then back to Rueben. Quicker than he expected, she went for the cartridge. He closed his hand and pulled it away.

"Who is it?" he asked.

"Who is what?"

"The target," he said, nodding at the red cloth. "Who you so damn mad at? Sure ain't no snake."

She slit her eyes at him. "It is a snake. The kind you never seen."

"I ain't teachin' you to shoot so you can go kill someone. I ain't gonna be part of that."

"Fine. I'll just teach myself. I don't need you anymore."

Allie marched toward Tag and mounted him. More and more she realized that this was her mission, no one else's. It felt like everyone simply wanted to control her, tell her what to do, even abandon her when she showed some spirit. She was now on her own.

"I want my gun back," Rueben shouted. "Don't want it bein' part of something bad."

Allie turned and threw the revolver at him.

"Geez, girl! You need help. Best get it before you hurt yourself."

"I don't need no help, especially from a skinny runt of a boy! I can protect myself."

Allie turned Tag to the trail.

"Wait," Rueben said, then paused. "Here. Take the gun. Just promise you'll be careful with it."

Allie looked at Rueben. Just when she was ready to give up on everyone in her life, he showed compassion. She grabbed the gun and stuffed it in her pants and then rode back to the ranch. Her dad, stumbling drunk and mean, flooded her thoughts. He'd slam open the front door and stand there, staring at his wife and daughter. Without a word he told them to shut up, to be quiet, not make a sound. He would hold himself in the doorway until he knew they heard him. He was the reason she was in Wyoming—without family... without her mother... full of rage and anger. She tried forcing in memories of her mother, but her father wouldn't allow it. He'd bust right back in. She wished he was dead in that prison, but then hoped he wasn't at the same time. Hard to kill a dead man.

17

CLAY LEANED BACK against his saddle as the fire burned low but bright against the distant hills of western Nevada. The fire crackled and spit. Coyotes howled in unison in the distance; too far to worry about them. The crescent moon lit low against the black of the night; stars quietly slipped in as if not to awaken anyone. The night still warm from the heat of the day. He slid down and set his head onto the saddle. He lay quiet. Life encroached. Unwelcomed. Thoughts seeped into his mind. Memories. Nightmares to some. Simply life to a Lind boy. He tried to ignore them, but they won out. Without a bottle there was no chance to fight back, nothing to numb the scenes that filled his head.

His mind jumped from Meg's killing and funeral to the thought of Daniel in prison all these years, to Allie, and to Keen. Seven years he'd been half-heartedly pursuing Keen. Seven years with nothing to show for the pursuit except wasted time and a wasted life. He shook his head. Regrets fell in. He tried to push them away, but they endured. *Killing*

Keen may end them, he thought. He vowed to set his life aside and hunt him down, vowed to find Keen and kill him. He felt energized by this renewed determination. But Keen still put fear in him; Clay knew the evil and danger harnessed to that man.

He closed his eyes and allowed his thoughts to move back to the warm quiet of the evening. He felt the soft patch of grass below him and remembered the time Daniel wrestled and held him to the ground when he was no more than eight. There was good in them then; he felt it, remembered it. Lost somewhere along the way, though. He wasn't sure when, or where, or how. And not a loss in a sudden manner like the time he sat on a mustang for the first time. "Tamed," they'd told him. "Smooth as ivory." Standing there the animal certainly looked tame and smooth, but just as quick as Clay mounted, he was bucked off, slammed to the ground without warning. *No, bad comes in slow*, Clay thought. He opened his eyes again and stared at the stars. It was never a particular beating from their dad; just a gradual shift from good and innocent to bad and guilty. Bad decisions. Some egged on by drinking, some with clear heads. Learning to pay the price was part of it. The first ones made them think. Gave them pause. The punishments soon just became part of the deal. He and Daniel were never caught by the law more than once or twice a year. Always worth the risk. He never saw Daniel kill anyone. Shot at plenty of men, though. Just not always good enough to hit. And being drunk swayed the targets anyway—something good that came of the bottle.

Clay closed his eyes again and breathed slow and tried pulling the sleep in and pushing the memories out. He remembered hearing Meg breathing heavy when she was in labor. Daniel sitting in some saloon doing the only thing he knew to do that was helpful. Clay hung around in the kitchen. Figured at least one man should be nearby. He, not Daniel, heard Allie cry for the first time; then he, not Daniel, saw her in tears at her mother's funeral—the endpoints of Daniel's relationship with Allie, with little good in between.

His memories shifted to fabricated images of Daniel in prison, half-dead from the work and heat and little food.

Clay sighed. The coyotes picked up their howling once again. Now closer. Cool gradually pushed the warmth of the evening away. He turned his head and peeked at the fire. It lay dying. He rolled his face back to the night sky, closed his eyes once more, and finally drifted to sleep.

In his dream he sensed someone behind him and tried running but couldn't. His legs were heavy. Lost in a forest of trees that stood high and thick around him, the scene swirled in black and gray and shades in between. He heard himself breathing. A young girl ran past him. She turned and looked back. It was Allie. No, Meg. Then both at once. A lion roared behind him and then jumped to his side. He felt its comfort and they began running toward the girl. Evil flooded the dream and the lion broke off. Clay felt pursued once more. He tried escaping into the forest, but his legs fell heavy again. He tried to scream, but only silence came out. He was stuck. Alone. The girl was gone. A rifle shot rang out. And then a second. Clay turned toward the sound. A man stood away from him with dead aim and shot again. Clay felt the hit and then the burn in his right eye. The man closed in. The forest darkened. Clay covered his eye as another rifle shot sounded.

He felt the pain in his cheek. He winced and dropped to the ground and curled up and waited for death. The man rode off into the night sky. The forest faded.

Clay awoke. The evil he'd felt remained as he lay in that moment between dream and wake, not knowing which was which. Crack! He felt another hit. It froze him. Then the fire cracked again. More cinders popped out and flew into his face and flickered and fell to the ground.

His heart pounded. He breathed in and held and didn't move. He looked with his eyes to the right. Then left. Then right again. He looked up. Then listened. Nothing. He closed his eyes tight and listened again. Slowly, quietly, he let out his breath. He saw the tilted moon hanging, resting on the tips of the trees. It had barely moved. He'd only been asleep for a few minutes, not much more. Without invitation the dream played again in his mind. Then again. And again.

He wrestled with it. Its meaning. The fear he'd felt. The evil it left behind still drifted thick and dark around him like a low and slow-moving fog, misty, even ghostlike. It settled above him and then poured over him as he lay awake and afraid to move.

Clay eventually sat up and took a long stick and stirred and spread out the coals. The fire glowed, then darkened as he let up. He set a pile of brush and twigs on the fire. After they took, he laid some thin wood on, then small logs, and waited for them to catch. He lay back down and immediately got up again. He grabbed his revolver from its holster and lay back with it across his belly. He pulled the shotgun closer to his side and kept its grip.

A second later Molly screamed and bucked and kicked

and screamed again, then jerked right and left to pull herself free from the tether. Clay tightened on the shotgun and jumped up. His revolver fell to the ground. He looked around but couldn't see anything. He readied himself to fire the shotgun. Molly bucked again and stood on her two hind legs and screamed and jerked with quick turns to the right and left and back to the right. The grass rustled at the horse's feet. A raccoon darted toward Clay's pack and the jerky lying open on top. Clay knew better than to leave food out. Daniel was always cussing at him for his messy camp. Without thinking, Clay stood and grabbed the pan of half-eaten beans from the rocks that surrounded the fire and threw it at the raccoon. The pan banged and bounced a full two feet from the animal, but loud enough and close enough to send it back where it came from. Beans splattered the ground and tree and Molly.

Clay dropped to his butt. He looked around for Daniel. He could hear him laughing. Innocent boys again. They could joke and laugh at each other and not get angry. Or get angry and just as quickly let it go. He missed his brother.

He wrapped the jerky and shoved it in a pouch, then wadded it up tight and stuffed it in a larger pouch and into his saddlebag.

He looked over at Molly. She returned the look, a little unsure of his aim. He stood and walked to her. "Sorry, Moll," he said, patting her. "Sorry, girl. Let's get some sleep and head into Reno tomorrow and get some proper food."

*

In the morning, Clay restarted the fire for coffee and bacon.

He would have finished the beans for breakfast as well but had lost those to the coon fight. He packed his things, loaded Molly, and rode south toward Reno. The dream kept up. Its fear and evil lingered still. He thought of the man in his dream. It felt like Keen. Clay remembered his renewed vow to focus on hunting down and killing Keen. He'd seen Daniel holding the gun on Meg that morning, but that evil in the dream, it was there that morning too. It felt right to Clay. It added up. If the man was there, he'd be after Daniel soon, and maybe even Allie. His vow to hunt down Keen set in hard. He needed to protect his brother, his niece, his family.

His ride into Reno shifted from food and comfort to a search for Keen. He'd look in every bar and brothel. He wouldn't mention Keen's name unless he had to. He didn't want to tip his hand. Then he'd head in another direction, to another town, and continue the search. His life would be pursuit, never a desire to see his brother or track down Allie. They had each other to worry about; he had the man to worry about, and to take care of. He owed at least that much to his brother.

Clay finally rode into the streets of Reno, Nevada. No different than Palisade off to the north and east. A wild town as well, just bigger and more of it. He and Daniel had ventured there many times. He knew most of the saloons. He'd start with the ones that had the cheapest whiskey and women. He knew the man well enough to know what he liked, and what liked him.

To begin his search, Clay would start on Virginia Street and check the bars the length of it, then move to the streets east and west. He strolled into the Reno Inn. Wednesday.

2:00 p.m. It was thin inside. Most men would be out working. Keen certainly wasn't like most men. Not like many men at all. He didn't work. He stole and killed for a living. He'd be easier to spot on a day like this than a Friday or Saturday night when the establishments would be packed full. Clay set eyes on every man in there, looking at faces and frames. Chances were slim of finding Keen so quickly, so his expectation was low. Purpose, though. He had purpose.

He walked down the street to the Western Tavern. Thin again. No Keen.

He skipped the Pacific Place. Too fancy. They wouldn't let Clay—or Keen—stand on the porch, let alone walk inside. On down the street to DeeDee's, then over to Barlowe's, where he decided to stay and have a drink. The crowd was heavier anyway, so it would take longer to catch every face.

He took a spot at the far end of the bar, near the corner. He'd have a full view of the saloon, the stairs to the second floor, the front door, and the front windows. He asked for a beer and settled in.

"Who you lookin' for?"

Clay looked at the bartender, wondering why he'd ask such a question.

"I say, who you lookin' for?"

"Just enjoyin' my drink," Clay responded.

"I don't mean nothin' by it, just saw you lookin' around, thought maybe I could help. Know all the regulars, and don't forget a face."

"Just a friend. Waitin' on a friend."

"You been here before, haven't ya?"

"Maybe. Couple years back."

"I'm Barlowe," the bartender said, continuing to clean beer mugs without looking away.

"Clay."

"First or last?"

Clay just looked at the bartender.

"Got it. Clay. Just Clay. Let me know if I can help. First one's on me. Kind of a 'glad to have you back' drink."

Clay raised his beer as a thank-you and nodded. He was happy to finally get a drink in him. He took in a long swallow. It tasted good and felt even better going down. Without Keen in sight and a beer in front of him, he started to relax and figured he'd enjoy himself before heading back into the streets.

As he took another sip, Clay noticed the group of four men that stood at the bar a few feet down from him.

"Worst thing I ever heard of," the cowboy said to the other men standing around him.

The man's loud voice pulled Clay's attention away from his drink. He glanced at him. A real cowboy, he thought. Chaps, authentic cowhide boots, and spurs. The man sat honest and had honest eyes to match. Clay listened.

"First he killed that stagecoach driver and his shotgun man," the cowboy continued. "Just two shots. Dead center in the head of both men."

"I've heard worse," the bartender said. "Hell, Joe over there killed three men just fallin' outta bed on top of 'em!"

All the men laughed; even Clay smiled at Barlowe's words.

"I ain't finished with my story yet, Barlowe. Can I finish or you gonna keep interruptin'?"

"Barlowe ain't just the owner and bartender," one of the three men said. "He's the entertainment too!"

"You been here thirty minutes," Barlowe said to the cowboy. "Ain't told a story yet worth a damn. And you been nursin' on the same beer. I ain't runnin' a place where you can sit and talk for free. If you wanna finish your story, it's time to buy another drink."

The cowboy look down at his near-empty glass. "Yeah, one more I s'pose."

The bartender grabbed the cowboy's glass and refilled it, then grabbed a clean one and filled it too. He set the two beers in front of the man.

"I think I heard you ask for two, ain't that right, boys?"

"Yep, that's the way we heard it," one of them said.

The three other men slammed their hands on the bar and stared at the cowboy. He looked at the glasses, at the men, then the bartender.

"You tellin' me that my stories ain't worth hearin' unless I'm drunk?"

"Drunk is a start!" Barlowe said.

The men laughed again. The cowboy picked up one of the glasses and drank it down, then wiped his lips. Clay enjoyed their antics. He and Daniel had behaved much the same on their rides, whether they were in a saloon or by a campfire.

"Like I was sayin'," the cowboy continued, "he killed the driver and his shotgun man, and there was five people inside the coach—three women and two men. They'd tossed their weapons out and their money and jewelry. The shooter ordered the two men to get out and dump the luggage onto the road. He shot open the safe, but only found fifty dollars inside. He'd caught the stage on the wrong side of the route.

"He took what he could carry and started to ride off. Then turned and asked the two men which of them deserved to live. Neither answered. He called one of the women out of the coach and asked her which of the two should live. She didn't answer neither. Then he just shot the older man clean in the forehead."

"That happened right here in Nevada, down between Goldfield and Tonopah," one of the men said. "My brother runs a ranch near there, and that was his wife and daughters on that stage."

"Did they find the guy who done it?" another man asked.

The cowboy shook his head. "No. But they know who it was. A couple long scars across his face."

Clay jerked his head so hard at the cowboy that it drew his attention. The men all stared at Clay, who kept his look on the cowboy. He could tell they were all sizing him up, as if he might be the scarred man, but quickly gave that up. Clay swallowed hard as he wandered his look from man to man and finally back to the cowboy. He thought whether it was smart to say anything or just turn back to his drink. He was desperate to find Keen, though.

"Name is…" the cowboy said slowly, still eyeing Clay.

"Keen," Clay said.

"You know him?" the cowboy asked.

Clay hesitated. He worried that knowing the name already told them he did. He felt trapped. He needed more information, though—anything to point him in Keen's direction.

"No... just heard about him," Clay finally said. "Those scars sure do give him away. Now you say this was down south near Tonopah?

"Yeah. The coach was headed to Goldfield from there."

"When?" Clay asked.

"Couple weeks ago."

Clay looked at the bartender. "You ever see that scarred man in this bar?"

"No, never," he said, shaking his head.

Clay turned back to the others. "You men ever heard of him or seen him in these parts?"

They all shook their heads. Clay looked over each man. They showed honest. *How the hell does Keen do it?* he thought. *Ravage a territory, a town, a stagecoach, and walk away clean?* Clay feared this chase, feared that it would lead to a showdown and Keen would come out untouched once again—and that Clay himself would be the one face down in the dirt with a bullet in him. But this wasn't about saving himself; it couldn't be. Not anymore. This was now about protecting Daniel and Allie.

Clay pulled a dollar gold coin from his pocket and politely tossed it toward the bartender and headed for the door.

"No need," Barlowe said. "Like I told ya, first one's on m—"

Clay was out the door before Barlowe could finish his sentence. He jumped on Molly and whipped her into a full sprint, heading south.

18

THE TALL WOODEN doors creaked inward and opened, one to the left, then the second to the right. Four men stepped from inside the prison. Just as abruptly as they'd opened, the doors closed. Daniel, the oldest and tallest of the four, stood and stared out at the Sierra Nevada Mountains to the west, then the lower hills to the east. The brown of the dirt and sand and dry prairie grass all around looked no different than the dirt and sand and dry prairie grass inside the prison walls. It was late August. The sun burned hot already, even in the early morning. Daniel shifted the cloth sack he'd been given by one of the guards from his right hand to his left. The guard knew of Daniel's journey and felt he at least needed some provisions. The sack held a half loaf of bread, a couple apples, and a bit of dried beef. The guard also gave him a well-worn cowboy hat to help shield his head from the sun, a thin blanket, and a canteen filled with cool well water. The clothes he was given were baggy, and the boots a full size too big. Standing on the outside of the prison doors Daniel set himself for the trek he had waited ten years to make. He took in a deep breath and let it out. He had thought maybe the air would feel cleaner or cooler outside the walls. It didn't.

The prison wagon stood ready to take him and the three other ex-prisoners to Virginia City. There they could look for work in the mines, take the train to another location, or wait for a family member to retrieve them. Daniel had no interest in Virginia City, or Reno farther to the north, or California, or where the hell ever else existed. He only cared about Palisade and Allie. Without a word he looked east and began walking.

As he headed away from the wagon, one of the prisoners he'd walked out with shouted to him, "Hey, Daniel. You ain't gonna ride with us? Best chance you got to start over."

He kept his head and stride east. A hundred yards out he heard the wagon wheels behind him crunch across the dirt and rocks as the driver turned and rolled the wagon north. In no time Daniel was walking in desert wilderness.

Just as quietly as he'd entered, Daniel left the Nevada State Prison in Carson City.

*

He and Clay had ridden this route dozens of times. He knew it well. The terrain was hilly and dry. Not much in the way of vegetation, at least that was edible. He would stick to side trails as much as possible—easier to find safe places to rest and sleep and hide—but track with the Carson River until its end, then head north to catch the Humboldt River and follow it the full way to Palisade. There'd be a dry distance from the Carson north to the Humboldt. He would have only his canteen water for a short time to get him through. Food would be difficult without gun or knife. Maybe he deserved it anyway. He earned a difficult trip, a difficult life. More punishment for what he'd done. A couple miles in he could feel the blisters start. They'd be burning soon, and for the next three or four weeks without letup.

Daniel's mind ran wild with memories. He scanned his life. From his childhood to the very steps he was now taking. He'd heard men say that when they were shot and thought they were dying, their life flashed before their eyes. He must be meant for a slow death, he thought, one where his life and regrets didn't flash in a second but repeated over and over in his mind, slowly and relentlessly. But he couldn't allow himself to die. He wouldn't. He needed to get to Allie and apologize—she needed those words, deserved them. He desired her forgiveness in return but didn't feel he deserved it. Daniel let life and regrets spill into his mind.

He remembered holding her when she was little. And he remembered not feeling anything. He tried, but after a few seconds he felt anxious to run, escape, get back out on the trail, be anywhere but there. He didn't feel much of anything in his life until Meg fell to the floor that morning. In that moment he felt the weight of his life, the weight of his actions, the weight of his choices. He'd missed it. Missed the life that could have been. That was gone now. Maybe, though, with his words, he could save Allie and give her a life.

Daniel could still see the Sierra Nevada peaks to the west and the familiar mountain peaks of the Virginia Range to the north. As dusk approached and his first day on the trail was ending, he slid into a grove of golden aspen trees. A low, rocky overhang across the river would give him comfort and safety. He drank down several handfuls of water and bit off a chunk of dried beef. His first bite since breakfast at the prison. He walked the banks looking for trout hitting bugs that rode the surface. He saw some activity, so he fashioned a spear from a long stick, then watched and waited. And waited. And waited. With no luck.

He gathered enough kindling and wood for a small fire. Nevada days were scorching hot, especially in August, but the nights could cool down. He slipped out of his boots, then took off his shirt, dipped it in the water, and wrapped up his feet. He took his blanket and tightened its roll, then set it near the fire and lay down.

Daniel wanted to jump up and run the rest of the way home. He was anxious to see Allie, though he doubted she would feel the same. Would she even be there? If she had gone to that orphanage in San Francisco, she certainly would have returned home by now. Yes... Allie was sure to be in Palisade. Daniel rested easier.

In the morning, he packed up what little he had, put on his boots, and set himself to another day of walking. His feet burned, but he kept his steps going and eased into accepting the pain.

As he headed back to the trail north of the river, he saw two riders heading toward him, with a third horse in tow. He read the faces at a distance and then more intently as they closed in. He readied himself to run. The lead rider wore a black cowboy hat and had the third horse tethered to his saddle; the rider that followed wore a tan hat and appeared younger than the first, no older than twenty or so.

Daniel sensed danger. He set himself to run into the trees but pushed the fear aside and braced himself.

"Mornin'," the man in the black hat said as they closed in.

Daniel stood staring, not wanting to stop or talk, watching for the danger he sensed.

"Lose your horse?" the younger man asked.

Daniel stared more. The two men looked at each other.

"I didn't mean nothin' by it," the younger man said.

Daniel hesitated a few seconds more. The men waited for him to respond.

"No, didn't lose my horse. Just headin' east," Daniel said.

He kept his sense of danger about the men. Ten years in prison trained him to expect the worst from anyone who approached. It had simply become a way of life, a way of seeing every man as out to harm him or take advantage of him in some way. He saw nothing in these two men that said he should treat them any differently.

"Closest town is near twenty miles back that way," the man in the black hat said, pointing behind Daniel, toward Carson City.

Daniel didn't turn to look. He didn't want to respond either. He now feared these men were bounty hunters. If they were, they might just drag him back to the prison, make sure that he hadn't escaped. That would be a good reward for them.

"Where you two headed?" Daniel asked.

"Carson City," the older man said, then leaned on his saddle horn and looked Daniel over, head to toe and back again. "You look like maybe you were there, in prison. Were you?"

Daniel didn't say a word, just studied both men.

"I'm thinkin' he was, Sam," the younger man said.

Daniel's fear of the two men being bounty hunters grew stronger. He now wanted out of the situation and started walking around them, angling himself toward the woods, prepared to run.

"Did you ever meet up with a Jessup Dunlavey in there?" Sam, the older man, asked.

Daniel stopped walking but held his look away from the men.

"He's our brother. We're ridin' there to pick him up and take him home."

Still unsure, Daniel turned and looked at each man. Neither seemed tense or desperate; neither showed an interest in reaching for their gun. They now read honest.

"You got no reason to fear us," Sam said. "We're just heading to Carson City to fetch our brother, nothing more."

"I never met him," Daniel finally responded.

"What were you in for? Thievin', horse stealin', cattle rustlin'?" the younger man asked.

"Leave it, Bill. It ain't our business," Sam said.

Daniel relaxed at knowing that he wasn't in danger, but still wanted to end the conversation. He turned from the men again and started walking away.

"Hey, you got food or protection?" Sam asked.

"No. I'm fine," Daniel said, continuing to walk.

The two men looked at each other.

"Where you from?"

"Palisade," Daniel replied as he walked on.

"Wait. Come back," Sam said. "Take this."

Daniel looked back to see Sam holding out a revolver.

"Go ahead. Take it. And some cartridges."

Daniel didn't move. He would welcome the gun for protection and small game.

"Bill, give him a couple pickled eggs and some venison," Sam said.

Daniel looked back and forth at the two men. The older brother showed himself sincere; he could tell that the younger brother didn't want to give up a weapon or food. Daniel slowly walked toward Sam to take the revolver.

"I'll get it back from ya. Leave it at the sheriff's office when you get to Palisade. Tell him it's for Sam Dunlavey. We'll pick it up on our way back through."

Sam flipped the revolver in the air and caught the barrel and extended the handle to Daniel.

As Daniel reached for the gun, the man squinted and pulled it back. "You weren't in for killin' someone, were ya?"

Daniel's eyes went wide and he jerked back a bit. He tried to stop himself from showing any response at the question but couldn't. He felt caught, and the thought of the men being bounty hunters hit him again.

Before he could decide what to do next, Sam laughed. "Just havin' fun with ya. Here, take it."

Daniel relaxed and took the revolver in his hand and looked it over. A Smith & Wesson Model 3. The shine was starting to go dull, and the wood handle was worn and nicked, but its weight felt good. He'd never held one before.

"Taggart," Daniel said softly.

"What's that?" Sam asked.

"Taggart."

"That your name?"

"No, that was the sheriff in Elko County. Is he still there?"

"Wouldn't know," Sam replied.

Daniel slipped the gun inside his pants and pulled his belt tight. He didn't want the bother of the gun but felt comforted by it.

"It'll be there," Daniel said, looking at the men and nodding in appreciation.

"Here, you'll need this too," the older man said, tossing Daniel a long blade in a sheath.

Daniel caught it. "Thanks," he said, feeling its weight much in the same manner he had the revolver. He'd never been given much in his life. Most of what he had only came from stealing, and he sure as hell didn't wait around to thank the owner.

"You a fool, Sam," the younger brother said. "You ain't never gonna see that revolver or knife again. The gun don't even shoot straight!"

"It shoots straight, Bill. You just can't aim worth a lick."

The younger brother tossed Daniel an egg and a bar of jerky. Then he bit off half an egg for himself and threw the rest at his brother. He kicked his horse into a full sprint, whooping as he rode away. The older brother kicked out after him, and they were gone.

*

Daniel didn't encounter anyone else for the next several days of his journey. He saw riders and wagons in the distance from both directions but made sure they didn't cross paths or see him. He wasn't afraid of anyone; just didn't want the company or the questions. He wanted to keep his pace for Palisade.

As he arrived at the Humboldt River and the trail that ran alongside it, he knew he'd likely run into even more travelers. It had been the most popular trail west for nearly fifty years. Most took the train west nowadays, but for those who were planning to mine or settle as farmers, they came in wagons, individually or in groups both large and small. He half expected to run into Sheriff Taggart or even Keen, either of which would be troubling. Running into Clay would be good fortune. Daniel kept his eyes east, heading off the trail only when necessary. It seemed every two minutes he was looking back from where he'd come, checking to see if anyone might be riding up on him unexpectedly.

A couple days into his walk up the Humboldt, Daniel made camp early. He crossed the river at a low point, putting it between him and the trail. He took off his boots and cooled his feet in the river, then moved deeper into the trees for better protection. He gathered tinder and kindling and small logs and set himself to building a fire. He rubbed a stick hard and fast into a dry log until it smoked and lit the tinder, then set the tinder under the kindling to burn. He wished Clay was there; his brother could turn dried leaves and twigs into an inferno in half the time. Once the kindling flamed up, he carefully put on larger and larger twigs and sticks and eventually small logs. He watched until each began to burn enough for the next. When the fire was burning to his liking, Daniel sat on a large rock a few feet away and took time to finally enjoy some of the venison the two brothers had given him. After his meal he set his blanket roll on the ground for his head and lay down. As soon as he was on his back and still, the pain in his legs from hours of walking and in his feet from the boot sores grew more intense. His muscles tightened and twitched out of control; the boot sores stung sharp. He winced once and then worked to ignore the hurt. Sunlight still lit low in the western sky as he closed his eyes. He listened to the night. Eerily quiet for a remote forest camp, he thought. No coyotes yelping or owls hooting, even in the far distance. As dusk gave way to full dark, Daniel fell asleep.

Scratch!

The sound woke Daniel. A match strike. He opened his eyes but lay still. His heart raced. He tried to keep his breathing calm, but his chest rose and dropped visibly. The flicker of a match's fire danced behind him and threw a tiny glow over his head. He smelled the burn, and then tobacco smoke as it floated to him. He listened for the clicking of a gun or the metal of a knife being taken from its sheath. He was now glad that he had Sam's revolver. He decided to make a move for his gun and take by surprise whoever was there. He closed his eyes and then in one motion turned onto his knees and reached for his revolver. It wasn't there. He ran his hands over the ground where he'd laid it before he fell asleep. Still nothing. He jerked his head to the figure sitting on a log behind where he'd been lying, easily seeing the man in the light of the fire. The man's gray hair shot out long and wiry from under his hat in every direction. As Daniel looked him over, the man removed his hat to reveal nothing above the wiry hair except bare skin. His beard and mustache shot out just as long and gray and wiry as his hair. He twisted a rolled cigarette in his fingers while sucking on it and puffing out clouds of smoke at the same time. He took the cigarette out of his mouth just long enough to smile, showing his missing front teeth, with the few left behind stained yellow and dark. Then the old man laughed as if a crazy scheme he'd hatched was playing out to perfection right before him.

"Who ya running from, huh?" the old man asked, the excitement in his eyes showing in the firelight. "The law? The husband? Bushwhackers?"

"Ain't runnin'," Daniel said, agitated but relieved that he didn't have a gun aimed on him or his throat slit. He figured he could take the old man, so he stood and showed his size.

"I been following you," the old man said. "You hide every time someone rides near ya."

"I'm just not that friendly. Prefer my own company."

"You runnin'," the old man said, whooping out loud. "You surely are."

"What do you want? Why you sneakin' into my camp?" Daniel asked as he looked around again for his gun and set himself to jump at the old man and wrestle him to the ground.

"Don't want nothin'. And ain't sneakin' either. I announced myself, but you likely didn't hear due to all the snorin'."

Daniel looked around the camp. "Where's my gun?"

"Oh, I gots it. You'll get it back when we part."

He stared at the old man, who continued to smile and show off his mouthful of missing teeth. Daniel shook his head and decided he was too tired to argue or care about his gun or the old man. He now wished he was still asleep.

"Ya see, young fella, I don't trust no one, but I do trust

myself. See? We'll both sleep better if I hold the pieces. Okay?"

"Okay, sure," Daniel replied. "You can lay over there, other side of the fire."

"I'll stoke it up so it'll keep going till mornin'. You just rest, Daniel."

Daniel froze. He felt a shiver of cold flood over him. His face went pale as he looked back at the old man. No, it couldn't be possible. He didn't know the old man; there was nothing familiar about him. He looked the old man over again and tried to see him as ten years younger, even twenty, but nothing showed familiar.

"Yep, I know ya," the old man said with a smile. "I remember when you kilt that woman and left that little girl with no ma or pa. Shame on you for doin' such a thing."

Daniel's breathing went heavy again. He looked around the old man and around the camp, trying to eye his gun in the glow of the fire. What was the man's plan? What did he want?

"I got yer gun. Don't let yerself fret. And I won't hurt ya. We all done bad things, so I can't say nothin'."

Daniel kept his look on him, now even more unsure of his intentions.

"You won't find the gun. Just forget it. I'll give it over in the mornin'. You got no way but to trust me."

Daniel gave in to the old man and lay back down but kept his eyes open.

"Were ya drunk? That's what I heard. Was she cheatin' on ya, or maybe you was the one doing the cheatin'? Easy to do in that town. I don't wanna be judgin' ya; no way I don't. Just makin' small talk so's we can pass some time."

"How do you know all this?" Daniel asked.

"Let's see. That was right at ten years ago now. I was up and down that line on the Central Pacific as a conductor, collectin' tickets and keepin' my trains runnin' on time. Yep. Peoples all talked about that day for six months. About you. That woman. That little girl. Your brother."

"What were they sayin'?"

"That you was drunk and killed her in a stupor. She done nothin' to you. Nothin' but keep food in your belly and that girl stayin' in Sunday school. You took guilty and got a short ten years. Shoulda got a rope, they all said. That brother of yours walked in right when you pulled the trigger and dropped her to the floor, blood all over you and her and that kitchen."

Daniel rubbed his eyes. Flashes of that morning rushed through his mind. He felt anguish for what he'd done to Meg all those years, ignoring her. Then what he'd done to Allie. His heart sank. He didn't know why she would even want to see him again. For a moment he lost hope. A sickness fell in his gut. He sat up and looked toward the Humboldt River, seeing himself walk in and be washed away.

"You okay, Daniel?" the old man asked him.

"Yeah, just thinkin' back, thinkin' about Allie."

"Allie... yes, that was her name. Where's she now?"

"I don't know. I'm headed to Palisade, hopin' she's there—or at least will come back to see me. I have some things to say to her."

"Yeah, you do at that," the old man said. "Ten years can

change things. Maybe she'll want you back even after what you done."

Daniel took a deep breath and let it out. "I need to see her, need to apologize."

He lay back down and covered his eyes with his left arm. He kept his thoughts on Allie. The old man let him have some quiet and went about fashioning his makeshift bed on the ground on the other side of the fire.

"I got throwed off the line," the old man said. "After that, I started roamin' these parts. Been out here four, five years now. Ya know out here ya meet people. People that say things, most of it horseshit."

Daniel was half-asleep when the old man started talking again.

"This one man," he continued, "this one man said he seen somethin' no one else seen that mornin'."

Daniel lifted his arm from his eyes. "What mornin'?"

"The mornin' you shot her," he said.

Daniel sat up again and looked across at the old man. "What man? What did he say?"

"That he was there. Saw it all. Who done what that mornin'."

"No. You're a liar, old man. There wasn't anyone else there. Just Meg and me. Even Allie was gone to Sunday school."

"He said he seen Meg with the gun first. She was full on mad at you. Wonderin' why you brought trash like him around."

Daniel stared in disbelief at the old man.

"Did she say that to you?" he asked.

"Yeah, she did," Daniel responded, looking away and

running Meg's words and that scene through his mind once again. Daniel knew that no one else could have known that except him and Meg. Someone else must have been there.

"Who was there, old man? Who did you talk to?" Daniel asked, almost in anger.

The man smiled big, proud and happy that he knew something about that morning that Daniel didn't.

"Hee-hee-hee. Said his name was Keen."

Daniel shivered at hearing the name. His body went cold. He didn't move. His heart beat fast and hard as he saw Keen in his mind, saw him there with Meg. He shook his head, not believing the old man.

"Keen? You sure?"

"Thin like a wire. Face all scarred up. Uglier than he is mean. Stealin' and killin' his way at life."

"Keen was there?" Daniel whispered to himself. "That's who she was pointin' the gun at. He must've been standing out the back door."

Daniel shook his head again and imagined the kitchen that Sunday morning, Meg standing and pointing the gun out the back door. But this time he put Keen there, Meg's gun aimed at him. He knew Keen didn't pull the trigger on Meg, so he wondered why he was even there. It didn't change the fact, though, that Meg was dead, Allie was gone, and he himself was guilty.

"Why'd you do it?" the old man asked him.

"Why'd I do what?"

"Take ten years of prison for somethin' you didn't do."

"I know what I did, old man, and I know why. It's mine

to carry and live with, no one else's. So if you got nothin' else to share, we're done talkin'."

The old man walked over to his saddle and reached into his pouch to pull something out.

"Yeah, I got this to share with you," he said, smiling and whooping and laughing, and then tossed Daniel a bottle.

After catching the bottle Daniel looked at the man, then removed the cork and sniffed. He wrinkled his nose. Although it reeked, he took a sip. As bad as it was, it was still the best, though only, whiskey he'd tasted in ten years.

"Thank you," Daniel said. He reset the cork and tossed the bottle back. "It's been a long while since I had a drink."

The old man caught the bottle and drank in three long swallows himself and put the cork back, then tossed it to Daniel again. Then he lay down and continued to talk about nothing and everything.

Daniel lay back down himself, looked up at the stars, and ran that morning through his mind a few more times.

"If Keen's alive…" Daniel whispered to himself.

His anger at Keen grew for being there that morning, but also for all the bad he'd pulled Clay and himself into. He realized that as he focused on Keen, he lost his thoughts of Meg and Allie.

Hell, I don't care what he saw or didn't, he thought. *I need to get to Allie. That's all I care about anymore.*

With Keen out of his thoughts and Allie back in, Daniel closed his eyes and drifted to sleep.

*

The morning sun lit Daniel's face. He felt its warmth and it woke him. He glanced around the camp. The old man was gone. The fire was burning strong. A couple slices of cooked bacon were lying in a small tin pan on a rock by the fire, and a cup of coffee next to the pan. Daniel's gun lay by his side, with a few dollar bills rolled up and stuffed halfway into the barrel. Daniel shook his head and smiled.

He ate, dressed, packed, and headed out again onto the narrow trail that ran along the Humboldt River.

The next two weeks were uneventful. Daniel wore more tired, and thin. His steps and progress slowed. His breaths were low and shallow. His rests and sleep grew longer. The soles of his boots were near paper thin. He'd stuffed torn blanket pieces into his boots to add cushion against the blisters and scabs. His beard was longer than he'd ever let it grow. He tried to bathe every few days, but that proved more and more pointless. Any food that he'd been carrying was long gone, and he was down to just two cartridges. He didn't have much left, except the desire to reach Palisade alive. He had every reason to die, and by all rights maybe should have by now.

As he progressed up the river trail, the terrain and sur-roundings and homesteads started looking more familiar. He was just a single night's sleep from Palisade. He felt the anxiousness rise up in him at the thought of seeing Allie again. The nervousness overwhelmed him. He stopped and leaned over. He allowed the sickness he now felt to surface. The pain that ravaged his body from the journey, and the hurt and regret that ravaged his life, surfaced as well. He didn't stop them; he didn't hold them back. His emotions exploded inside. The feelings that he'd kept buried his whole life flooded up and out. He had barely shed a tear in thirty years. This was thirty years' worth of tears—of the beatings and shame from his father for showing emotion or making a mistake, and often for no reason at all. The yelling. The anger. The evening where he sat in front of the fire next to his mother jumped to his mind. He'd not once thought about that memory until this moment. He was eleven years old. His father had gone into the kitchen, grabbed a bottle of whiskey, blew out the only lantern in the house, and went to bed, leaving Daniel and Clay and their mother alone in the dark. Only the glow of the fire gave light to the cabin, throwing lurking shadows across the room and onto the far wall. He didn't know where it came from, but he now remembered the hurt he felt and the tears it brought. He cried out loud at his mother's feet. Almost immediately his father stormed out of the bedroom and up to Daniel, towering over him.

"Shut your cryin', boy! How many times have I told you? Ain't no Lind boy gonna cry in this house! That's not what men are made of."

His father's anger grabbed and shook him so hard that he stopped breathing. His father stepped closer and set to backhand him.

His mother jumped up and pushed his father's hand away. "No! You leave him be, Mac! Go back to bed. See if you can find a man at the bottom of that bottle of yours."

As Daniel stood there on the side of the trail, his father was still yelling at him. He heard the voice. Felt the anger. The fear shook him once more. He spun around, expecting to see his father, but no one was there. His father's words echoed again: "Shut your cryin', boy!"

He tried shoving the hurt and pain and tears back down, but he couldn't this time. He took in a deep breath and tried again. The emotion overwhelmed him. Daniel wept. A train whistle blew loud in the distance.

He yelled back at the whistle as if it was his father: "No, I won't stop crying! I was hurting and I needed you. Needed you to teach me how to be a man. All I learned from you was bad. You failed me. And because you failed me, I failed Allie. I don't miss you! I don't miss you one damn bit!"

Daniel fell to his knees and closed his eyes. He imagined how Allie might look now at seventeen. He wished to know. And he desperately wished to know her, know his daughter. His heart softened. For her. For Meg. And for himself.

The train whistle blew again. He didn't hear his father or feel the anger this time. The steam rose just a few hundred yards off, white and pure and rushing up to heaven. He thought of the old man he'd met a couple weeks earlier, who worked on that rail line as a conductor. He thought of Meg's parents who traveled up and down the length of that same line, probably sipping wine in their plush car as he stood near death on the other side of the valley. As Daniel watched the steam of the engine rise, dark clouds burgeoned from the west, consuming the soft blue of the sky above him. His nerves and heart and breathing settled, even as the storm clouds rushed in, consuming more and more of the blue. Raindrops began to tap at him. He didn't hear the rider until he was right on him.

Daniel stood and looked up at the man, who had stopped his ride just a few feet away. At first he thought it a mirage or dream—the weeks of walking and little food and the emotions of those last few moments playing tricks on him. The rider didn't speak at first; he just stared down on Daniel as his horse shuffled its feet to a full stop. Daniel squinted and strained to take in the horse and rider. Sweat and rain shoveled dirt down the man's face, unveiling the scars. They were less visible now, tangled and twisted with age lines cut into his face from a life afflicted with brutality. And they showed Keen uglier and more evil than Daniel thought possible.

"You see an old man back your way?" Keen finally asked.

Daniel didn't answer. He continued to take in Keen, a man he hadn't seen in ten years, and hoped he'd never see again. He began to fear that Keen would recognize him and put a bullet in his head, or not recognize him and put a bullet in him anyway. That was Keen, after all. Daniel thought of the revolver tucked inside his pants. It was loaded, but Keen was too fast for him. Besides, getting to Palisade and seeing Allie was more important. He needed to stay alive, which meant he needed to pacify Keen. A gust of wind whipped sideways and threw more rain at the two men. Neither said a word. Daniel lifted his arm and wiped rain from his eyes and face with his shirtsleeve. Thunder rolled up from behind Keen, joining the storm clouds and rain and dark.

Without an answer, Keen leaned forward onto the horn of his saddle and showed his anger. "I said, you seen an old man back your way?"

Keen didn't recognize him after all. The long beard, half-grayed hair, thin-as-a-whip look—nothing about his appearance so much as whispered *"Daniel Lind."*

"Yeah, I seen him. A couple weeks back, near the

start of the Humboldt." Daniel pointed the direction he'd come from.

"I just come from that way. Didn't see him. Where was he headed?"

"Don't know. He moved on without sayin' where to."

Keen scowled at Daniel.

"What ya got in your sack there?"

"Just some camp fixins."

"Lemme see."

Daniel opened the bag and lifted it up.

Keen leaned and peered in. "Ahh!" he grunted, then kicked the bag and knocked it to the ground. "Where you headed?" he asked.

"Salt Lake," Daniel replied. "Got kin there. Comin' from Reno."

"Mighty long walk, ain't it?"

"My horse got bit by a rattler and died a few miles back. Had to leave most everything behind with it."

Keen looked back down the trail he and Daniel had just traveled. Daniel hoped he would ride back that way, hoped even more that he wasn't headed to Palisade. He thought of Allie and the danger she would be in if Keen found her. And he thought again about pulling out the revolver. But Keen would put a bullet in his head before he even got a hand on it. He decided to stay calm and learn Keen's plans.

"Where you headed?" Daniel asked.

"Palisade. I'm still lookin' for that old man. And got a score to settle there with a couple brothers. Scores I shoulda settled when I had the chance. We lost track of each other, and I'm gonna find them."

Rain began to fall harder. Keen looked at the sky, then to Daniel. Without another word he pulled the reins and kicked his horse east, toward Palisade.

A panic pierced Daniel. If Allie was in Palisade, Keen might find her before he arrived. Daniel wouldn't get there until tomorrow, and that could be too late.

19

Allie—

Your father was released from prison on August 21. I'm sorry. We knew this day would come. He served his time. I just wished for your sake that it was longer. I don't know where he is headed nor his plans. He gave no notice to the warden. He does not know where you are, so you are safe. I sent a note to the US marshal's office in Cheyenne. They are aware of the situation with you and your father. Write back to let me know you are well. I will visit if you wish. Be safe.

Sheriff Taggart

ALLIE SAT ON her bed and stared at the letter. Tears slowly rolled out. Memories she wished would stay buried returned. The ten years now seemed as ten minutes. It happened too fast. She ripped and crumpled the letter and threw it across her room.

Becky stood beside her. "You're here now, with us. Your father won't harm you. I promise."

"You can't promise that," Allie shot back. "You don't know him or men like him. How bad they can be."

Becky turned Allie's face up to hers. "Yes, I do know men like him. I know what they're capable of. Have you seen a man in this house since you've been here?"

Allie went silent.

"You know that I was married to a man named Del, the boys' father. But he couldn't settle down. Ran off to who knows where. Haven't seen nor heard from him in all these years. He shoulda been here to help us, take care of us. He abandoned me, abandoned his kids."

"I know. You told me about him awhile back."

"And my brother, Jim—the sheriff who brought you here, the one you think is a savior and a saint—he's a drunk and lets his drinking get in the way of his work. Didn't know that, did you?"

Allie shook her head.

"A badge on a man doesn't make him a man or a protector. I know. He shot my little girl."

Allie was shocked. She lost thought of her father and focused on Becky and her loss.

"I knew you had a daughter, but didn't know what happened to her," she said.

"Yes... I did. Jim was visiting us. It was twelve years before you arrived. Anna was six, and our oldest. She went to hide in the barn and surprise her uncle. He was packing to leave and then headed to the barn to saddle his horse. He had already been drinking, which was about all he did the three days he was here. As he walked into the barn, Anna jumped out from behind some hay bales and started pretending she was shooting. She was holding her father's handgun. Jim said he only saw the gun, so he pulled his revolver and shot her without thinking. He was too damn drunk to know where he was or what he was doing or that it was just a six-year-old little girl playing with her uncle. I heard the gunfire and ran to the barn just as he was stumbling out carrying Anna. 'She's gone.' That's all he said. 'She's gone.'"

Allie's eyes went big. "That's what he said to me that morning my mom was killed!"

"I hate those words," Becky said. "I still hear them and his voice."

"Me too," Allie said. "They just keep repeating over and over in my head."

"The words will never go away, Allie. We can't push away those moments that are so devastating to us. The more devastating and hurtful they are, the more they stay with us."

"I'm so sorry, Becky. I had no idea this happened—that you lost your little girl this way."

"Jim stayed that night but was gone the next morning. Didn't even wait around for the funeral. I didn't see him again until he showed up with you. Gone twelve years without a word. And Del left a couple years after that. Had Davey and Jacob to tend to by myself."

"I'm so sorry."

"It's not your fault. Not your burden to carry. It's mine; you have your own."

Allie's heart ached for Becky, both for losing her little girl and for having a broken relationship with her brother as well. They both knew what it felt like to have someone they deeply loved die, and then also have the person who caused the death to live on. It still didn't seem fair. It felt like a cruel joke to Allie. As she sat on the bed with Becky standing next to her, Allie felt as one with her. She imagined both of them hearing the sheriff's words relentlessly echoing in their heads and hearts: "She's gone." Becky's loss of her daughter made her more human, more real. She reached and hugged Becky.

"I'm sorry that you experienced these things with your husband and brother," Allie said. "They made life tough on you, just like my dad made life tough on my mom and me."

"But just know, Allie, we're all capable of bad. Even you and me. Lying, stealing, not honoring your parents are sins just as much as killing. All sin separates us from God, no matter how big or small we might think it is. And because we all sin, we all need forgiveness the same too."

"Have you forgiven Del and your brother?" Allie asked.

Becky started to respond but stopped, leaving her mouth half open. Allie could tell it was a question that Becky had never been asked.

"Umm … Uhh … I don't know," Becky said softly. "I've tried. I think I've been, uhh … maybe I've been too bitter about what they did to me." She paused mid-thought. "I'm not a very good example for you, am I?"

Allie smiled for Becky. "It's difficult to forgive, so I don't blame you for struggling with it. At least you're trying. I'll never be able to forgive my dad for what he did. Never. So I'm not even going to try."

"Oh, Allie. Give it more time. I promise to keep trying myself."

Allie continued to think about Becky's words on being bad and needing forgiveness.

"I lied," Allie said.

Becky looked surprised at her words. "What do you mean, you lied? To me?"

"No. I lied to my mom and dad once. I took a dollar piece off of the table. I said I didn't do it, even promised them I didn't."

Becky sat down next to Allie on the bed and held her close and stroked her hair. "Go ahead, tell me more. I'm listening."

"I wanted to see inside that place where my dad always went, the one that seemed so much more important to him than me. I gave the dollar to my friend Charles. He said he could sneak me into that place and we could look from the balcony. I watched my dad drink and laugh. He drank at home, but I never saw him laugh. I saw a different man down there, a happy man—away from me and my mom."

"Oh my, Allie. That is sad to hear. But men don't always know how to show love to their family. Maybe more like they don't want to. It's not manly to them. They let their rough-and-tough side shine. That's what other men respect, so that's what they let show."

"Doesn't make it right," Allie said.

"No, it certainly doesn't make it right."

"It's hard to see my dad's ways and what he did to my mom as no worse a sin than me lying."

"It's all sin, but the damage sure is different. We desperately need to forgive one another, but even more, we each need God's forgiveness and grace to cover our sins."

Becky pulled Allie's face to hers and looked her in the

eyes. "I'm sure your father did the best he could at the time. His raisin' was likely worse than yours. He needs grace and forgiveness just as much as you do for that lie, as much as I do, and as much as Del and my brother do. We all need it. Desperately need it. We get buckets of grace and forgiveness from God if we would just accept it. But we need to give it just as much, especially to those who hurt us most."

Allie tried again to imagine herself forgiving her father. She saw herself standing in front of him, small and scared and hurt, him full of anger. The words wouldn't come out; she could tell fear kept them down. It was as if he told her not to speak, threatened her with his eyes to not say, "I forgive you." Like it weakened a person to say it, and worse, weakened a man to hear it.

"I don't know, Becky," Allie said. "He was bad. I've told you some of the things he did to my mom. And he took her away from me. Nothing is worse than that. I ain't had her all these years. Hard to forgive that."

"I didn't say it was easy, just that God asks us to forgive others if we want to be forgiven by Him."

Allie looked at the crumpled letter on the floor. Anger returned. She just couldn't forgive him. Her mother was lying in a box far from her and he was out of prison. She clenched her jaw and looked away.

"Are you okay, honey?" Becky asked.

Allie's anger was exploding inside her and she didn't care if Becky saw it.

It's not fair! she thought. Her father was now free—free to live and breathe. Her mother was dead. *It's not fair,* she kept thinking. *It's just not fair.* The more she sat there thinking of her father out of prison and free, the greater her anger grew. She could see him smiling and laughing as he left prison, riding to the first saloon he could find, getting drunk, and then heading to Palisade to reunite with Clay so they could return to their bad ways.

Allie leaped from the bed and ran out of her room. "I need to leave!" she yelled.

"Allie?... Allie! Where are you going?"

She didn't respond. She ran from her room, out the front door, and into the barn.

The time had come. His prison term was over and she was ready to make the journey she'd fixated on the last several years. Confident that her father would be in Palisade with Clay, likely at the old house and up to their old ways, Allie began preparing for her trip. Her emotion shifted from anger to anxiousness at the prospect of finally confronting him about what he'd done to her mother. Becky's talk about grace and forgiveness wasn't enough to sway her. She was now on a mission to confront her father, and she wasn't going to let anything, or anyone, stop her.

Allie ran into the barn, then climbed up the ladder and to the corner where she kept the revolver hidden in the hay. "I'm going to do this for you, Mom," she whispered. She felt the anger that had burned in her for years. She pulled out the folded paper that lay beneath the gun. She ran her finger down through the stations along the Union Pacific and Central Pacific lines: New York, Chicago, Omaha, Kearney, Cheyenne, Laramie, Medicine Bow, Rawlins.

"Yes, Rawlins. That's the closest station," she said aloud. "There's a train that leaves at 11:20 a.m. every day."

She was certain her father was headed to Palisade and would likely arrive before her, given the delay it took in receiving the sheriff's letter.

"Sunday," Allie said. "Two days from now. I'll have Rueben ride me up to Rawlins."

She put the gun back and headed to the house, returning to her room and avoiding Becky along the way. The travel bag that the sheriff had given her when they left Palisade still lay beneath her bed. She pulled it out and filled it with the clothes she would need, leaving room for the revolver.

*

Allie was out of bed and packed Sunday morning before the sun; everyone else was still asleep. She knew it wasn't right for her to leave Becky without a good-bye, but she had to. Becky had taken such good care of her since she arrived unannounced ten years earlier. And now she was leaving just as abruptly, no different than Del or her brother had. She knew that Becky had come to rely on her help with the farm and with house chores, and that was about to end. Allie was another mouth to feed, no doubt, but helpful at the same time. But she needed to make this trip and didn't want anyone trying to stop her. The note she left was simple:

Need to go home. Thank you for all you've done for me. —Love, Allie.

She placed the note on the kitchen table, along with some of the money she'd earned, and walked out. Although Allie felt rushed, she stopped in the barn to say good-bye to

Tag. She needed to spend those few minutes brushing and petting and talking to him before she left.

The sun was still low but gave enough light to see the path to the main road north to Rawlins. Rueben promised to meet her right at sunup where the two pines stood watch over travelers as they headed south to Savery Creek or took the road north to Rawlins.

She watched as Rueben rode up to her and then jumped off.

"Hey, Allie."

"Hi, Rueben. Thank you for doing this for me. I appreciate it."

He helped Allie up and onto the saddle, then stepped up and sat in front of her and kicked his horse into a trot.

"When you comin' back?" Rueben asked her.

"Don't know. May not. May stay there, or head into California. Not sure yet."

"I'd like to see you again, Allie. That is, if you do get back this way."

"Rueben, you've been sweet. And helpful. And fun. This just doesn't feel like home to me. My heart has always been elsewhere. But I truly won't know until I'm back in Palisade."

"I understand. Maybe I could come see you? Would that be okay?"

"I don't know. Wouldn't want you to get there and learn I moved on. I'll write and let you know."

They rode the rest of the way with little conversation. Allie had her arms around Rueben loosely, but as they got closer to Rawlins, she held more tightly. Her thoughts went to how well he had always treated her. Respectfully. Rare for a man given the world she grew up in.

"You need a break?" Rueben asked.

"No. I'm doin' fine. And I don't want to risk bein' late, so let's just keep riding."

"Sure thing," he said, then kicked the horse into a faster trot. "Let's pick it up, big guy. Gotta get Allie to the train and home."

As they entered the edge of Rawlins, he settled the ride to a walk, then near the station rode up to a hitching post and wrapped the reins around it. He helped Allie down, then grabbed her bag, and they walked the remaining half block to the station. The smell of steel and steam reminded Allie of Palisade. The bustle of the platform made her anxious to get seated and settled for the long trip home. Inside, the station sweltered. The agent was fanning himself with a folded route map. He continued even as they approached.

"Where you two headed?" he asked.

"Oh, not me, just my friend. She's goin' to Palisade," Rueben responded.

The agent tilted his head down, peered at Allie, and snickered. "Not a place for a young 'un, especially a little girl. If you was passin' through, I'd tell ya to stay on and don't venture out. You might get yourself hurt."

"I can take care of myself," Allie said.

Rueben stared the man down. "One ticket. One-way. Palisade."

"One-way to boot! I guess you *won't* be comin' back, then!" he said, laughing.

Allie grabbed Rueben's arm and pulled him tight. She

was anxious and excited and scared all at the same time. She now wished Rueben was going with her. He would comfort her and help keep her safe. He had that way about him.

"Train's boardin' now," the agent said. "You've got less than five minutes to say your good-byes.... Maybe your last good-byes."

Rueben and Allie ignored the man and walked out of the station, then headed across the platform to the train.

Rueben stopped short of the steps and looked at the station clock—11:18. "Hey, Allie. Wait."

She turned and looked at him, read his face, then looked away. Smiling. "Rue…"

He took her hand and folded it into his, then slid their fingers together. She liked the feel of her hand in his. Even in the heat of the afternoon Allie felt the warmth pour through her body. She looked down and smiled. Rueben had never been forward like this with her—no boy had. It felt nice and good but odd at the same time. The train whistle blew, stealing away the moment with Rueben. She needed to go.

"Well, this is good-bye, then, I suppose," Rueben said.

"Yes, I can see that," Allie said, now looking away but still smiling.

He looked the opposite way. She glanced at him and could tell he didn't want her to leave.

"I need to do this, Rueben," she said.

"I know, Allie. I didn't expect to feel this way. I'm going to miss you."

"I'll miss you too. Bye, Rueben."

He turned to her just as she started walking away, and as her hand slipped from his.

"Good-bye, Allie," he whispered to himself.

*

Allie dropped her bag on the floor and fell into her seat. She set her stare out the window and onto the platform.

"All aboard!"

The train whistle screamed, the wheels turned and inched forward. Before she knew it, they were at full speed in the western Wyoming territory. The ground outside her window sped past, the far horizon held still. Reality struck. She was on her way to Palisade. She was going to face her dad. She picked up the bag that held her revolver, set it on her lap, and pulled it close.

The train rocked back and forth as it rolled at full speed. The wheels click-clacked against the tracks. She wondered how different Palisade would look. Would she even recognize it? Would she even recognize her dad?

"Tickets!"

Allie handed hers to the conductor without looking at him. Her effort to prevent another preaching about traveling alone. He moved on without a word. She relaxed, then reached into her bag and pulled out a slice of bread and began to eat.

"Mind if I sit here?" a voice said, nodding to the seat across from Allie.

Allie looked up to see a woman with warm brown skin and dark eyes. Allie nodded.

The woman set two large bags on the floor and fell into the middle of the seat. Her black hair was pulled straight back and lay tight against her head. Streaks of gray in her hair gave her quite a distinguished look. The black straw hat she wore looked shiny and new, and the silk roses that bloomed on top looked as though they'd just been picked. The woman smiled at Allie.

"I've been sittin' in the next car up, but that cryin' baby sets me off."

She looked at Allie, as if to reassure herself that she wasn't a baby, and then returned to talking. "I've been ridin' this line since the beginnin'. You'd be surprised the things I've seen. I can put up with most anything, but cryin' little ones is just too much to bear. You agree?"

Allie didn't know how to respond. Didn't get the chance to either.

"You ain't much from the baby carriage yourself. You look like a quiet one, though." The lady laughed at herself. "You quiet, ain't ya, girl?"

Allie started to talk but was again interrupted, "No mind. It's okay. I talk enough for two people."

Ten people is more like it, Allie thought.

"Had to talk a lot. And fast. Eleven kids in my family. If you didn't speak up, you got no word in otherwise. And if you didn't eat fast, well, you starved. A band of fightin' pigs at a new slop. That's what we looked like! Ha!"

Allie held back a laugh.

"You know what else? People live on this train. On the train! Got no other place. Got their own car too. Fancier than any hotel room you or I ever stayed in. With a water closet! A danged water closet on a train! I don't know where it goes, though. I'm afraid to ask!"

Allie looked at the woman and wondered where all of the words were coming from.

"You headed somewhere on your own, girl?" the lady asked. She leaned her head toward Allie, giving her permission to finally speak.

"Yes, headed to... um... California," Allie said, not wanting to give the lady a chance to question her choice of heading to Palisade by herself.

"Me?" the lady continued. "I'm headed to Carlin, then Palisade. I clean houses, bars, hotels, restaurants. If it's dirty, I clean it. God's gift to me and my gift back to God. Not sure it's an official gift of God, but I surely got it. Love it too. Not always the cleanin', but the afterward, what it looks like. Sparklin'! That sure satisfies me enough."

Allie continued to eat her bread, though slowly, and in small bites. She kept her eyes on the lady so as to not disrespect her.

"Know how I know about that fancy car? The one in the back here? I clean that too. Every week. Just finished as we stopped in Rawlins."

"Do you know them?" Allie asked.

"The ones livin' in that car?" She nodded. "Sure do." The lady leaned toward Allie. Looked to her left, then whispered, "They're not nice people. Never say much as a word to me. Like I'm not even there or good enough to be talked at. Oh, they sure tell me if I missed a spot, mind you."

"What's their name?" Allie asked.

"The Gants. Mister and Missus Arrow Gant." The lady laughed. "That's what I call 'em. Not to their face of course!" She slapped her knee and laughed again.

Allie wanted to know more but didn't want to show herself prying.

"Their daughter got shot awhile back. Tsk, tsk, tsk. I did feel for 'em then. Her husband did it, you know. Spent ten years in prison. I'd a strung him up. Save a lot of time and money and good air, if you ask me. He just got out, I heard 'em say. Likely headed back to Palisade."

Allie jumped in her seat. Her heart leapt. Her breaths deepened. Eyes went big. Skin paled.

"You okay, girl?"

She forced herself to breathe, slowly in and slowly out. "Yes, I think. Yes, I'm fine. I'm okay."

Allie now knew. Her grandparents were on the train. And they knew that Daniel was out of prison. Allie panicked again. She'd visited them a couple times in their car when she was little. She remembered how nice it was. She hadn't been allowed to touch anything. Just sit and behave. She wanted to run up and down through the cars and explore every nook and cranny. But those other cars were for "little people," as her grandmother called them. Allie was certainly now one of those little people.

"She had a young girl too, ya know—the lady that got shot. Heard she was sent away to an orphanage. So sad. Grandparents didn't want her. She'd be better off anyway. Not nice people, and livin' on a train ain't no way to grow up."

Allie's heart pounded. "Do they ever talk about that lady, or her little girl, the one at the orphanage?" She could barely speak but hoped to hear of her grandparents' hurt and sadness for their daughter and granddaughter.

"No, all they talked about back then was the man that

shot her. How bad he was and how they say Meg—That's it... Meg! That was her name!"

Allie's face lost all color—her skin went white. And she couldn't hold back the tears any longer. It was the first time she'd heard her mother's name spoken in all these years. Hearing her name made her real again, brought her back to life. But just as quickly she was gone again. Allie once more felt the pain of losing her mother. She longed for her, longed for her voice, longed for her reassuring presence.

"You okay, girl? I'm gettin' you some water. Maybe a sweet. You wait here."

The lady left. Allie let the tears flow, then wiped them and forced herself straight. She wanted to hear more from the lady but found the words hard to take. The hurt she so often felt was closer now. Her grandparents were right here on the train, driving spikes into her heart and gut. Allie figured they enjoyed it, like they were getting the last laugh at Meg for what she'd done to them, with no worry about what they'd done to her. She saw the lady scurrying back and gave one last wipe of her eyes.

"Here, drink up. And here's a cookie. It'll bring some life back into ya."

"Thank you, ma'am. I'm okay."

The water was warm, but it refreshed her. It also gave her something to do, as well as time to compose herself. Allie felt rattled but wanted to hear more.

"Let's see, where was I? Oh yeah... Meg. I never met her. They never talked about her, least not till she died. Then it was only how she'd messed up her life with that man. Seems they may have been right."

"What happened to that little girl, their granddaughter? Didn't they try to find her or see her?"

"Lordy no. It's like that whole family was bad to them. That little girl no different than her dad."

Allie's heart sank. The hurt fell heavy on her. She was a nobody to her dad and to her grandparents. And her mom had been a nobody too—to her husband and to her own parents.

The lady noticed Allie's sadness but continued anyway, a little more gracefully, though: "I'm sure she's doin' fine. Children tend to be strong and resilient like you wouldn't believe."

Allie leaned to set her glass of water on the seat next to her, but as she did, it fell out of her hand and spilled. She jumped to her feet, knocking her bag to the floor. The revolver fell halfway out. The woman looked at the gun—her eyes and mouth wide open—then at Allie.

"Umm, it's my daddy's," Allie said as she leaned and shoved the gun back into the bag and sat again. "I'm takin' it to him. He forgot it." She looked away from the woman.

The woman looked at Allie, looked deep into her. She finally noticed her, finally saw the young girl across from her. Allie was no longer just a thing to talk at but was now a human being who was hurting and maybe even in trouble.

"What's your name, sweetie?" she asked with concern.

Allie didn't answer. She kept her look away.

The lady looked her over head to toe; she fully took her in. "Where's your momma? Your daddy? Are you on this train alone?"

Allie didn't answer. She glanced at the woman, who now

studied her intensely, maybe putting the pieces together—their conversation and Allie's emotions and curiosity about Meg and her parents, and that little girl in the orphanage, how old she was then and how old she would be now, and that the father was getting out of prison. And the gun.

Allie watched as the woman's eyes grew even wider.

"You ain't goin' to California, are you?" she asked flatly.

Allie looked away again, pulled the bag tight to herself, and shook her head. The woman lightly gasped. Allie could feel her staring. She knew what was coming next. She took in a breath and waited for the words.

"You're her, ain't you? You're that little girl."

Allie stayed quiet and kept her gaze out the window.

The lady put her hand to her mouth. "Palisade. You're goin' to Palisade. And with that gun. Oh my, child…"

20

After leaving Barlowe's saloon in Reno, Clay had spent those next three years fully focused on hunting Keen. He survived the only way he knew how—stealing. He tried honest jobs at times but couldn't get used to the daily routine. Eventually he'd take something that wasn't his and move on. He tried to keep most of his work in Arizona and Utah and even California, anywhere away from northern Nevada. He knew Keen spread out his travels all over the west, even down into Mexico. In that tenth year of his brother's prison sentence, in mid-September, Clay was in western Nevada and decided to ride into Carson City, to the prison, to see if Daniel had been released. He'd never visited his brother, not in all those years. He'd ridden through several times but could only stand on the outside staring at the walls, trying to find the courage to walk in. Part of him was scared of being recognized, but mostly he didn't think he could look at his brother in prison clothes. Jail was one thing; prison another.

He stopped his ride across the road from the prison and

once again stared at the walls, still searching for courage. Thirty minutes turned into an hour, and then two. He watched and waited and wondered and hoped. Clay was no closer to walking into that prison than he had been the last time he rode by a couple years earlier. He watched as a wagon pulled up and stopped by the front doors. A line of prisoners walked out and one by one stepped into the wagon. They were being released. He looked intently at each man, searching for his brother. He wasn't among them.

After another twenty minutes he saw two men entering through a small door at the corner of the prison. A few minutes later two different men walked out. This was his chance. He rode up to the men and dismounted.

"Afternoon, gentlemen," Clay said. "Are you guards?"

"Yeah. What ya want?" one of them asked.

Both men gripped their revolvers.

"I'm not here for trouble," Clay said, slightly raising his hands. "Is Daniel Lind still inside?"

"Daniel Lind? Oh... yeah. He was a quiet old man. Don't think I heard him say more than ten words the whole time I was around him."

"Was?" Clay asked.

"Yeah. Let out about three weeks ago."

Clay's skin shivered. He closed his eyes and let out a full breath, as if he'd been holding it for those ten years. He looked around, wondering what to say next.

"You know him?" the other man asked.

Clay hesitated. "Yeah. He's my brother."

"I never seen you visit."

"Nope. I didn't visit. Did anyone?"

The two men looked at each other and shook their heads.

"No, not that I recollect," the first guard responded.

"Me neither," the second added.

"Know where he went?" Clay asked.

"Most men take the ride into Virginia City to look for work in the mines," the first guard said. "I was helpin' the prisoners into the wagon that morning. Daniel just walked away. Looked like he was headed east. That was the last I seen or heard of him until now."

Clay knew that Daniel would be headed to Palisade and was likely there already, unless he walked the full way, which he doubted his brother would survive after ten years of prison labor.

"Thank you, gentlemen. Appreciate it," he said, tipping his hat to them. He grabbed Molly's reins, mounted, and kicked her into a full sprint toward Palisade.

Clay was now worried, afraid that he would fail in his mission to protect and save his family. He wouldn't be able to live with himself if he let Keen hurt Daniel or Allie.

"I gotta make this ride home and fast," he said aloud to himself. "Gotta protect Daniel from Keen, and maybe even from himself. I need you, Molly—need you to hang in there until we get home." He reached down and patted her side. "C'mon, girl, help me out with this ride."

Clay rode hard out of Carson City and away from the prison, up the trail that followed the Carson River. He knew he was weeks behind his brother, and likely behind Keen as well.

*

Keen was indeed far ahead of Clay. Even as Clay was deep into his ride east, Keen already sat at the edge of Palisade, atop a hill to the west. After leaving Daniel in the rain the day before and sleeping along the river under a grove of trees, he had stopped his ride and took in the town. Main Street was filled with the rush and flow of people in and out of shops and restaurants and saloons. A train of the Central Pacific line sat next to the station as passengers loaded for the next ride out. The slow-moving Humboldt River ran alongside the tracks as far east and west as he could see. Houses and buildings fanned out every direction, but only for a handful of blocks. Dry desert lay beyond the town, full of nothing but sand and sage and ruts deep enough to trap a horse.

Keen rode down the winding path to a hidden section of the Humboldt. After stripping and bathing, he dried himself in the sun and dressed again. He trimmed his beard as best he could with his knife and slicked back his hair. He didn't want to be seen by the sheriff or the deputies, so the less he looked like the trouble he was, the better. He mounted again and rode into Palisade. He tied his horse to a post at the back of the Landing Hotel and walked in.

"A room. Upstairs. On the corner," Keen said to the keeper.

"Two dollars a night," the keeper said. "Name?"

Keen turned the book around, grabbed the pen from the keeper, and placed an X on the next open line.

"Any other questions?" Keen asked.

"No, and I don't want no trouble."

"You ain't gonna get any if you leave me in peace."

He slammed the money on the desk. The keeper handed

him the key and Keen walked upstairs and into the room. He tossed his guns and belt on the bed, hat on the dresser, then stepped to the corner window and opened it. He looked east, then west, from the street below out to as far as he could see each direction. Twenty minutes of watching turned into forty, then a few more. He pulled a chair to the window, sat, and leaned forward, keeping his look out at the street and town.

Daniel was sure to show up, he figured, along with Clay. He regretted letting those brothers get away and now wished he'd killed them long before Daniel went to prison. He didn't usually make mistakes like that, leaving witnesses to his killings, but had enjoyed their company on many rides, so figured they were close friends, or at least as close as he'd allow.

"I'm fixin' that damn mistake," he muttered, "and ain't makin' it again."

He glanced at his guns on the bed, just to assure himself he was set to follow through on his promise.

Two trains arrived and departed in the time he sat and kept watch. Each arrival brought another round of travelers flooding into the streets. The rail passengers mixed in with the regular flow of horse riders in and out from both sides of town as well as those arriving by stagecoach throughout the day. Dust of the streets never found the chance to settle. Saloon music from below banged so loud in his room that it felt like the piano was right next to him.

The sun began to fall farther to the western horizon. It didn't seem to cool the air, though. Sweat rolled steadily down his face and neck. He stepped to the dresser and washbasin to rinse his face with a few splashes of water. He dried himself and sat again.

Back in his chair less than a minute, Keen jumped and leaned to the window. He squinted and made out Sheriff Taggart down the street. He watched as the sheriff crossed the street at an angle and moved toward the hotel.

"Damn sheriff," he said out loud. "Gonna mess this up for me."

Keen knocked the chair away and grabbed one of his handguns from the bed, checking that it was loaded, then walked out to the hall and peered around the corner and down to the front desk. Normally calm regardless of the situation, Keen now felt anxious. He knew the sheriff was a good shot and quick as hell too. His only chance to beat him would be to surprise him—or if he'd been drinking, which was a pretty good bet any day.

He watched as the sheriff and manager talked at the front desk, but the noise of the saloon that filled the first floor of the hotel drowned out their voices and words. After only a few seconds the keeper nodded and pointed to the stairs.

Keen pulled himself back to hide. The anxiousness he already felt shot higher. He weighed his chances to run. "Damn," he said. The sheriff would be sure to have a warrant for his arrest—dead or alive. He could kill him on sight and have the right to do so. "Damn," Keen said again. He walked toward his room and reached in for the doorknob, then quietly pulled the door closed. He walked to the next room just past his and turned the knob. Locked. He moved across the hall to another room. He turned the knob and slipped inside just as the sheriff hit the top of the stairs.

Tap-tap.

Keen could hear the iron of a gun rapping the door of his room across the hall.

"Keen," the sheriff said in a low voice.

Tap-tap.

"Keen, you in there?"

He heard the sheriff calling to him. Keen didn't answer, though, just kept his revolver raised and finger on the trigger. He waited patiently, hoping the sheriff would quit the situation and move on.

With no response the sheriff slid to the side of the door and knocked again.

Tap-tap.

"I'm comin' in, Keen," he said.

The sheriff turned the knob and pushed the door open. It swung and banged against the wall inside. He peeked and looked around, then stepped in.

Keen heard the door bang open and relaxed. He was certain that when the sheriff saw the empty room, he'd holster his gun. Keen smiled and set himself to surprise the sheriff.

Inside the room, with no sign of Keen, the sheriff holstered his revolver and walked to the window and peered out into the town, looking up and down the street.

Keen quietly opened the door of the room he'd hidden in and moved into the hallway and then to the doorway of his room. The sheriff stood gazing out the window.

Keen enjoyed this situation. He had the upper hand on the sheriff and was about to surprise him. He stood quiet. Still. Gun pointed dead on the sheriff's back. He wasn't in a hurry, so he waited. A man and woman walked out of a room from down the hall. Seeing Keen with a gun, they hurried past him and down the stairs and into the disorder of the saloon below.

The sheriff spun around at the noise of the couple running—only to see Keen with a gun aimed on him. He quickly reached for his own gun but knew it was too late. He gave it up.

Keen savored the sheriff's unexpected circumstance. He watched as the sheriff looked him over, first his eyes, then his stance, then his finger set fixed and firm on the trigger of his revolver. Most men shot with their body or eyes first, then the trigger, flinching or blinking just before they fired. *Of course, those men are all dead,* Keen thought. He showed himself ready to fire.

Stepping into the room, Keen booted the door closed behind him.

"You got somethin' on me, Sheriff?"

"I got enough on you to put you away till you rot."

"Ha! Then why ain't you or any other lawman done it yet? I been around."

The sheriff snickered.

Keen tightened his grip and set himself to fire at the sheriff. "I don't believe you're in a position to be laughin' at me," Keen said. "You're standin' on the wrong side of a loaded gun for that."

"You won't get away with killin' me, Keen. Don't do it."

"You're scared, lawman. Scared of me and scared of dyin'."

"I ain't got the patience for your mouth. Pull the trigger or get the hell out of Palisade."

"Oh, I'll get to killin' you, Sheriff. But can't leave town.

I got plans to meet up with some old friends. You remember the Lind boys, don't ya? Good folk, they are. Good folk."

"You stay out of that, Keen. Ain't got nothin' to do with you."

Keen laughed. "You never were much of a lawman, Taggart. Smart, but stupid at the same time. All that killin' and stealin' right under your nose, but you can't smell it for all the whiskey you keep poured in you."

The sheriff looked down. Keen knew the sheriff's weakness and knew his story. He might not have to kill him, after all, he thought—*Might just need to shame him to death.*

"Yep, I thought so. You shoulda quit the law when you shot that little girl."

Keen walked up to the sheriff and tapped the nose of his gun against the sheriff's temple and whispered, "You got it all wrong about Daniel. He might be a drunk and a thief, but hell knows he ain't no killer."

The sheriff looked hard at Keen, not believing his words.

Keen smiled and nodded his head. "First you kill that innocent girl in Wyoming, then you let an innocent man go to prison. What next—gonna let all the guilty ones go free?"

"What are you sayin'? That Daniel didn't shoot Meg?"

"You the lawman. Figure it out yourself. I'm guessin' you have... what, maybe a few hours? Then all hell will break loose in your town."

Keen watched the sheriff swallow hard.

"You still tryin' to figure it out, are ya? If Daniel didn't do it, who did? Keep thinkin, lawman."

"He had to of done it," the sheriff said. "No other explanation for it."

"Gonna drive you crazy, ain't it? Tryin' to figure this one out. What happened. Who shot that woman."

Keen leaned his face into the sheriff's. He paused and waited, his breathing flooding over the lawman. He savored the power he held in that moment.

"I seen it,... I was there," he whispered.

The sheriff jerked back from Keen. "No. No you weren't," he said. "That don't make sense."

Keen grinned. He reveled in knowing what the sheriff didn't, what he'd never been able to figure out on his own.

"Daniel lied to you, lawman."

"You? Did you pull that trigger on Meg?"

"No... no I didn't. I'm gonna let you chew on this some more, Taggart. I got a couple brothers to hunt down—I mean, meet up with."

"Why do you need to hurt them boys? Just leave 'em be."

"They know too much," Keen said, slowly backing away from the sheriff, gun still aimed at him. "It's here, Sheriff. It's happening. Now. In Palisade. In your town. On your watch."

"Keen... don't. Just leave. Head out. Let it go."

"I don't let nothin' go. I play it to the end."

The sheriff set his hand on his revolver. Keen stepped back in and pressed his gun into the sheriff's temple.

"No," Keen said.

With his other hand, Keen pulled the sheriff's hand away from the revolver. He took hold of it himself and slid it out from its holster. He pointed the gun up and spun the cylinder, spilling the cartridges to the floor, then tossed the revolver onto the bed. He kept his own revolver pressed into the side of the sheriff's head and pulled the hammer back.

"Good-bye, lawman."

Knock-knock!

Keen wheeled around. He was caught by surprise at the knock on the door. He looked at the sheriff and held a finger to his lips.

"Shhh."

"Sheriff? You in there? Sheriff, it's James and Jeb." James pounded the door again.

Keen smiled. "Your girls are here," he said to the sheriff, then walked to the door and swung it open, his gun already pointed at the two deputies. He waved them in.

"The sheriff and I were just havin' a friendly chat," Keen said.

They saw the cartridges on the floor and gun on the bed. They moved to stand next to the sheriff.

Keen walked into the hall, smiling the whole time. He was getting away and there was nothing the sheriff or his deputies could do. He would now be free to hunt Daniel and Clay and kill them both.

"Enjoy the room, ladies," he said. "It's on me."

"Keen," the sheriff said, stopping him as he started to close the door. "I'll hunt you down. I'm not afraid of you."

Keen kissed the tip of his gun and blew it at the sheriff, then pulled the door closed and headed downstairs to the back of the hotel and walked out.

*

"You okay?" James asked the sheriff.

"Yeah, I'm okay," he said, frustrated that Keen had bested him once again. He bent over and picked up a cartridge and threw it against the wall. Then picked up rest of the cartridges and walked over to the one he'd thrown and picked it up. He grabbed his gun, sat in the chair, and reloaded.

"You want us to go after him?" James asked.

"No... no. I'll do it. But be on the lookout for him. He threatened to kill the Lind boys. You have authority to kill on sight."

The deputies looked at each other.

"You ain't never give us that order before," Jeb said.

The sheriff wanted to keep James and Jeb safe, and that meant away from Keen. But he also needed their help if they happened to run into him. He realized that he was putting them in harm's way. *Oh, hell,* he thought, *time for them to become real lawmen anyway.* He wouldn't be around to hold their hand forever.

"Just do as I say. You two go look for the Lind boys. Stay in town, though. I think they're headed into Palisade. Might be here already. I want 'em in jail. They'll be safe there. I don't want any more bloodshed on this matter."

The deputies stood looking at their boss. He looked up at them. Without another word they left the room and headed out into the streets of Palisade to look for the Lind brothers.

The sheriff dropped his head into his hands and rubbed his face hard. He wasn't just frustrated; he was now scared. Keen was tough and vicious. He'd kill a lawman just as quick as he would an enemy. *Men like Keen make no distinction.* He breathed in deep and blew the breath out hard, then stood and leaned his head into the window and looked out onto the town. His mind jumped to the fact that Keen was there the morning Meg died and that Daniel hadn't pulled the trigger, that he hadn't killed Meg but confessed and went to prison for it. Who was he trying to protect? Keen? That didn't seem possible. *Why'd you do that, Daniel Lind? That's not the selfish brute of a man I remember.*

He thought back on the early days of the case and how frustrated he'd felt at the time, and then figuring the case was resolved with Daniel pleading guilty. Now, ten years later, he was back to frustrated. He squeezed his eyes closed and banged his head into the windowsill, then turned and walked out of the room, back to the jailhouse to get his rifle and shotgun.

"At least Allie is safe with my sister," he said to himself.

*

Daniel hit the edge of town and headed for the closest water well he remembered. He sat on the trough and pumped cool water onto his head and into his hands, catching enough for a few sips. He shook his head wildly side to side to cast out the excess water and squeezed his fingers back through his hair to push out more. The drinks filled him, but it had been a couple days since he'd had much of anything to eat. *What now?* he thought. Nearly four weeks walking to Palisade and almost dead from the pain, heat, starvation, and exhaustion. All that time to think and plan, and now no idea for what to do next. He knew he wanted to find Allie, to at least learn if she was even in town. He also needed to eat. The old house sat on the other side of Palisade. He headed to the back of town and started the walk.

A block up, he watched a man run out of the back of a hotel, then jump on a horse and ride hard in his direction.

Daniel began to find a place to hide. As the rider approached, Daniel could see the man didn't notice him, or at least didn't care to. The man rode past at a full gallop without a glance at Daniel. The dust trail the horse kicked up led west and faded with the rider. It was Keen.

A whistle blew loud from the east and pulled his attention from Keen and back to his walk. Steam billowed high and brakes squealed as the train rolled to a stop. He thought about the possibility of running into Allie on his walk to the house or even at the house. Excitement, anxiousness, and fear mixed inside him and fought with his hunger and pain and tired body. Seeing his daughter for the first time since the day before Meg's killing seemed real. Very real. He knew she was there in Palisade. Knew it for certain. A bolt of nerves killed the hunger he'd carried for two days. He stopped his walk. Regret set in. He now wished he'd taken the wagon to Virginia City. Wished now that he'd never made this walk to Palisade. His belly would be full and he'd be deep in a silver mine, his life buried in a hole. Allie could live her life without her worthless father tearing it apart again. She surely wasn't here anyway, he thought, and even if she was, he would be the last person she would want to see. He looked back to the west, toward Carson City and Virginia City, and thought about how far he'd come. He turned back toward the east, toward the old house, and slowly started walking again.

21

ALLIE HELD TO the railing and paused at the last step. She looked out and over the station and then up and down the full length of the train. The eastern horizon already darkened, the western slipping from the light. People spilled from all of the exits of the train and crisscrossed the platform. The engine quieted and settled as the steam rose up and then melted away. Palisade.

"I'm home, Mom," she said quietly to herself.

It surprised her that home had such a feeling, especially Palisade. It felt warm and comforting; she was expecting an evil, even dead-like feeling. She thought of Savery Creek and how much she loved Becky and her life there. This was home, though.

Two young boys burst from behind Allie, bumping her forward and onto the platform below. They stopped and turned. "Sorry, ma'am." And off they went as abruptly as they'd arrived. She watched them as they ran on. They looked the age she'd been the last time she was here, the day she left for San Francisco with Sheriff Taggart. At that thought she remembered why she was back in Palisade. She lost the feelings of warmth and comfort that had just filled her and clutched her bag tight to herself, then began walking toward the house.

She took in the station as she walked. The single-story depot building looked the same as it had ten years earlier, though now smaller than she remembered. Its wood siding showed worn and grayed by the years and engines relentlessly arriving and leaving, an iron river traveling from there to here and on again, suiting its purpose. Detail of the station once long gone in her mind returned—two windows to either side watched over passengers as they arrived and departed, the benches below the windows where the old men sat and stared ahead and talked without ever hearing each other, the single door to the inside that split the benches and windows.

The walk to the edge of town, to the house, would be over a mile, one she'd walked hundreds of times in her short life in Palisade. She took a breath and began the final steps toward home and the end of her journey.

The sun began to fall away as the glow of the station lit brighter into the evening. Allie moved to the far side of the depot and studied the eyes of each person she passed. None studied her. She looked into one of the windows. Wondering. Anticipating him yet expecting no one at the same time. He certainly wouldn't be in there. In no hurry to get home, she began to wish time would slow down. Maybe even stop. She felt her bag, felt for the hard steel of the revolver to reassure herself. Inside the ticket office the spectacled man stood politely speaking through the narrow window with the couple in front of him, pointing to the schedule written in chalk on the blackboard behind his desk. Several people queued after the couple and waited patiently for their turn. Men stood straight and proper, seemingly unbothered by the heat or the line; ladies vigorously cooling themselves with unfolded fans.

"Yes, and from there heading on to Cheyenne," the agent said, his voice fading in and then out as she walked by.

The town itself appeared beyond the station. It felt familiar, yet odd and distant at the same time. Like she'd been here before, but only in a dream. The wind kicked and threw dust at her. The same hot, dry, dirty town.

She stepped onto a short side street that led to the center of town. The station noise faded as she entered the dark and quiet break between it and the noise and lights of Palisade's saloons and hotels. Music and men and women poured into and through the streets; the smell of whiskey and beer and cigars followed. She turned onto Main Street and headed east, to the house. The buildings of the town now seemed tilted and running crooked, not the perfectly rowed streets and structures that her childish mind remembered. Palisade was broken down, haggard, graying; a boom town slowly fading away.

The stores and hotels and saloons of the town quickly ended. Houses approached, then thinned out. The road curved up and out, east to the final outskirts. Lamps flickered and glowed in the homes, their light rushing out to welcome and guide Allie home. She slowed her steps and stared ahead. Then stopped.

There it was. Allie stood and took in the house. It fit the town. Even with the setting sun she could see the sagging roofline. The rocks of the chimney had fallen and slid to the ground. The windows on the first floor were all boarded up; those on the second were busted. And the front door was cracked open at the bottom, hanging by the top hinges alone.

Emotions flooded Allie—the warmth and comfort of being home returned. But the broken and abandoned look of the house filled her with sadness. She felt the memory of her mom—the happiness they'd brought each other. In that moment Allie wanted it to be her home again, to be walking in from Sunday school or from a visit with a neighbor.

As she stood there deep in thought, the shadowy image of a man appeared from behind the house. He walked to the road and toward Allie. Her nerves jumped. She froze and held her breath as he continued walking. She squinted to study his shape and make out his face. He closed in. She slipped her hand into the bag and gripped the revolver. She now wondered if she could go through with it. She shut her eyes and readied herself to pull the gun out. *Please don't let it be him,* she thought.

As his steps grew closer, she opened her eyes. Her heart raced.

"Evenin', young lady," the man said, tipping his hat.

Allie relaxed.

He stopped next to her and turned and looked at the house.

"Been trying to get the Franks to sell this place to me for years," he said. "They just let it go to ruin. Such a shame."

"No one lives here?" Allie asked.

"Not for ten years or so," he said, shaking his head.

"Gonna put in one more bid to 'em on Monday. Just taking a final look. Then I'm givin' up."

Allie kept her stare on the house. "Yes, that's a shame," she said. "Well, I best get home," she continued, not wanting to raise his suspicion.

"You have a nice evenin' now." He tipped his hat again and turned and headed toward town.

"You too, sir," Allie said.

It hurt to hear that the house had sat empty all these years, that no family had moved in to make a home of it. It did seem such a shame. But she smiled on the inside, happy that it was preserved as her home and not spoiled by another family, one that might not have cared or known that her mother had died here.

As the man walked away, Allie crept closer to the house. Her heart beat hard and fast. Her breaths were deep. Fear fell on her. She didn't know what to expect. She leaned to the window and peered between the boards that covered it. Empty. Quiet. She pushed on the door, but it didn't budge. Through the thin opening between the door and the frame she could see that it had been boarded and nailed shut from the inside. She walked around to the rear of the house. Fear followed. She set her hand on the revolver again. The back door was boarded shut from the outside, and the windows as well. She tried pulling boards away, but they were nailed tight.

The barn and pen still stood next to the house. The hogs were gone. The barn leaned toward her and seemed in the act of falling. Dark filled the desert beyond the house, consuming the last sliver of light from the western sky on the other side of Palisade.

Allie stepped inside the barn and searched for a place to lay for the night. The barn creaked. She sensed the sway of the structure. It creaked again, and again.

"This isn't safe," she whispered to herself.

Back outside Allie looked around and then walked to the road. Worry set in. She needed a place to sleep and wondered if she'd find one. And it needed to be safe, where she wouldn't be seen.

The night cooled. She looked around and felt lost. The Martens' light was on, but it didn't seem right to ask for help or a bed so late and without notice. She quietly walked around the side of the Marten house, to their back barn. She eased the door open and closed, then headed up the ladder to the loft where she'd played so many times. She crawled past a few bales of hay, pulled the revolver out of the bag, set it aside, and put the bag under her head. The light of the moon, high and bright and full in the night sky, splintered through cracks in the barn's siding and lit up the hay around her. She rolled to her left and peered out a window into the night. Allie wondered if her father was looking at the moon at that same moment. Her mind quickly moved to memories of looking out her bedroom window at night as a child, her mother holding her and comforting her. She felt safe curled up in her mother's arms. At that thought, Allie curled up with her arms tight around her and fell asleep.

*

The barn doors banged open—first one door, then the other. Allie heard heavy steps below. The ladder jostled as the footsteps climbed to the loft where she lay. She held her breath.

Her heart pounded, harder than those times she played hide-and-seek with the Marten boys. She would bury herself deep in the crevasses between the bales. Her giggles always gave her away. Innocence long gone. The footsteps ended; the ladder stilled. She saw the hand reach for a bale a few away from where she was hiding, then yank it down to the ground below. The hand reached and grabbed another bale and yanked it down. Then another. And another. Only one remained before Allie would be revealed. The hand reached and grabbed the last one and pulled. It shifted away from Allie. The horses below nickered loud.

Mr. Marten stopped and looked down. "Yeah, I know. I hear you. I'm comin'," he said. "That should do it for a few days anyway."

He let go of his grip on the last bale shielding Allie and descended the ladder.

Feeding time. Allie relaxed and slowly let out her breath, but she remained deathly still. Her heart continued to pound hard and fast.

The barn doors closed and the steps faded.

Allie relaxed, then quietly gathered her things. She stood and brushed the hay from her hair and clothes and climbed down. She snuck out a side door and walked around the back of a few houses toward town. She had plenty of money to buy some breakfast. If asked, she decided she would tell a story that her parents were on their way from the hotel and would soon join her. She walked the wood planks of Palisade's town and chose a newer restaurant, one where it seemed only visitors would frequent.

She sat at a table along a wall that had a good view of the

full room and front doors. She didn't see any familiar faces, not even among those who worked there. Allie finished her meal, set a dollar on the table, and sat for a few minutes. She took in the restaurant, the people, the moment. Her thoughts went to her plan. She knew what to say, what to do. She wouldn't have time for his words, for his excuses. Her anger intensified as thoughts of finally confronting her father after all these years sank in. She began biting her lips and looking around. Energy and rage swelled inside her. Allie bolted for the door and headed back to the house. If he wasn't there, she would return to town and check the saloons. If night came and she still hadn't found him, she would sneak into the Martens' barn again to sleep.

When she neared the jail, she moved to the boardwalk across the street. She didn't want to take the chance of being recognized by anyone, especially the sheriff. The town was busy with both locals and travelers. Allie walked slowly, studying each person as they passed. None looked familiar. Older men especially brought an anxiousness to her. She would stop as one approached, study them, and slip her hand into her bag, onto the revolver.

She wandered the town into the late afternoon, eventually moving on to where the buildings thinned and transitioned from businesses to homes and then to small farms. At the far edge of town Allie turned up the side road that led to her house. In the distance she saw a disheveled man walking her direction. She could see that he was a vagrant. Homeless. Helpless. Her heart went out to him. She let go of the grip she had on her gun. *No need with this one.* She'd seen many men, and even women, with no place to go or stay or manner to feed themselves in Palisade and even around Savery Creek. She saw that in the old man headed her way. She wondered if he'd been struggling just recently or if this was his way of life. Maybe a line worker who lost his job and hope when the rail work ended, or a miner—or even a cowhand—too old for the strenuous work. As Allie neared the man, she squinted to see him better, to see his eyes, to read his face.

As they closed in on each other, she began to smile, a way to encourage and warm him. Something about this man was different than the others she'd passed. She felt it. He caught her look and stopped walking a few yards from her. He squinted himself and studied her. Allie kept moving forward. His squinting and furrowed brows made him look angry, she thought. Allie continued her smile, though with some nervousness now, as she set to pass by him. His eyes looked familiar but not the rest of him. He was too thin and old and frail to be her father. This man looked near death; her father was big and young and healthy. She passed the man and continued walking. He turned and watched her as she moved by.

"Allie?" the man said.

She froze. Her body shuddered. She tried to turn and look back at him but couldn't. It wasn't him; it couldn't be. Maybe it was the sheriff, or one of her old neighbors. She didn't want it to be her father.

"Allie," he said again.

She knew the voice. The familiarity of it. It rattled her. An evil haunting in the flesh. It *was* him. She closed her eyes. Her mind raced. The years. The anger. The yelling. Her mother crying and weeping. That morning. The years of waiting and planning in Savery Creek. Memories rifled through her mind. She gripped her bag tight and slipped her hand onto the revolver. She felt the weight of it, the cold of the steel, its purpose. Her hand easily slid around the grip; her thumb onto the hammer—she set herself to pull it back and yank the gun out and aim it on her father. She clenched her jaw and stood resolute, ready to fulfill her mission and journey.

Allie turned and faced her father.

They stared at each other. She saw that he was starting to tear up, even as anger rose up within her. She remembered the countless times that she was the one in tears and he was the one raging with anger. "Now it's my turn," she whispered to herself.

Allie pulled the revolver out and let the bag drop to the ground. The heart she'd just had for the disheveled man fell away.

"Allie, please. I want to say something—"

He stopped talking when she pointed the gun at him and slowly shook her head.

"No. N-No. N-No," she said, rocking side to side.

Anxiousness and anger vibrated through her words. The courage and bravery she'd carried for ten years now betrayed her. She wanted to just start pulling the trigger on her father, but knew she needed to be in control first. Allie took a deep breath and settled herself. She remembered Rueben's words: "Slow down.... Pull smooth on the trigger.... Let the gun do what it wants after."

Tears began to fall as she spoke to her father. "You don't get to talk," she said. "There's nothing you can say that will bring her back. You took her life. You took *my* life. I hate you. I hate you. I just hate you."

Daniel dropped his head at her words and let tears fall. A moment later he lifted his eyes to her. "Before you pull the trigger… you deserve the truth."

Allie's anger raged in her like she'd never known. "The truth? I heard and saw the truth for the seven years I lived in that house! I heard and saw it in my head every day for the last ten years. You just figured it was time to finish the job that morning. And now you want to apologize so you can be free of the guilt. Ain't that right?"

"No… no." He shook his head. "That's not what happened. I hurt your mother, I did. I'm sorry. There's no excuse for that. But I didn't kill her. I just didn't protect her. That's all. That's why I chose prison. I didn't pull that trigger, but I did bring it about. I didn't protect her, or you."

Anger flooded from Allie. Her nerves ran high. She started rocking side to side again, ready to shoot and wishing she could, but not finding the courage. She wiped tears away with her left hand, keeping her right hand on the gun and trigger.

"I didn't kill your mother, Allie. I thought prison would give me the punishment I deserved. But it didn't. I'm still guilty. The pain is still there. The hurt. It will never go away. I know that."

"You're a liar!" she yelled, shoving the gun toward him, tears pouring out.

"I'm here just to apologize to you, Allie. All I wanted to do was tell you the truth and apologize. I have nothing else to say. My life ended when your mother died."

Allie's eyes went wide. "Your life ended? Your life?... You selfish bastard! Mine never started! Do you get that? Do you have any room in your selfish heart for someone else's life?"

Allie's hurt ran deep and he didn't seem to see that. Her anger grew.

"I loved your ma, Allie. I loved you. I just didn't know how to show it."

Allie shouted, "No, you loved your brother! You loved your drinking. You loved your life of lying and cheating and stealing. Not me. Not my mother. Ten years for her death... and mine. That's it. That's all you got. How does it feel to walk out a free man knowing your daughter is still in a prison?"

Daniel set a hand on his eyes and wept.

"You killed her and you're a coward for not having the guts to admit it. I hate you for that."

"Allie... please, can I talk?"

"No, you don't get to talk. You get to listen. Then you get to experience what she experienced."

"Allie, just listen—"

She screamed and then lowered the gun. "You're so damned selfish! It's always about you. *You* get to talk. *You* get to leave and abandon people. *You* get to devastate people. You! You! You! It never ends. It never will end until I end it."

Her words felt good; they felt honest and gave her a freedom and strength she'd never known before.

"You're right, Allie. I deserve this."

He closed his eyes, looked down, and raised his hands.

She lifted the gun again and set both of her thumbs on the hammer and pulled it back, then took aim at her father, her hands and the gun shaking.

"Why? Why did you kill her?" she asked.

Daniel lifted his head and looked at his daughter, hands still in the air. "I didn't do it," he said softly.

"I'm guessin' you were still drunk from the night before and don't remember pullin' the trigger. Sounds about right, doesn't it?"

"I'm sorry, Allie. I'm just sorry. I'm sorry I hurt your mother. She was good to you. Good to me. I just couldn't see past myself and my own selfish ways. I just didn't know any better. I was the father to you that my father was to me. I didn't know how to stop it. I'm sorry I hurt you, sorry that I killed you on the inside, took your life away. No other way to look at it. I failed you. I failed your ma. I'm so sorry."

Daniel took off his hat and dropped it, then closed his eyes and looked down again.

Who is this man? Allie thought. *He keeps surrendering, giving up, not fighting back. All I've ever known is fight in him, pushback, selfishness, anger. And now nothing but surrender.*

She looked at her father as he stood there, eyes closed, head down, ready for his life to end.

"I won't stop you," he said. "Do what you came to do."

Allie wiped the tears from her cheeks with her shirtsleeve and rubbed her eyes. She steadied herself and lifted the gun again and aimed.

The disheveled man—the vagrant she saw walking toward her earlier—now stood before her. She had felt for that man on the road when she didn't even know him, but hated the man now before her, one she knew all too well. But it was the same man. She wanted the vagrant to have life and joy and be set free from suffering, and her father to suffer and die. The vagrant was now her father. A tinge of hurt for him rose up in her. She pushed the feeling away and forced her anger back in. That's why she was here, after all: to kill her father for what he'd done to her mother. Becky's words snuck in as she stood, gun in hand, aiming at her father: "He needs grace and forgiveness too. We all need it." Her heart started to soften for him, but she stopped it. Cold. Allie forced her anger back in once more. She chose anger over mercy, killing over forgiving, hate over grace. She looked out beyond her father, to the hills in the distance. She set her finger tight against the trigger, closed her eyes, took a breath, held it, and pulled. Then pulled again and again and again.

BANG! BANG! BANG! BANG!

Allie had let the gun go wild. She barely controlled it. With her eyes still closed she lowered the revolver and waited. She listened for her father but could only hear the loud ringing in her ears from the gunshots. Slowly she opened her eyes. Her father was bent over with his arms crossed tight against his chest. Then he fell to the ground and onto his side and groaned.

Allie gasped as her father lay still in the dirt. Then she watched as he sat up and ran his hands over his body, feeling for wounds, for blood seeping into his clothes.

The shots had missed. They'd sailed into the side of a hill in the distance, right where Allie had aimed. While she wanted him to know and feel what her mother had experienced that morning, she wasn't a killer. It wasn't her true heart.

Allie dropped the gun and looked at her father. After firing those shots away from him, she was now unsure of her feelings. It felt a bitter mix of anger and sorrow. She paused a minute longer, then walked over and knelt and picked up the old hat he'd been wearing. She softly brushed off the dirt and grass, then set it on his head. He kept his look down. She returned to where the gun lay on the ground and stared at it.

All of those years in Savery Creek, she thought, all of that planning and hate and vengeance eating at her, gone in just a few seconds. Pointless. As if it was all a waste of time and effort, a waste of a life—*her* life. She didn't know whether to hold onto the anger for her father or be angry with herself for not having the courage to avenge her mother's death, or for allowing hate and vengeance to take root in her heart to begin with.

Allie picked up the gun and her bag and walked away.

22

THE SHERIFF STIRRED the coals that had nearly burned out. The morning sun had already risen far above the horizon. He had wanted to be out riding by now, continuing his hunt for Keen, but instead lingered, enjoying the peace of the camp. The thought of setting more wood on the fire crossed his mind, but he knew he needed to head out. As he played with the coals, he thought of his chances of actually finding Keen: *Zero.*

He stood and began packing. Sleeping under the stars was his way of escaping the town, its problems, and himself. The ride through the county gave him the break he needed. He loved northern Nevada—not so much the people or the towns, but its beauty and nature. He desperately needed this ride away from Palisade. The desert and surrounding hills had been here long before he showed up and would be here long after he was gone. They gave him a real sense of his own mortality.

He lifted Gal's saddle and settled it into place.

Snap!

The sheriff heard the twig snap deep in the woods and knew someone was there. He slipped the saddle back off and set it down, then crouched low and moved over to where his shotgun lay against a tree and grabbed it. He held still and listened. He'd give whoever was out there a few seconds more to announce themselves before firing a warning shot. He wasn't in the mood for company, especially the rude kind that barged into a man's camp unannounced. He mostly hoped it wasn't Keen.

"Hello!" a voice from the woods yelled.

The sheriff stood. "Who's there?"

"Clay Lind, Sheriff. It's Clay Lind," he said, emerging from the trees.

The sheriff clicked both hammers back and raised the shotgun at Clay. "Stop. I need to see your hands. You better not be bringin' trouble."

Clay raised his hands. "They're up. And my weapon's back with my horse."

"Keep 'em up and turn around. I need to see you're not carryin'."

Clay turned slowly to show he had no weapons.

"We've been looking for you and your brother," the sheriff said. "Keen is here, in the county. You're all tryin' to start something, but I'm out to stop it."

"Is Daniel in Palisade? Have you seen him?" Clay asked.

"Haven't seen him yet, but my guess is he's already there or headed there. He probably thinks Allie's going to be there as well."

"Allie? In Palisade?"

"No, she ain't. She's safe, though. Not even in the state."

"That's good to hear, Sheriff. Wouldn't want her in the middle of this trouble gettin' hurt."

"What do you want, Clay?"

"I ain't here to harm you, Sheriff. Just here to find Keen before he gets to Daniel."

The sheriff waved Clay into the camp with his gun, then let the hammers back and set the shotgun down. He rested his hands on the revolvers still holstered around his waist. Clay lowered his hands and walked in.

"I saw Keen," the sheriff said. "He's after you and your brother."

"Where'd you see him?"

"In town. Yesterday. At the Landing. But he got the best of me and run off."

Clay remained stoic.

The sheriff was surprised that Clay hadn't said anything smart at him for being bested by Keen. He looked the younger Lind boy over. He hadn't aged much in those ten years. At the moment, though, he looked worried, a side of Clay he'd never seen before.

"Let me get you somewhere safe, Clay."

"No, can't, Sheriff. I gotta help my brother."

"He was there that morning—Keen was. Did you know that?"

Clay looked down, remembering the evil he'd felt in his dream, and felt that Sunday morning. "You sure about that?" he asked, looking back at the sheriff.

"Yep. Told me so himself. And I didn't see lyin' in his eyes."

Clay nodded that he understood.

"And there's more…" the sheriff said. He paused and watched Clay brace himself for the sheriff's next words.

"Keen said Daniel was innocent. Didn't shoot Meg." Those words were hard for the sheriff to get out. It meant that he hadn't done his job. That he'd not only failed Allie and Meg and Daniel, but Clay as well.

"What?" Clay said, shaking his head in disbelief.

"I'm sorry, Clay."

"Are you sure?"

"Yeah. I'm certain of it now."

Clay walked over and sat on a stump near the fire, took off his hat, and dropped his head. "I ain't got no clue or reason for it, Sheriff—why he'd confess and take ten years for something he didn't do."

"Only Daniel can answer that, Clay. Look, I can't force you to sit in jail and be safe, so you're on your own. I'm out to stop more innocent blood. If you take a bullet, it's not on me, got that?"

"You know I have to do this, Sheriff."

"I know. So we're both huntin' Keen, then?"

"Reckon so."

"Well, he's gotta get both of us to save himself."

"With you on my side, I'll take those odds, Sheriff."

Crack!

The shot echoed across the low valley.

The sheriff winced hard and grabbed his right shoulder as he twisted to the ground. He'd been shot twice before, both times in the thigh. Those were bearable—up and walking in a few days. This shot cracked his shoulder blade. It hurt like hell.

He glanced over at Clay, who was now hiding low behind a cropping of sagebrush.

"You okay, Clay?" he yelled.

"Yeah. You?"

"Just a flesh wound. I'll be fine." He scanned the area, then pushed himself up just enough to crawl toward a nearby tree for better cover.

Crack!

The sheriff grabbed his right thigh and gritted his teeth as the pain from the two bullets pierced his full body. He twisted onto his back and lay still.

"Ahhh! Damn thigh shot again," he said. "Clay! Stay down."

"You damn sure bet I will."

"You see anyone yet?"

"Gimme a second."

Clay kept low and peered through the brush. "Yep, I see him! It's Keen. Up on that bluff. Got his rifle in his hand and ridin' down this way."

"Go on, get outta here," the sheriff said.

"How bad you hurt?" Clay asked.

"Not bad. One in my shoulder, another in my leg."

"Yeah, I think you'll make it," Clay said. "Ain't never heard of no one dyin' from bein' hit in the shoulder."

The sheriff laughed. "Go. Get out," he said. "Save yourself."

"No. Can't do it. Let me load you up and haul you to town."

"I'd slow us down and he'll just catch up. You need to protect your brother. Now go, get outta here."

"Nope. I'm stayin', gonna fight Keen with you." Clay crept from the sagebrush to the sheriff.

"No, dammit. You can't help your brother if you're dead. Get the hell outta here."

"This ain't my day to die, Sheriff. I got—"

Crack!

The bullet screamed above Clay's head. He dropped and rolled low again to the sage but stayed close enough to be able to reach the sheriff's hand. Clay started pulling him as the sheriff rolled to his stomach and pushed with his left leg.

Crack!

The next shot nicked Clay's left hip, and he let out a groan.

Crack!

The sheriff screamed. He let go of Clay's grip and curled up, then tucked his arm tight to his rib cage, but the blood still rushed out.

"Damn," Clay grunted.

Tears ran down the sheriff's face. *This can't be it,* he thought. *Not now.*

The sheriff closed his eyes tight. Scenes from his life flashed through his mind. Some had always been with him; some he'd forgotten. In the woods in deep snow hunting with his father. The time he'd taken a swing at him. The look and feel of his first rifle. The smell of his mother's cornbread. Her holding him after he'd fallen out of a tree he'd been climbing. Racing his sister through the pasture behind their cabin. His first kill as a lawman. His first drink of whiskey—its taste and burn. JT Treeman's eyes on that train. Holding Anna lifeless in his arms. Becky standing in shock before him. Allie waving good-bye to him from the back of the wagon in Rawlins.

The images were clear and real and vivid and flashed like a lightning strike. There, then gone. His life. That fast. Regrets set in just as fast and hard. Pulling the gun on Anna. Abandoning his sister. Not marrying. Never being able to push the bottle away for good. The anger he had for others who didn't deserve it. Taking time to just be instead of always on the move, always running away.

The sheriff now wished to start over, to not die like this, sudden and unexpected and at the hands of a man like Keen. He desired more time. More life. He worked to hold on but felt himself slipping away. His mind raced between memories and regrets and hopes. Even as the pain of the first three shots still surged in his body, with Keen still out there, he raised himself to his knees.

"No!" Clay yelled. "Stay d—"

Crack!

The next shot hit the sheriff in the chest. He took the round and held for a second, then fell to his back, his head hitting hard onto the ground and bouncing once, his arms falling limp. Blood seeped into his shirt and spread out, then trickled from the corner of his mouth. He gasped for a breath and coughed. He looked up and saw Clay rising. The sheriff squeezed his eyes shut in pain.

Clay ran and grabbed the shotgun and blasted a round at Keen. Then another.

"Keen just rode off," Clay said, coming back to the sheriff. "I got a couple shots at him."

The sheriff felt Clay grab his hand; he held tight to him.

"I'm… sorry," the sheriff said.

Clay set his other hand on the sheriff's chest wound and gave some pressure to stop the bleeding.

"I'm… sorry, Clay. I… I did the best I could. I'm so sorry."

"Hang in there. I'll get you to Doc. Don't you worry."

Clay started to stand but the sheriff pulled him back.

"Too late, Clay… Let me be. Just let me be."

Clay knelt back down and held the sheriff's hand.

The sheriff fixed his eyes on Clay. "This is my cursed life: I'm dyin' and… got nothin' but ugly… lookin' down on me."

He tried to laugh at his words, but only moaned in pain.

Clay smiled and gave a quiet laugh. "You ain't dyin', lawman. Too many people need you around."

"No. This… This is my time. God wants good men here, not… the likes of me. I tried but fell short."

Clay squeezed the sheriff's hand. "I know what you did for Allie, Sheriff. Daniel knows too. You rescued her. That makes your life worthy."

The sheriff forced a smile. "You… really believe that?" he asked, his words barely with sound.

"Yeah, lawman, I do. I truly do."

The sheriff shook his head and groaned, then tensed his body and fought back tears. "I shoulda let go the reins a long time ago… stop my runnin'… stop hidin'."

At those words the sheriff looked up. Blood stopped flowing down his cheeks; his tears trickled to a stop. Becky and Anna filled his final thoughts. Then Allie. "I love you…" he mouthed. His body warmed as his mind gave way to gray and then black and then dark and then quiet.

23

AFTER FIRING THOSE shots into the hillside beyond her father, Allie walked away and headed to the house, farther up the road. She'd failed in her journey to kill her father and avenge her mother's death. No resolution for her mother, or for herself. Now she had little reason to stay in Palisade. The town and her father were dead to her. She'd spend one more night in the Marten's barn, then head back to Savery Creek.

The next morning, Allie decided to visit the house before she left. As she walked up the path, she could see that someone had tried to break open the front door. The gap at the bottom was wider, but it still showed boards nailed to the inside; its top hinge held tight. She pushed on the door, but it still wouldn't budge. She walked around to the back of the house. The boards that once sealed the door shut were scattered on the ground. She pushed and the door easily swung open.

Allie stood at the entrance and listened. Nothing.

"Hello?" she whispered.

Then a little louder: "Hello?"

The house was empty. The kitchen table and what little furniture the Lind family had was gone. Allie stepped in and set her bag on the mantle. As she did, dust floated and danced in the sunlight that raced in through the back door. Dirt layered every surface but couldn't bury the moldy, musty smell.

It took a few seconds, but everything from her memory fell into place. The front door nearly straight across from her still held the heavy wooden latch she could barely lift as a young girl. The fireplace stood along the back wall, to Allie's left, its large rocks framing the vacant firebox. She could now see the top of the mantle, which once held knickknacks from her grandparents' store as well as oddly shaped rocks and sticks she had collected from her adventures into the desert behind the house.

To her right—the kitchen where her mother had been killed that Sunday morning. Allie went cold and shivered. She'd not been in the house since that early morning. She watched and waited and listened, expecting something more. A knowing. A sense of what happened. Relief. Or finality. Maybe even her mother's voice. But nothing. The scene was long gone. She walked to the corner of the kitchen and ran her hand over the counter, trying to feel her mother. She stood a moment longer, then turned away.

Across the main room the railing of the stairs to the second floor lay broken on the ground. The stairs leaned heavily away from the wall and toward Allie, as if inviting her up.

She walked across the room and to the landing. Glancing

to the top of the stairs, she placed her hand on the wall for balance and set herself onto the first step, then gently gave it her full weight. Then the second just as carefully and gently. Then the third. Each step creaked but with a different pitch, as if they had their own story to tell. Allie ascended the stairs then turned left and walked down the short hall to her room. Empty. Cold. Lifeless. She tried to imagine her bed in the corner, with the lumpy straw mattress and itchy wool blanket resting on top. And her small dresser, always taller than she had been, next to her bed. The window along the back wall was shattered, allowing all of those sounds and shadows that so scared her as a child to come and go as they pleased. Not many nights did she fall asleep with sweet dreams dancing in her head—darkness and evil lurked outside the window, sometimes down the hall, and too often both.

Allie closed her eyes and felt her childhood. She could smell her mother's bread warming the house. Her steps across the wooden floor below with those hard, black shoes clip-clopping back and forth. The sounds comforted her. Her mother was always busy. Always active. Never resting. Her voice would call her downstairs: "Allison! Allie, dear!" Her mother's presence and smile as warm as the bread she baked.

Those memories and quiet of the room fell on Allie. Her heart sank. She felt the loss. The loss of what had been taken from her. The loss of her mother and her childhood. The loss of joy. Her room—this house—now stood as lonely and abandoned as she had that Sunday morning out on the road in Sheriff Taggart's arms.

Thoughts of her mother pulled Allie back down the hall to her parents' bedroom. One look inside and the feel of her mother fell away. Fear poured in and drenched the room. The smell of whiskey followed and stirred the fear. She felt her father's suffocating presence. A quiet man of few words. He didn't need words though to unnerve Allie. She wondered now if her mother had felt the same way. Or maybe her mother hadn't known how to feel, or didn't want to, or stuffed it down and pretended herself strong. Allie held her arms to her stomach and slowly backed out of the room. She had reached her limit.

Allie descended the stairs and returned to the kitchen and comfort of her mother. She stood in the corner where her mother last lay. The blood on the cabinets had dried to a dark brown. She reached out to touch the blood when she heard a noise. She spun to see a man standing just inside the threshold of the door. They each stared. Neither moved. The fear she'd felt upstairs returned and shook her. She tried to scream, to say something, to even just make a sound, but her voice locked. She was frozen.

"You must be Allie," the man said, his words slow and drawn out.

She didn't move. If evil had a look, it would be her father's the times he came home drunk; if it had a voice, it would be this man's. It told her to fear him; his dark eyes and scars down his face told her to run. Escape. Now. But she couldn't. The front door was boarded shut. The only way out was through the back door, which the man blocked. And he'd surely grab her if she bolted for the stairs.

"I'm Keen," the man said through a crooked smile. "I knew your momma."

Keen stepped deeper into the kitchen. Allie pressed

herself back against the corner of the counter as tightly as she could. As she reached down to brace herself against the lower cabinets, she felt the stain of her mother's dried blood. Tears filled her eyes.

"You're Daniel's daughter, ain't ya?" Keen asked.

Allie didn't respond. She glanced at her bag on the mantle. *He's too close,* she thought. *I'll never get to the gun in time. He'll just grab me.* She didn't want to die, not now, not this way. And she knew her mother hadn't wanted to die either. Allie regretted her trip to Palisade. Regretted wanting to kill her father. It made her like him. She wasn't. She wasn't like him.

Allie cried. Keen snickered.

"You look like your momma. She was a pretty one. Good that you take after her and not your pa. That woulda been a cruel shame." Keen laughed, then stepped back and leaned against the counter, opposite Allie.

Please, God, get me out of this, Allie prayed. *Please, help me.* Keen's move to the counter gave Allie a clear path to the mantle. She eyed the bag again.

"I visited your momma once. It was dark, late in the night. She was in bed; you were in your room. Your dad drunk in a saloon with his brother. I peeked in on ya. You sleep quiet-like. I liked that. But I wanted something in your momma's room."

He smiled again.

Allie's heart raced; her breathing quickened.

"I walked to her room," Keen continued. "She was awake. That don't make things easy, ya know."

Allie took a deep breath and tried to push out a scream, but her throat hardened. She tried again. Nothing.

"I found the money your pa hid in his dresser. Your momma started cryin' and tellin' me to get out. I walked over to her—you know, to comfort her."

Allie closed her eyes tight and threw her hands over her ears and screamed loud inside her head. She wanted out, away from this man. She wanted his voice to stop, his words, the images he brought.

"I was gonna ask her for a kiss. No harm in that, right? Takin' your daddy's money was easy; well, maybe other things might be easy too. I grabbed her wrists and pulled her in."

Stop! Stop! Stop! Allie screamed. She was ready to flee. She inched her feet toward the gun. *I'll just turn it on myself,* she thought. *At least he won't be able to hurt me then.*

"That's when you cried out to your momma," Keen continued. "Do you remember that? Somethin' woke you and you just started cryin'. I let her go and walked out nice and easy. No harm done at all."

Allie ran for the gun.

Keen jumped in front of her and shoved the bag off the mantle. The bag hit the floor and the revolver tumbled out. Keen eyed it, then Allie. He turned to her and raised his hand, ready to strike.

"Were you gonna try and shoot me?" Keen growled. He lowered his hand and grabbed her arm and pulled her into his face. "Or maybe you were thinkin' of doin' what your momma did that mornin'."

Allie shuddered.

He nodded and smiled. "Yeah. I was there when it happened. I seen it all. Who done it."

Allie's eyes grew big. Anxiousness now mixed with her fear. *Who is this man?* she thought. *Why was he there?... Did he kill her? What happened?*

"I came back that next morning for another friendly visit. But your crazy momma tried to kill me. Aimed her gun right at me. Not very neighborly, if you ask me."

Allie didn't move. She fixed her eyes on Keen.

"I was standing right where I am now," he said. "Ain't that funny? First your momma, now you standin' here in front of me. I must be livin' right." Keen's crooked smile returned. "Your ma, she picked up a revolver that was sittin' on the table and pointed it at me. She pulled the trigger, but nothin' happened. Wasn't loaded. Like I said, I must be livin' right."

Allie stood there, still frozen, caught between fear of this man and anxiousness about knowing what happened that morning.

"Your momma grabbed a box of cartridges from the table. They all fell to the floor. She snatched two up and loaded them in. Hands shaking the whole time. I just watched. Didn't see her havin' the guts to pull the trigger again. Your daddy started comin' down the stairs. Well, stumblin's more like it. I figured he was in a jail cell. Guess I got that one wrong."

As Keen talked, Allie saw the figure of a man step to the back door. The sunlight at his back cast him into a shadow. He stood quiet and still. The grip of a revolver leaned out from his gun belt.

"As your daddy came down the stairs, I backed out of the house; decided my social call was over. I still watched, though. Saw it all."

"Did... Did you kill her?" Allie whispered through tears.

"She pointed the gun at me, then at your daddy. Asked him why he let trash like me in the house. Like I said, not very friendly."

Allie lost her patience with Keen even as the tears continued to flow. "Did you kill her?" she yelled.

He shook his head. "No, Allie, I didn't. Daniel told her to put the gun down. He went over to her. She didn't set it down. Turned it on herself. It went off just before he got to her. Your daddy didn't kill your momma, either. No, missy... he didn't."

Allie pulled away from Keen and fell back to the counter. In that moment she understood her mother's last minutes. She closed her eyes and felt her mother's torment. She watched in her mind as her mother turned the gun on herself and pulled the trigger, right where Allie now stood. Her mother had been driven into a corner, trapped by evil.

"And that's when I ran in the front door," Clay said from behind Keen.

Keen spun around to see Clay standing in the back doorway, revolver pointed dead on him.

"Allie, I want you out here with me. C'mon," Clay said, waving her out.

She didn't move. Her mind was numbed by the revelation that her mother had taken her own life. Keen still stood just a few feet from her. And now Clay, attempting to play hero, stood at the back door. The moment overwhelmed her.

She held herself against the cabinet and stared first at Keen, then at Clay. Her eyes begged her uncle to make sense of this situation.

"Allie, now! Out here with me," Clay said.

With Clay's gun still aimed on him, Keen didn't stop Allie, nor did he try to make a move.

Allie slowly walked to where Clay stood, moving far around Keen, and then out the door and behind her uncle.

Clay looked at Keen. "Why are you here? Haven't you caused enough trouble for one lifetime?"

"Unfinished business," he said with a hard, straight look at Clay, unfazed by the gun on him.

"Allie ain't part of your business. Sheriff Taggart wasn't either. You had no reason doin' what you did to him. You shoulda hit me instead."

Keen smiled. "I was aimin' for both of ya. The sheriff got what he deserved. And I know I hit you too."

"Not even close. If your aim was any better, you mighta nicked me," Clay said. "Now drop your gun belt. Left hand only. Keep your right away."

Keen didn't move. He slowly shook his head. "I ain't going nowhere till I finish what I came for," he said, looking out at Allie.

Clay waved his gun at him. "Off," he said.

Allie felt saved, rescued. They weren't out of danger yet, but she was relieved and heartened by her uncle's actions.

Keen unbuckled his gun belt, pulled it off, and held it up with his left hand. "Come and get it," he said.

"No. You toss it over there."

Allie watched as Keen showed no sign of surrender. She

backed farther away from the house, unsure of what he or Clay might do next.

"Last chance, Keen. I ain't waitin' any long—"

Before Clay finished speaking, Keen threw the belt at his face and without hesitating fell to his right and pulled a knife from his boot, then grabbed the blade tip and flipped it at Clay.

Bang!

In a single blur of motion, Clay knocked the belt away and fired a shot at Keen as the knife flew by him and struck the wall by the door, dropping to the ground.

Allie screamed and backed farther away from the house.

Keen rushed and tackled Clay through the doorway and onto the ground. Clay turned and busted Keen's head with the butt of his revolver. Keen rolled to his side in pain. Clay stood and kicked him in his ribs. And then again and again. Then he stepped back and aimed his revolver on Keen.

Allie held her mouth closed as she watched Clay pull the trigger.

Bang! Bang!

Both shots ripped into Keen's chest. He cringed and curled to his side and held tight to his body. Blood gurgled in his throat as he tried to gasp for a breath.

Clay stood over Keen. Gun still on him. He pressed his boot onto the man's shoulder and shoved him over, faceup.

Blood filled Keen's mouth and covered his teeth. He fought to smile. "You're a… bad aim, Clay." He sucked in a breath, gurgling. "I… woulda killed you with one shot." He coughed, spitting up blood.

"One shot is too charitable. I wanna see you suffer, Keen. Enjoy your last moments this side of hell."

Allie knew her uncle had just saved her life, but it didn't take away from the brutality of those few minutes, from being in the presence of evil to learning the truth of her mother's death. She stood there, trembling and in tears, wrestling with that truth—and this moment.

Clay turned and walked over to Allie. He pulled her into his arms and held her. Behind them Keen started to let out a groan but never finished it.

"It's over, Allie," Clay said. "Ain't no one gonna hurt you now."

Allie let Clay hold and comfort her as her mother's death and her own experience with Keen in the kitchen came full circle. She welcomed knowing what had happened to her mother, but it jolted her at the same time, triggering words and images that would forever be cut into her. Now she only wanted out of Palisade, out of the evil that the town brandished and forced into her life.

She finally pulled back from Clay and told him what Keen said about her mother's death, about that morning, and the night before. And how she had run into her father the day before.

"We wasn't good, Allie—me and Daniel—I know that. You and Meg, you didn't deserve this. None of it. You shoulda had better. We only saw ourselves, nothin' else. And that's wrong. We had bad carved into us from the day we was born. And it was carved deep. We had no choice in the matter. And even when the cuts heal, they're still there to remind you of where you come from, who you are, who you'll always be."

Allie looked away. She wanted to tell Clay no, that he wasn't bad, and that her dad wasn't either. But she couldn't. The truth was right there in the way. The way her father treated her mother, it was there that morning, all the way to this moment.

"I didn't ask for this life," Allie said. "It was thrust on me. I should have had a normal childhood, but my dad took that away from me." She pushed away tears.

"Think on all the good times you had with your momma," Clay said. "Carry those with you, not the bad."

Allie smiled at the thought of always carrying memories of her mother with her, but even standing there in those good thoughts, her father overshadowed them.

"Can't separate them from the bad," she said. "They're right there together. It's all part of me."

Clay hugged her. "I'm sorry for what you've been through in your life, Allie. And I'm sorry for my part in it."

"Thank you for saying that, Uncle Clay. It helps."

He pulled back and asked, "Where's your dad now?"

"I don't know. Back in town maybe. Don't suppose I'll see him again."

Allie looked over at Keen lying dead on the ground.

Clay followed her gaze. "I gotta ride in and tell the deputies about Keen," he said.

Allie looked at her uncle. "I heard what he said—that Sheriff Taggart got what he deserved. He's dead, isn't he… the sheriff?" she asked, already sensing the answer.

Clay looked away and rubbed his mouth. Then lightly nodded and sighed. She knew he didn't want to say the words; he'd prefer to protect her from more pain.

Finally, though, he said, "Yeah, I'm afraid so. I'm sorry, Allie. We can talk about it tomorrow. No need to worry on it now."

Allie turned to the east, toward Wyoming and Savery Creek. She wiped the tears from her eyes. She thought of Becky and knew she'd have to be the one giving her the news about her brother.

"Hey, let's get you to a hotel for the night," Clay said. "We can meet up there in the morning."

Allie nodded but kept her eyes east.

24

ALLIE STOOD AT the front window of the hotel and watched as people passed by. Hoping to see him again but knowing she wouldn't.

"Mornin', Allie," Clay said as he walked up behind her. "You sleep well?"

She ran the sleepless night through her mind. It felt good to be in a bed, but it was a long, restless night.

"Not really. Too much to think on. Got my mom and the sheriff and his sister Becky all racing around in my head. But mostly thinkin' about my dad and what will become of him. And wishin' now I could see him one more time. Just not sure why or what to say, though."

"You and me both. I ain't set eyes on him in ten years. Not sure how I'll feel if I see him or what I might say either."

"Go with what's on your heart, Uncle Clay. That sure won't hurt none."

He smiled. "Maybe good advice for both of us, don't ya think?"

Allie smiled too and then nodded.

"Knowin' my brother, he's back at the house, likely spent the night there. Wanna ride out and take a look?"

She looked away from Clay and back out the window. The emotion of the moment fell hard on her. Only seventeen but feeling like she'd already lived a lifetime. It still didn't seem fair to put so much weight and responsibility on a young girl. Allie took a deep breath and held back the tears. She was now *wanting* to see her father. There was something in their interaction the day before that stuck with her. She saw something in him that was pulling her back.

"Yes," Allie said, "I think I do."

They walked out of the hotel. Clay helped Allie up onto Molly, then they rode slowly through town.

"What are you gonna do after all this?" Clay asked.

"Head back to Wyoming, I suppose, to Becky's place. I got nowhere else to go. She's been good to me and it does feel like home."

"It's good to have a home," Clay said.

"You? Are you gonna stay here in Palisade?"

"It don't matter what I do, Allie. Need outta here, though. I always did like the Arizona Territory. Maybe head down to Tucson. It's warm there all year round. Can't beat that."

"Warm is good," Allie said.

"Maybe someday you'll let me come and visit you in Savery Creek."

"Sure, Uncle Clay. I'd like that. You'd be welcome anytime."

Allie's thoughts, though, remained on her father, what she would say to him. She still felt stuck between anger at him and sorrow for him. She began to hope he wasn't there;

that would make things easy. She could just leave town and not have to face him again.

Clay rode Molly to the back of the house, then he and Allie dismounted and walked to the door, past the spot where Keen lay dead yesterday evening, his blood now black and dried and mixed with the dirt around it. Allie studied the spot for a few seconds, then gave it up and returned her thoughts to her father. Her stomach knotted at the prospect of facing him again. A queasy, near sick feeling swelled up inside her. She pulled her bag to her stomach and walked into the house. The events of yesterday screamed at her as she stepped in. She closed her eyes and held her bag tighter, then walked to the corner of the kitchen once again.

"Daniel?" Clay said. "Daniel, you here?"

The house was quiet. Clay looked at Allie, who was still facing away into the corner of the kitchen. She hoped it would stay quiet, hoped he wasn't there, but she braced herself.

"Daniel?" Clay said one more time.

Allie looked at him and lightly shook her head.

"I'm gonna look upstairs, Allie. You okay down here?"

She nodded. As Clay started to move, they heard creaks coming from above them. Clay froze. He looked at Allie. They both raised their eyes to the ceiling and listened. They heard the sounds again. They kept their eyes on the ceiling. Then footsteps mixed in with the creaks—slow and moving toward the stairs. Clay walked over and stood next to Allie. She grabbed his hand.

The footsteps stopped. Allie looked to the top of the stairs. A shadow darkened the wall. Allie gasped. It held still, then began to dance back and forth as the footsteps descended. Allie squeezed Clay's hand tighter and tighter as Daniel finished his walk down and turned his look to Allie. She peeked up at Clay. Tears streaked down his face.

*

Daniel looked at his brother. "I ain't a ghost," he said.

"I know, I'm just takin' you in. Prison wasn't good on you, brother."

"It did it's best to kill me. Hopin' to see Allie again was the only thing that kept me alive." He paused, then said, "I ain't much for words, Clay. Didn't plan what to say to you."

Clay softly shook his head. "Nothin' to say. It's good that I get to see you before headin' out."

Daniel searched for the words, something meaningful for his brother to carry with him, something healing and hopeful. The words weren't there, though. He looked at Allie, then around the house, to the kitchen, at what he'd brought about. He chose the truth:

"I wasn't good, Clay. I hurt Meg, hurt Allie. I see that clear as day now. Wish I could change it all but can't. I'll live with what I've done rest of my days."

"You and me both, Daniel. You wasn't in this alone."

Daniel looked at Allie again, hoping she heard his apology this time.

"Do you miss him?" Clay asked. "Pa, I mean. Do you miss him?"

Daniel hesitated. He remembered yelling and cussing at that train whistle a couple days earlier, at his dad. He remembered all the toughness he'd whipped into him and his brother. Tears welled up in his eyes and hung there.

"I miss our momma," he said, still looking at Allie. "I sure do miss our momma. And yeah… yeah, I miss him too. I suppose maybe I understand him a bit better now. He had it tough too, ya know."

"He did at that," Clay said. "And understandin' things is good."

Daniel looked at the floor, then up to the ceiling, gathering his thoughts. "I surrendered, Clay. I surrendered my life. I gave up on me and my selfish ways. I'm free from all that bad. Just wanted you to know that."

"Seems like you let go the reins." Clay said, smiling.

"That I did," Daniel said, smiling himself.

"Hey, brother," Clay said, "I'm headed down to Tucson. Think I'll stay on there. You come and visit me soon, you hear?"

"You know I will," Daniel said, knowing they'd likely never see each other again. He kept his gaze on Clay for a long moment.

Clay turned to Allie and gave her a hug and kissed her head. "Give my brother here a second chance," he whispered. "We all deserve it."

Then he walked to Daniel and grabbed his hand and pulled his brother in tight and held him.

"Love you, brother," Daniel said.

"Love you too, Daniel."

Clay backed away from his brother, keeping his eyes on him, then turned and walked out the door and over to Molly for his ride south.

Daniel looked at Allie. A mix of hurt and anxiousness filled him as he fought whether to speak to her or follow Clay out the door and out of his daughter's life. Would she talk to him? Would she be the one to walk away? Would she pull her gun on him again?

*

Allie watched her father as Clay walked away. She wondered whether to talk with him and maybe give him that second chance, or walk away herself, as he had done to her so many times in her life.

Daniel turned to his daughter. Without thinking, she backed into the corner of the kitchen where she had stood the day before.

"I tried to stop her," Daniel said. "She pulled the trigger before I could get to her."

Allie slid to the floor and sat, her thoughts now fully on her mother. She ran her fingers over the floor and felt her closeness.

Daniel walked over and leaned back against the cabinet next to Allie. Neither spoke. She appreciated that he let them be quiet so she could soak herself in her mother's lingering presence. After a few minutes he slid down and sat next to his daughter, then put his arm around her and pulled her close. Allie sat still, unsure of what to do: pull away, stay still, or lean on him. She wanted the closeness, but still feared him at the same time. Allie fought to stay still, to not move in or away. She closed her eyes and cried, then finally let go and laid her head on his shoulder.

As he held her, she felt her father for the first time. She knew then that she needed him, needed a father.

"I know that your life ended that day too," he said, "not just your mother's."

Allie stayed quiet. She felt the anger still inside her, the rage, though it now burned low. She pulled herself back and took a long look at her father, his eyes, his honesty.

"You didn't pull that trigger, did you?" she asked.

He shook his head slowly. "No, Allie. No. I'm a failed, broken man who lived a bad life. I'm just trying to be honest for once."

"Then why did you confess? Why leave me believing that you had killed her?"

"I *was* guilty, Allie. Guilty of not protecting her. Guilty of being mean. Guilty of being selfish. I needed to be punished."

She let his words sink in. He seemed to fully understand what he'd done to her mother and to her.

She pursed her lips, then said, "But punishing yourself was just another selfish act. I was hurt and lost all those years that you were in prison. I needed you. I needed a father."

Daniel nodded. "I wish I could reach deep into your heart and pull out all of the pain and hurt and anguish I caused you, Allie, and set you free."

She kept her look on him a few seconds more, then slowly leaned back onto his shoulder.

"I want it all back, Allie. I want the time back. Desperately so. I want the chance to do it all over again, to do it right. The chance to make better choices, to be the father that you always needed."

"It doesn't work that way, Dad."

"I know… I know. Can you give me a chance to get it right from here on out, though? A second chance?"

Allie felt conflicted. She wanted him back, but still carried the anger and hurt. It seemed too fast, too easy. She needed time.

"I think I can, but not yet. I'm just not ready. And I can't stay here either. I can't be in this house, in this town. There are too many painful memories, too many ghosts."

"I just want my daughter back however I can get her."

Allie let her father hold her a moment longer, then she stood up. Daniel started to follow.

"No. Not now," she said. "Not yet. I'll send for you when I'm ready. Just give me a little time."

Allie saw the hurt and sadness in her father's face. She wanted to give him what he wanted right then, without delay, but it felt wrong in that moment. She knew it would come, but it couldn't be now.

Daniel looked up at her, then smiled and nodded. She smiled back in appreciation of his understanding, then reached toward him. He lifted a hand and she squeezed it, then turned and walked to the door.

"Allie," he called to her. "What color dress were you wearing the day before?"

She stopped and turned back to him. "The day before Momma died?"

"Yeah."

"Why do you want to know?"

"Because I missed you, Allie—missed actually seeing you, or even knowing you. I always did. You were there but you weren't. I just wanted to remember you on a day you and your momma were still together."

Allie smiled. She remembered. "Yellow. A yellow dress with white flowers and a white collar."

Tears filled his eyes. He leaned his head back to the cabinet. "Yes, I see you now," he said.

Allie turned and stood in the back doorway, looking out. She thought back on her life in Palisade as she soaked in the view and this final time in the house with her mother and father. She searched her heart for what she truly needed most in that moment. She thought of her life in Savery Creek. Of Becky and her boys and Elsa and of course Rueben. She missed Tag and desired to be with him riding free in the open ranges of southern Wyoming. She thought of the sheriff and her Uncle Clay, and how they'd both saved her. She thought of her mother and the memories of her that she'd always have. And she thought of her father, Daniel Lind.

Still at the back door, looking to the desert, she said, "Dad… will you walk with me into town?"

EPILOGUE

NEARLY SIXTEEN YEARS after Allie Lind left Palisade at the end of her journey to avenge her mother's death, she returned. The town no longer a passenger stop, but simply a watering hole for the steam engines that still ran the Central Pacific line. Most of the people were gone, along with the hotels, saloons, shops, and homes. There was no longer a reason to venture out. Travelers who did have a reason to visit needed to depart in Carlin, a few miles to the east. Allie and her family had made the trip from Rawlins, Wyoming, to Carlin in early June 1904.

Once in Carlin, they hired a horseless carriage for the short ride to Palisade. Rueben held Allie's hand as she stepped from the carriage. Their two young children followed. Allie had turned thirty-three a few months earlier; the same age as her mother when she'd passed away. The ghosts that Allie thought long dead and buried had returned with that birthday. Sleepless nights and long cries without warning or reason followed. She felt lost and abandoned once again. Rueben had encouraged her to make the trip home and face her past, face the memories and demons that still gripped her.

Allie braced herself as she stepped onto Main Street, uncertain of what might happen, what she might see, what she might remember. Allie and her family wandered the dusty, empty town. She shared stories of her childhood, what they were seeing, and what was no longer there.

Palisade now stood as a ghost town. Run down. Lifeless. Dead. The occasional activity at the train station barely hinted at the remnants of a bustling town now long gone. The store her grandparents owned still stood, along with stores on either side. The glass window remained unbroken, with *Franks' General Store* etched across it. She wiped dust away and peeked into the store but made no mention of it to Rueben or her children. They moved down the street, to the jail cell where her father sat for several weeks in the summer of 1878. Two of its stone walls stood upright, but the jailhouse had otherwise crumbled. Bertie's Palisade Hotel across the street, with its crooked balcony, had fallen in on itself, floors and walls and broken furniture piled high. The other buildings on that row had also fallen—nothing remained but dirt and rubble. The cemetery was still there, across the trail behind the town. The prairie grass, tall and dry and golden, swayed among the few headstones that remained. She eyed Sherriff Taggart's marker just inside the entrance. Always the lawman, he continued to stand watch over Palisade. She told her children of this caring man, how he'd taken her on a trip west to San Francisco and then back east to Wyoming. How he'd saved her by bringing her to Becky's home, and how she'd waved good-bye to him from the wagon when she was about their age, not knowing it would be the last time they would see each other.

Allie stood at the foot of his grave, then leaned down and laid a yellow rose for him. "Sheriff," she said, "Becky wanted me to tell you that you are worthy of forgiveness, always have been, and that you deserved it long before now. You are missed and forgiven and dearly loved."

She found her mother's wooden marker at the back of the cemetery. She knelt in front of the grave and pulled her children and husband close and talked about the woman her mother was. "She was always full of love, and a bright spot in a very dark place." Allie said a prayer and then set a white rose on the grave. "I miss you, Momma, and love you, and always will."

Her father's grave lay beside her mother's. He had passed away a year after leaving prison. He did make the trip to Savery Creek, though, at Allie's request, to be with her on her eighteenth birthday. She gave him the words he so longed for, words of forgiveness. He told her how he was healed on that trail as he yelled at the train in the distance, but truly felt whole and fully healed hearing her words. He returned to Palisade a few days later, to their house. Deputy James had called on him soon after to see how he was getting along, only to find him curled up in the corner of the kitchen. Allie didn't hear of his passing for several days and so missed the funeral. A few days after she received James's message about her father, a package arrived. It was a box full of letters, the letters her father had written and sent to Allie while he was in prison. The sheriff had kept them all—120 of them—one for every month her father was in prison.

Allie reached into her purse and pulled out the little yellow dress with white collar that she was wearing the day before her mother died, the dress her father couldn't remember. She unfolded it, kissed it, and laid it on his marker. "I miss you, Dad, and love you. I'm happy that you found the peace and freedom that so eluded you your whole life." She held a moment longer by her father's grave, then took Rueben's hand and they walked with their children back to town. Allie thought of the last time she'd walked that little trail—leaving her mother's funeral all those years ago. She felt again the loss and hurt of that day. She had hoped for a different feeling walking away this time—a sense of comfort or even peace—but the loss and sadness of her life in Palisade remained.

Back on Main Street, they headed east, to the edge of Palisade, then off the main road toward the house. In the distance she could see Esther Jorgensen's place, and Rose Marten's next to it. They were still there, still standing, but barely. Both were grayed and tattered and empty. The rock fence in front of Esther's house was fully flat, with no sign that flowers had ever bloomed there. The barn behind the Marten house, where Allie had played as a little girl, and later hid, had fully fallen to one side.

Then, across the road, to her house. Gone. The barn gone too. The view to the back across the high, brown hills was far and clear. Allie's heart sank at the vacant sight. As she stood staring and running memories through her head, the house found its way back in. She stepped closer and squinted and watched. The heat of that Sunday morning all those years ago returned and held her. Allie didn't move. The baby blue dress she wore fit tight against her once more. Her mother's Bible curled up in her hand. The front door opened and then closed. Allie gasped as the sheriff began to move toward her, as if out of a mist. Without hesitating she dropped her Bible and started to run past him, to the house, to her mother. Then she stopped. She quit. She chose not to fight this time. Allie surrendered. The sheriff continued walking toward her. He looked strong and certain, a lawman that had a job to do. He kept his look fixed on her. She closed her eyes and waited—waited for the words to hear again that her mother was gone. Her heart raced, but she held still and allowed the hurt, the loss, the sadness to fall over her. She made no attempt to push it away. She simply accepted it.

As the sheriff neared, a gentle, warm breeze swept into her, then through her, then past her, and away. A calm fell over Allie. A stillness. A peace. She relaxed and smiled, then stretched her hands wide and set her face to the sky. She let the sun wash over her, then breathed in long and slow and deep. She held the breath for a moment, then let it all go.

When Allie opened her eyes the sheriff was gone, but the calm remained. The house had faded into the mist, leaving only the desert beyond, running wild to the farthest horizon—boundless and open and free.

ABOUT THE AUTHOR

John D. Hughes is a writer, author, speaker, and recovering CIO (Chief Information Officer). He was born in Aspen, CO, grew up in Ohio, and now lives in Washington state. Let Go the Reins is John's third book, and his first novel. He previously wrote and published Haunting the CEO, a leadership fable, as well as Unselling, his guide for introverted independent consultants. John and his wife live a simple, small-farm life in western Washington.

Visit www.hugheswriter.com for more information about John and to connect.

Made in the USA
Columbia, SC
11 August 2019